Personal Protection

Tracey Shellito

CREME DE LA CRIME

First published in 2005
by Crème de la Crime.
Crème de la Crime Ltd, PO Box 523, Chesterfield,
Derbyshire S40 9AT

Typesetting by Yvette Warren
Cover design by Yvette Warren
Front cover photography: Guy Moberly. Image supplied by
Alamy Ltd, Abingdon, OX14 4SA

Printed and bound in England by Biddles Ltd, www.biddles.co.uk

ISBN 0-9547634-5-9

A CIP catalogue reference for this book is available from the
British Library

www.cremedelacrime.com

About the Author

Blackpool-based Tracey first turned to writing when she was diagnosed with asthma as a child. She claims she was always fated to write crime. "While my mother was pregnant she developed a fascination with the television detective programme Hawaiian Eye. I was named after her favourite character, Tracey Steele," she says. "The rest, as they say, is history!"

No one writes a book in isolation. Wordsmiths scribble and type the final words alone, but ideas, inspiration and support from family, friends and even strangers play an important part in the finished article.

Thanks go to Simon Teff, Anna Paterson, Liz Serjeant and Mike Savage, my first readers, whose comments told me it was a story worth writing; to John Dawson, biggest critic and biggest fan; to Vincent Hamer, friend, muse and inspiration; and to everyone at Crème de la Crime for giving me this chance.

To my parents, Fred and Jean Shellito, who always believed in me. This one's for you.

1

"That's the best thing about dykes. They're not afraid to get their hands dirty."

"Cheers for that, Craig. Pass me the spanner."

"Which one's that?"

I glared at him between the slats. He grinned and handed it over. I torqued the bolt.

"That should do it. Try now."

"Don't you want to come out from under there first?"

"Nope."

"The whole fucking lot could collapse on you!"

"I have every confidence in my work. Besides, I need to see how the suspension holds up with some weight on it. Best place to do that is from down here."

"You're mad."

"Probably. If it does go, I'm sure you'll do the decent thing and dig me out."

He threw himself on to the steel framework. I admit I flinched. (Scared? Me?)

The thing held. I gave a few final twitches to the screws and bolts then slid out from under, leaving Craig to wrestle the mattress back on to the futon sofa.

"You wouldn't have this problem if you bought furniture you could actually sit on, instead of stuff that just looks the business," I pointed out, on the way to the kitchen and a bowl of soapy water.

Though I have to admit the house does look good. Wood laminate floors, Persian rugs, minimalist furniture and art deco prints. A perfect snapshot of queer man at home.

The sound of furious keystrokes grew louder as I approached the kitchen. Dean was still in his home study under the stairs, pounding the laptop I'd bought him for his birthday. He didn't even look up as I passed. I sighed and went in to scrub off grease, wondering how long it would take for him to forgive me.

Craig paused to say something nice to his partner, then propped his long, designer-clad body on the door post to watch me, the power of the pink pound never so obvious.

His oh-so-expensive aftershave wafted over me as he shifted to a more aesthetically pleasing position. There is nothing gay men do in company that isn't carefully considered, even when nobody is supposed to be watching. Especially then.

"Thanks for coming."

"No problem. I hadn't got anything else on."

"I wasn't sure if you and…"

"She's visiting her mum."

"Oh." He flicked imaginary lint off his immaculate denim shirt. "Do you think you and she will..?" He gestured around him at the house.

" Matching clothes and shopping at Ikea on Sundays? Not my scene. No, I'm happy as I am."

"Is she?"

"What is this, twenty questions? Yes, if you must know. I'm well aware of the standing joke - the thing most lesbians do on their second date is rent the furniture removing van; but I did that scene with Gina. It was a contributing factor in our break up." (Along with her going back to dating men, but the less said about that the better.) "I won't make the same mistake again. I'm not cut out to live with anybody, Craig. I'm too fond of my privacy and getting my own way. I don't do cohabitation."

He carefully looked at the floor, so that I wouldn't have to see his disapproval. I dried my hands and flipped the bowl up to let sudsy water spill into the shining chrome of the sink.

"I know it wouldn't suit everybody, but it does suit me. Besides, who'd want to come home to the smell of gun oil and a bullet-proof vest on a tailor's dummy every night? It's not exactly calculated to add an air of permanency to a relationship, is it?"

When I came out of school I didn't know what to do with myself. I had qualifications, but nothing special. Nothing appealed at the job centre. I was young, restless and bored. One night, after trying to talk my way out of it, I got into a fight at a club. Somebody who knew what they were looking for saw me. They approached me and offered to sponsor me on a training course. As a bodyguard.

I turned out to be good at it. I try to avoid fighting unless it's absolutely necessary, though I have to know how so I can defend myself and my Principal if the need arises.

Some of the training sounds a bit psycho unless you're in the military or armed response police. Getting hypothermia as you stand around practising surveillance techniques. Team reconnaissance, intelligence, endurance, observation, recognition and identification of threats and threat levels. Formation walking. Ramming cars. Aggressive and evasive driving. Having the stuffing beaten out of you. Fighting and talking your way out of a fight. And shooting and being shot at comes with the territory.

I take my job very seriously. Unfortunately so do my girlfriends. With the usual result that, after the novelty of having a bodyguard as an affair wears off, they start wondering how much of a future there can be with someone who could take a bullet for a complete stranger.

I've learned never to lie about my job. Most of my prospective partners don't believe me anyway. Then I take them home. Seeing the Kevlar with a few holes punched in it is usually enough to make my affair bite the bullet too. But better sooner than later, after I've learned to care about them.

This one was different.

Perhaps it was because she had a job that wasn't calculated to inspire security in a relationship either. As far as I was concerned it was a marriage made in heaven. We'd been together three months. She had her home, I had mine. We got together to do all the things couples do and stayed the night at one or the other's place having great sex. What more could a girl want?

"Why didn't you tell me she was an exotic dancer?" my working partner Dean had screamed at me, after said revelation prematurely terminated last month's dinner party.

"Because I didn't think it mattered!" I'd yelled back.

It didn't, to me. Hell, that was how I'd met her! I'd gone to the place with some straight clients, who wanted to kick back after the job was done. And there she was. A lap dancer. When she saw how I looked at her and that I wasn't a guy, she was at my table all night. I took her home, and the rest, as they say, is history.

It was a big turn-on for me, the idea of her showing off her beautiful body to those sad acts who'd never get to do more than look. I was the one she came home to.

For all his liberal views, Dean had a different take on the sex industry. Dating someone who took their clothes off for money was too much for his delicate sensibilities.

It was too much for his dinner guest, too. Being

confronted – and recognised – by the object of his sexual fantasies over the dinner table was his nightmare come true. How was I to know the husband of the couple Dean had invited hung out in lap dancing clubs, my girlfriend's in particular? His own wife hadn't!

So now the wife was filing for divorce, Dean's status as a socialite was in jeopardy and I was persona non grata. Luckily for me, the lady who'd been the cause of it all thought the whole pretentious set-up was a major cause of hilarity, otherwise I might have found myself girlfriendless as well as friendless, through no fault of my own.

I was glad that the fall-out hadn't been worse, but life was too short for this crap. I wished it would blow over so we could get back to normal. Dean's frosty attitude made working with him a real trial. We work out of a squatty two room office suite in the town centre as a private detection and protection agency.

While I was getting qualified as a bodyguard, clever clogs was passing his Bar. A part-time job 'serving process' as the Americans would call it, (subpoenas, skip tracing, etc) gave him a way to use the dry facts of the law and exercise his nosiness, gossipy queen that he is. He began taking instruction in the field as a private detective.

We'd known one another off and on for years. We first met in school, then afterwards on the scene. (That was weird. I was really surprised how many people I went to school with turned out to be gay.) But it wasn't until he'd qualified, set up the business and was looking for something to make his services unique that we got together again. Offering a bodyguard service was certainly unique, and some clients found a female bodyguard an extra fillip.

To begin with I worked for him, the business taking a

percentage. It didn't take him long to see my part of the job brought in bigger bucks than surveillance on cheating wives and philandering husbands, even if there was less work.

He offered me a partnership; I jumped at the chance and bought in. Now I help on cases where he needs leg-work, while getting qualified as a detective under his mentorship; and he helps on the odd occasion when I need back up. When it's not expected to get too messy, that is; we wouldn't want him to break a nail or muss his hair, would we? As a rule, I'm the muscle and he's the brains.

"Fuck!"

Craig and I turned.

"This fucking thing is eating my report!"

"Has he backed it up?" I asked.

Craig threw his hands in the air. "God knows! Since you persuaded him that all things computerised are not works of the devil, he's been a law unto himself on that thing. He won't let me touch it."

Which is as well, since Craig is a nurse and knows bugger all about computers.

We wedged ourselves under the stairs on either side of Dean, peering over his shoulders. I started to reach for the keyboard to stop the problem, but Dean snapped, "I don't need your help."

I backed off. Craig must have seen how much it hurt, because he went into facilitation mode. The great compromiser in action is really something else. It took him seven minutes to get his partner away from the infernal device and into the kitchen to the cappuccino machine. By that time the screen was an ominous blank. I slid into the seat Dean had vacated and set about rescuing the disappeared data. I suppose a month isn't long enough to learn it all. He had backed everything up. Thank God.

When laughing boy came back with his bowl of coffee, the printer was chattering. Dean scanned the print-out.

"Thanks," he told me grudgingly.

"You're welcome."

"Thanks for putting the futon back together, too."

"'s OK."

"How did you..?"

I showed him how I'd restored the data. "Nothing is completely lost unless you switch off."

He muttered something which was probably as close as I was going to get to an apology about the party fiasco.

"Look, I didn't know Mr Clean Cut Family Man was sneaking off to lap dancing clubs. I didn't deliberately set out to ruin your soirée."

"You should have told me what she did."

"So you could un-invite us, you mean?"

"No, of course not, but we could have said..."

"I'm not going to edit my life for you, Dean."

"I never asked you to!"

"As near as damn it! You're my friend and business partner, not my mother!"

We glared at one another.

"You never asked what she did. You were just happy I was shagging somebody instead of moping around. And you didn't have to toss my leavings out of my flat any more."

He had no answer to that. He retreated behind the bulwark of his delicate sensibilities. "I don't know how you can live with her taking off her clothes in front of other people."

"Drop it, Dean," I advised.

Craig intervened. "Randall's a big girl, Dean. If she can live with her girlfriend jiggling her bits in naff blokes' faces, that's all that matters. Just be happy she's found someone she likes who likes her too."

A backhanded compliment if ever I heard one. Since Craig had come down on my side I'd been waiting for the other shoe to drop. It's comments like that which tell me he's being genuine in his support. He still doesn't like me much, but since I went out on a limb to keep his partner out of the firing line last summer he's warmed to me.

It was his idea for me to come round and fix the sofa. Mend a few fences. I wouldn't have put it past him to have unscrewed the bolts himself. He's a sneaky bastard is Craig.

"I suppose it isn't any of my business," Dean muttered.

"You're right, it isn't!"

The camaraderie was starting to cool between us, as our 'discussion' escalated towards 'argument'. We were literally saved by the bell. My pager went off just as their mobile rang. Craig answered the mobile and handed me the house phone before acknowledging the call and handing the mobile on to Dean.

"For you," he told him unnecessarily. Dean's mouth thinned into a tight line of annoyance. He snatched up the phone and stomped off into the kitchen talking as he walked.

"You're not helping," Craig pointed out as I dialled.

"Neither is he. I have nothing to apologise for."

The phone rang twice before a distraught, unfamiliar, female voice answered.

"Randall McGonnigal. You paged me?"

"Thank God! It's Tori's mum. You've got to come! She's been raped!"

2

I have only ever driven that fast four times in my life. Twice on an Aggressive And Evasive Driving Course (once to rehearse, once to pass), once with a client doing it for real, and that nightmare journey to Tori's mother's house. A journey that should have taken three-quarters of an hour took thirteen minutes. I know; I was counting. And it still seemed too damn long.

As I drove I tried to remember all the things I'd learned about the crime of rape. There are four main motivations. Misogyny, revenge, mental aberration and opportunity. Misogyny, revenge and crimes of opportunity are all about power. Men who hate or fear women. Those who want to dominate or punish a specific victim or a victim by proxy, who reminds them of a hated figure who they cannot attack. Those who are inadequate in their own sex life, as a way of working out their anger at their impotence or premature ejaculation. Whatever the reason, it's a fact that about eighty percent of rapes are perpetrated by abusers known to the victim. Almost sixty percent never get reported, because of that. Rack my brains as I might, I couldn't think of anyone who'd fit the bill as Tori's attacker.

The good fairy must have been looking out for me, because I made it to her parents' Cleveleys bungalow without police interference. But getting through the door was another matter. Her grey-haired, septuagenarian, West Indian father with a belly like Buddha brought to mind Xeno's paradox; I was determined to get in, he was determined to keep me out.

"Get out of here, go on! Haven't you people have done enough to my Vicki?"

You'd think I'd be used to homophobia by now, but it never gets any easier.

"That's enough, Rafe, come away now, come inside."

The woman who coaxed the shuffling man inside and plucked me off the doorstep was white but not much slimmer. She fastened the door behind us, pushed her still muttering husband into the living room and closed the door on him, before she turned back to me. She took a step away and looked me up and down.

"This is not the way I'd hoped to be introduced," she admitted, sticking out a hand. The voice from the telephone. "I'm Tori's mum."

I accepted her hand and shook it firmly.

"You must have flown to get here."

"I came as quickly as I could. Please, where is she? Can I see her?"

She nodded and beckoned me to follow. The house was long and low, big for all that. The corridor she led me through doubled back on itself like the letter J before terminating in a set of loft ladders leading to a conversion, an addition to the building.

"We had it done when Victoria came along. She was a late child, not expected, loved all the more for that." It was as if she read my mind. Or perhaps she just needed to talk.

"She hasn't told us much. She won't let us call the police. She says she can't bear to go through all that being poked and probed, doesn't want to be humiliated any more." She bit back a sniffle.

"I'll speak to her about it," I promised.

"She doesn't know I called you. But I couldn't think of

anyone else."

"Thank you for trusting me."

"Now that I've seen you I think I did the right thing."

I didn't know what to say.

"That bolt might be on. But it's loose. I dare say a good push might do the trick…"

I squeezed her hand and climbed the ladder, leaving her at the bottom watching me hopefully. I knocked gently on the trap door. There was no reply to my first overture. I knocked again more loudly. A muffled sob and an equally muffled "Go away" were my reward.

I tried the door and found it bolted as her mother had suggested. Hoping that she hadn't decided to haul a piece of furniture over it to ensure her privacy, I turned my head, retreated a step then applied my shoulder to it. The door smacked back satisfyingly.

Tori gave a shriek of fear.

This was not the best way to make an entrance after what had just happened to her. I ducked the candlestick she threw only just in time. When nothing else followed, I climbed up the rest of the ladder into the tiny bedroom.

I could see why she had retreated to this place: perfect for a child, low-roofed, cosy. Memories of its security must have been very strong. She was curled up on the rumpled single bed, surrounded by bedraggled stuffed toys, illuminated by a single anglepoise lamp on a child-sized formica desk. Her auburn hair lay in a tangled snarl across a lace trimmed pillow. She'd made a vain attempt to peacock-tail it, as she must have done when she was a child. A sparsely bristled hairbrush on the rug covered wooden floor testified to her attempts to turn back time. To when things were innocent and safe. And here I was recalling her to the present. I wanted to go to her and hold her, but I had no idea how welcome I'd be.

"Tori, it's me."

I ducked the low beams and walked slowly across the floor toward the bed, showing my open hands, the same way I would a sniper in a hostage situation. And was this really any different? Tori might be the victim, but she was every bit as volatile.

I knelt down in front of the bed, picked up the hairbrush and set it aside. I offered her my hand. Tentatively her fingers crept across the coverlet towards the warmth of mine.

Sensibly, I didn't move. Like any frightened animal, I let her make the choices, let her come to me. I was careful to have nothing on my face, in my eyes, but how much I loved her. Whatever had happened, that wouldn't change. She was no different in my eyes unless she chose to be. I didn't want her to think of herself as soiled, or responsible for what had happened. I needed her to know she was not to blame.

"Tori?" I whispered, putting all of that into my voice as best I knew how. With a sob she fell into my arms.

I held her uncomfortably like this, without complaint, until the first storm of weeping had passed. Then I climbed over her on to the bed, wedged myself beneath the eaves so that she wouldn't feel trapped, so she could go at any time, and lightly put my arms around her waist, letting her decide how tightly she wanted to be held.

She snuggled into me, her head under my chin, her arms around my neck, even though her body was stiff against me and only just touching mine. I didn't know whether that was usual or not. I had never personally dealt with a rape victim before.

I could smell something earthy in her hair, a tantalisingly

unpleasant but familiar cologne – not hers – along with the sharp scent of blood. She hadn't washed, just fled straight here after her ordeal. Though I was desperate to know what had happened, to find someone to blame and hurt for this, I steeled my anger with patience. I waited. She would tell me when she was ready.

Afternoon turned to evening through the skylight. She drew strength and courage from my undemanding comfort. Then, between one moment and the next, from silence came a torrent. The words rushed out of her without pause for breath or punctuation. Sorting out the tangle of the tale took all my skill.

"Walking and walking and walking... Singing and walking. 'Hello Mr Postman, nice to see you! I didn't think you still did this round...' So very old, see how grey his hair is now! Old and grey. Like a merry Santa... Bungalows... low, flat and... No! Don't want to! Don't want to see! NO! Hurts! Worse than a migraine, worse than concussion, worse than... DON'T! PLEASE!"

I was deafened by a blood-curdling scream. God knows what her parents and the neighbours must have thought. I stroked her filthy hair and crooned nonsense words to her until she stopped whimpering and the monologue cut in again with frightening clarity.

"If you like pricks so much, then have some!"

The words of her rapist. I shivered. Had one of the clients at the dance club followed her? That's what Dean had suggested, and he would be unbearable if he was proved right. I cursed myself for thinking about that at a time like this. But how do you stop? Even when somebody else's life hangs in the balance, you can't help thinking about how that death will impact upon your own life. Rape was no different.

"Rubber and wood, metal and vegetables..."

At first I didn't understand what she was saying, then the chilling realisation hit me. She'd been raped, but not in the conventional fashion and not with anything DNA typing would be able to convict the perpetrator with. Pseudo penis? Dildo? Phallic objects, sharp and blunt. My mind shrank from enumerating the possibilities.

"Tori?"

"Fucked and fucked and fucked…"

"Tori, who did this to you?"

"Fucked and fucked and…"

"Tori?"

Her voice degenerated into sobs.

This time I did hold her tight. And told her over and over that I loved her and that I'd get the bastard who did this and make them pay.

Somewhere amid this litany I started to cry. A mixture of anger and frustration, pain and horror, pushed me over the line from big bad bodyguard to as much a victim of this crime as she. All of us would have to live with this; in the aftermath we all became victims.

Then I found myself comforted; she was kissing my tears away and stroking my face. Sanity had come back into her eyes.

"You won't make me go to the police?" she whispered in a small voice.

"I'll never *make* you do anything, Tori. I promise you that."

"But you think I should go."

"I won't push you to tell me, but without knowing more about what happened I don't know if that would do any good."

She looked away.

"Let me help you. You know I'd do anything for you! If you don't want the police involved, fine, we won't involve them. Tell me what you know. I'll deal with it for you."

She reached down. Drew the gun from my waist holster, synched behind my back for driving. No, I'm not getting paranoid. I'd been expecting to hear from a client while I worked at D & C's. That's why I was wearing the pager. That's why I was carrying the gun. Thanks to my original sponsor's clout, I can legally carry a concealed weapon. (Don't ask; it's complicated.) I have a Glock 26, subcompact. With the full magazine of fifteen 9-millimetre parabellum rounds it's no lightweight.

She held it between us, pointed towards the roof. The unaccustomed weight of it made her small wrist tremble.

"Would you shoot them for me?" she whispered.

I went cold inside. Would I? Could I? The Glock was distinctive. I couldn't get away with it. She probably knew that too. She wasn't really thinking straight. Hell, I can't say I was.

"You said you'd do anything for me." She threw my own words back at me.

I flinched. "Do you hate me that much?"

The question brought her up short. It wasn't what she was expecting.

"Of course I don't hate you! What..?" Then she looked at the gun. "Jesus." She swallowed hard and nodded her understanding. "This... this is not America. There are only so many guns in the country... Your licence is for this..?"

I nodded. "It would only be a matter of time before they found me. Then I'd spend the rest of my life in prison. I don't think I could live like that, Tori."

I really couldn't. I'm not good with authority.

"What's the euphemism? You'd eat your gun?"

"Yes."

On my black days, I had more than once contemplated that particular form of suicide. It was quick, if you knew what to aim for. I do.

She saw the look in my eyes and caught her breath. "But if I asked you, really asked you and meant it, asked you to kill them?"

"Yes, I'd do it."

She shivered and slid the gun into the holster at my back. "You're scary." She cuddled into my shoulder and this time laid the full length of herself against me. "Tell me again why it is that I love you, scary lady."

"Because I love you. Because we have good sex. Because I'd do anything for you. Any or all of the above."

She sighed, almost contentedly. "It doesn't make the pain go away, but it does make it easier to bear. Thank you. Thank you for dropping whatever you were doing and coming here. For making me that offer. For being you."

"I wish I could have been there to stop it. I wish it wasn't just comfort and consolation I have to offer you."

I felt her smile against my shirt. "You'd have kicked her ass but good."

"*Her?*"

She looked up at me. "I thought it was. Now I'm not sure. You probably think I'm useless…"

"No! No, it's shock." And not wanting to remember. I couldn't blame her.

I let out an explosive breath. It was a reasonable assumption. Who else would use a fake prick? Smell of perfume? God, maybe it was one of her exes! I don't know why I didn't think of it sooner. This is why I'm the brawn of our outfit.

"You thought it was one of the men from the club?"

I hated to disappoint her, but now was a time for honesty. "The thought had crossed my mind."

"That's what Mum and Dad thought too. I couldn't talk to them. How could I explain that another woman might have done that to their daughter when I was coming here to talk to them about you? You've probably met my dad. You can see what he's like. If he knew who'd done this…" She shivered.

I could sympathise. Coming out to your parents is always difficult. Many of us leave home to avoid the necessity. I did.

"I just wanted to get in a cab and go home, but I wasn't in a fit state. Anyway, whoever it was stuffed me in a sack and dumped me on the doorstep so it wasn't as if I had any choice. They even rang the bell." She began to giggle hysterically.

I held her again, until the laughter turned to tears then faded away.

"God I hurt," she whispered wretchedly.

"There is something we can do about that. Get you in a bath."

"I don't want to do that here. I want to go home. Will you take me?"

"If that's what you want. But I think you'll find it uncomfortable to sit in a car so soon after…" I bit off what I was going to say.

"I have to deal with it."

"But not so soon. Please, Tori, take a bath here. You can have another one when you get home, if that's what you want. You need to feel better about yourself. You can't do that if every time you look in a mirror what happened to you looks back."

"I don't have any clothes here," she protested. But her resistance was weakening.

"You can have some of mine; you know I always keep spares in my car."

"In case of blood and bullets." She swallowed back giggles that would have become as hysterical as the last.

"Yes," I agreed simply. Why varnish the truth?

"All right," she agreed.

Then another thought struck her. "I don't know what I'll say to Mum and Dad."

"Leave that to me."

I have an idea now what police officers have to go through when they make house calls to tell people that their loved ones are dead. Sitting in that pristine living room, facing Tori's homophobic father and partisan mother, I told them as much of the truth as I thought they could stomach. That their beloved daughter had been molested: abducted, bound, gagged. I didn't specify her attacker's gender. I said they'd done it with implements other than what nature gave them.

Her mother cried and her father raged. When I left them to fetch Tori my spare clothes they were both crying, feeling as helpless as I had, confronted by the truth and the fact that they had not been there to save her. Most parents never think of you as anything but their baby, no matter how old you grow. It is a mark of their love when they still want to protect you from the evils of the world, no matter how you might have disappointed them. While I didn't have that luxury, Tori was fortunate. Her parents thought the world of her, had always supported her, no matter how they disagreed with her choices.

It might have been wrong to let them think that the

attacker was a man. But the opportunity to give Tori their complete support for what she was, why she'd chosen as she had, was a chance not to be missed. I had no desire to make her father feel that his gender was evil, that he was the same by default. I truly hope that was never what he thought. Having come so far along the road towards acceptance, not to drive the bolt home just when she needed them most would have been a crime bigger than the one she'd just suffered.

I knocked at the bathroom door, thinking that she'd been in there too long. There was no bolt on this door. She was squatting in the water, crying and bleeding into the bath.

"Tori, you have to come out, let me get you dry."

"N...n...no! I... There are *things* stuck in me!" she cried.

I scrubbed a hand across my face. Shit, shit, shit. "Then I'll get them out," I told her.

There followed one of the most harrowing episodes of my life. Tori, on her back on the bathroom floor, my jacket raising her lower back and beautiful behind in the air, legs spread as if for a cervical smear, while I employed tweezers, water, a magnet and my fingers until we were sure there was nothing left inside her that could harm her.

Then I stripped myself and put her under the shower, washed her hair and scrubbed her until she was clean, until both of us were wrinkled like prunes and the water was going cold and there could be no further reasons not to come out.

"I've ruined your jacket," she said quietly as I towelled her dry.

"Doesn't matter."

"It matters to me!"

I stopped what I was doing. "Then you can buy me a new one."

She nodded vigorously. "Yes, yes, I will."

"OK." I went back to drying her.

Her mother was just coming down the loft steps when we came out of the bathroom. Bed linen lay in a heap at the foot of the stairs and the light was out above.

"I've remade your bed, love. If you need to come back, you know we'll be here."

She hugged her mother tightly and managed not to cry.

"Thanks, Mum, I will, I promise. How... How's Dad taking this?"

"You know your father. He'll get over it. It'll take a while, but he will. Don't fret about it."

Then she saw my gun. Her eyes opened wide. "You really are a bodyguard."

"I feel like a pretty useless excuse for one today."

She gripped my hand. "You couldn't have known. None of us could. You hear about this sort of thing on the news, but it doesn't come home that it's real until it happens to you. Won't the person you're guarding be wondering where you are?"

"I was on call. He didn't call." Of course it was that moment that the bloody pager went off. I didn't even look at the number. I quite deliberately plucked it off my belt, turned it off and dropped it into a pocket of the ruined jacket. Tori's mother's hand gripped mine even tighter.

"Go and say goodbye to your father. Let him see that you're all right."

Tori swallowed hard, then, steeling herself, walked into the living room and closed the door behind her.

"Thank you for coming. For telling us everything."

I nodded. I couldn't exactly say it had been a pleasure.

"You'll take good care of her, won't you?"

"Count on it. I only have one job right now, that's protecting Tori."

Now it was her turn to nod. She looked at a scuffed bit of wallpaper and smoothed it back against the wall. "You're going to get them for her, aren't you?"

"If I can."

"Does she know who it was?"

"She's still in shock. She might remember more later. It's too early to say."

"Will you come and tell me when it's done?"

I nodded. Tori came out. She had been crying again, as had her father. I hadn't expected anything else. I didn't expect him to take my hand, though.

"You take care of my little girl."

I realised I was being given the sacred trust. Father to son-in-law, acceptance, the passing on of responsibility. Tori heard it in his voice and caught her breath. I returned the pressure on his hand with a little more than my accustomed force, showing him my strength, my worthiness of the faith he was placing in me.

"With my life, sir," I told him and meant it.

"You are not what I wanted for my daughter, what I expected when I learned who…"

"I understand. I'll do my utmost to prove to you that she hasn't accepted second best." Even though I know you'd rather she was with a man, I thought.

His rheumy eyes took in every facet of my face. "You'd better, because even if I don't know where to find the bastard that did this to her, I know where you live!"

"I wouldn't expect anything less, sir."

He nodded and went back into the living room with great dignity.

I looked at both women in wonder and found them smiling. My chivalry had found an echo in my lover's father. If I let him down, I'd hand the gun to him myself. I'd deserve it.

I got Tori into the car, cushioned on a duvet I keep in the boot for stake-outs, and pointed the bonnet towards my home. I wasn't sanguine about the security at her house. I hadn't been there when she needed me. I wouldn't let her down with ignorance now.

I'd discover who the perpetrator was. And when I did, I'd find out everything there was to know about them and a way to pay him or her back. Shooting would be too quick. What I had in mind would be much slower and more thorough. They were going to pay.

3

The Illuminations twinkled as I drove along the promenade. Tori, swathed in my old sweatshirt and jumper two sizes too big, against the cool September night as well as her internal chill, pressed her nose against the window. The bulk of the newly refurbished Miners' Rest Home twinkled invitingly with lights enough to rival those set up for the tourists.

"Are you going to check your pager?"

"No."

She turned away from the window. Though I kept my eyes on the road I was aware of her scrutiny. I jumped when her hand touched me, which was entirely the wrong thing to do. She recoiled into herself, curling into the tiniest space possible, trying to disappear. I slapped on the indicators, took us into a side street, pulled over, then reached out to her.

"I'm sorry! I didn't mean to react like that. You just startled me."

I managed to coax her into my arms. Somebody blew their horn at the car and I gave them the finger in the rear-view mirror. She looked into my face.

"It isn't your fault that you weren't there. I don't blame you."

"I know, Tori, it's just that…"

"It's your life, it's what you do, protecting people. Not to have been there when I needed you makes you feel helpless. For such a small woman, you have so much presence, so much attitude." She stroked a finger along my jaw. "I almost expect to wake up some mornings and find you've grown stubble overnight and that there's more between your legs than there was when we went to sleep."

Don't think I haven't dreamt about it. I'm one of those lesbians who loves women because I felt I was destined to be a bloke. I got given the wrong body. I'm not a dyke because some guy did me wrong. I like blokes – I just wouldn't want to sleep with one. Maybe I think of them as brothers, or the competition? Tori seemed to be suggesting as much.

"I'm sorry. I don't mean to come over all macho, it's just how I am."

"I know. I wouldn't have you any other way. You make me feel safe."

There's not much you can say to that. It's one hell of a compliment. I hugged her.

"You can't put your life on hold because I got hurt. You have a job to do."

"I can't just leave you and go haring off after some stranger!" I protested. "Let them call somebody else! You're more important."

"Dean will fire you."

"He can't. He's not my boss, he's my partner. I'm only responsible for myself."

That was crap. If I let the business down and the client base abandoned us, he could sue me for negligence.

"Please," was all she said.

I swore softly and got out the pager. I dare you to refuse anything to a woman who speaks to you in that tone of voice, with that look in her eyes. I turned the thing on and it updated. Four more calls. Every ten minutes. All the same number. Dean.

I picked up the car phone and dialled.

"Finally! How is she?"

"As well as can be expected. Thanks for calling, Dean."
I meant it.

"What kind of a shit would I be if I didn't? If there's anything I can do…"

"Not just now, but if you're up for getting who did this…"

"That sounds like quite a story," he said, cautiously.

"We'll talk later, OK? Can you call the client and tell him something came up, that I can't take the job?"

"Of course. He still hasn't been in touch?"

"Nope."

"Maybe he doesn't need your services. I'll call and make sure."

"Thanks. I appreciate it."

This conversation was going nowhere. He said, "I'll let you get back to whatever you were doing. Keep me updated?"

"Always."

"Ciao for now, then."

"Ciao."

I hung up.

Tori smiled at me, her bruised-looking eyes spoiling the image. "That wasn't so painful, was it?"

"All right, I was acting like an adolescent boy. I'm sorry. Just kick me if I do it again."

"No way! You might kick me back! And your martial arts training gives you an unfair advantage."

"I'd never..!" I stammered, horrified.

She pulled me close and held me tight. "I know you wouldn't. It was meant to be a joke. In very poor taste. You'd never do anything like that. I never meant to imply you would."

I never physically fight with my affairs. I don't always

know my own strength but I do know what I'm capable of. Even play-fights can degenerate into real violence. I never want any woman to accuse me of that. Another reason why this crime was all the more heinous. That a woman might have done this.

Even my lovemaking tends towards the vanilla. I only penetrate a woman if that's what she wants, and then I only use my hands. Or my tongue... And nobody gets to penetrate me. Don't get me wrong, I'm not a stone butch. I like somebody to return the favour. There are just some things I won't do. Fucking a woman with a foreign object is one of them.

I realise this makes me old-fashioned. I mean, what is a lesbian without her brightly coloured silicone strap-on? Put it down to age. If a woman wants cock she can be with a bloke. I'm in sex for sex, not power.

Tori brought me out of my introspection. "Will you take me home?"

"We're going to my place." She was going to give me an argument if I didn't nip this in the bud. "We don't know whether they've found out where you live. Perhaps they've staked it out, and are waiting for you to come back. I'm not happy with your security." I'd been trying to persuade her to upgrade her alarm system for weeks, without success. "I don't want to be jumping at shadows all night and neither do you."

"I wouldn't with you there to protect me."

"Low blow, babe. You know I sleep like the dead. If I stay, I'll have to spend the night on a kitchen chair to stay awake."

She sighed.

"I don't want to wake up in your bed only to find someone trying to stave in my skull with a baseball bat."

That was enough to convince her, so back to my place it was. My apartment is like Fort Knox: one of the benefits of working in the security business. Nobody gets in without the keys and the codes.

She settled back into the seat and watched me drive. I was hard pressed to keep my mind on the road. Being stared at by someone who loves you and is undressing you with their eyes is a wonderful, highly erotic thing. It's also very distracting. I ran two red lights before she smiled and turned her face out of the window again to let me concentrate. The last thing we needed was to be picked up by the traffic detail.

I don't live in Cleveleys. I work in Blackpool, but live in St Annes, about twenty minutes away down the Fylde Coast, with high property prices and subsidence problems. One day, like Venice, we'll all wake up to find ourselves afloat.

I shared the top floor of a long low building off St Anne's Square, in a quiet area near the park, with Ashley Hayes, (tall, blond, interesting, but male) a mature law student. He seemed OK, but I often wondered how he afforded the place. Every student I've ever met either had rich parents or didn't know where their next meal was coming from. Maybe he had a nest egg that allowed him to go back to school or something? Or perhaps his barrister lover, Cecily Richmond, was keeping him. He and I had only spoken in passing so my curiosity remained unsatisfied.

Cecily is one of my exes. Her flexible sexuality had as much to do with our break-up as her predilection for bondage and sadism, and we didn't have an equable parting. Her taking up with Ash had led to some ugly scenes on the landing.

Luckily my downstairs neighbour (and owner of the property) was more into security than Tori was. Persuading him and Ashley to find a third of the cost of the alarms and locks I'd installed hadn't been too difficult. If I could get him to chill out and cheer up (he was always banging on the ceiling complaining about the noise) the place would be perfect.

I installed Tori in my apartment and went back to the car for the quilt and her ruined clothes. I didn't imagine we'd get any evidence from them, but Tori might want them, if only for a ritual burning.

When I returned Cecily was blocking my way. Her hand came out to toy with my tie. The bitch once choked me into unconsciousness with a tie she'd bought me as a Christmas present. Waking handcuffed to my headboard, because I wouldn't fight back for fear I'd hurt her, to find her standing over me with a paddle, is one of the low points of my life. Sometimes my feelings about violence towards women are as much a hindrance as a help.

"Hi, lover. Busy?"

"I'm always too busy for any sick little game you have in mind, Cecily. And I haven't been your lover for a very long time, if I ever was. Get out of my way."

"So butch! Grown a dick yet, have we?"

She reached for my crotch. I took an involuntary step back and almost fell down the stairs. She smiled as I struggled to get my balance.

She looked like the perfect designer dyke: long blonde hair and red lipstick, power suits and high heels. That was what had attracted me in the first place. (So sue me! I like high-maintenance feminine women!) But her obsession with dungeon sex made my skin crawl then as much as it does now.

There's some history between my past and present ladies. The lesbian population in this town is fairly small. Eventually you find a few girlfriends in common with your current beau. I wasn't sure what went on between Tori and Cess. Tori's job meant she didn't get out on the scene much, so where they met I had no idea. All I knew was it was around the same time Tori started going out with me. Nothing came of it. Every time they meet the claws come out. It's like being trapped between two sparring cats. All spitting and raised hackles. It would have pissed me off if it hadn't been so damn funny.

My encounters with Cecily were less humorous. I never knew what to say to her. I pushed past her and slammed into my apartment. The echo of her vicious laughter made my ignominious retreat worse.

In the apartment Tori saw my expression. I turned away, too furious to try and explain. She was having none of it. She plucked the bundle of cloth from my arms tossed it aside and caught my chin, tilted my face up and back, then stepped away consideringly. "Cecily?"

Still beyond words, I exhaled noisily and nodded.

She came back and slipped an arm around my waist and pressed herself against me. "What am I going to do with you?"

She scraped a fingernail along my jaw. I shivered with desire. Her hand cupped my skull, fingers feathering through my cropped hair. She drew my mouth down to hers.

Her other hand dropped between us to unzip my fly. My eyes, which had closed when she kissed me, snapped open. I tried to pull away but she tightened her grip. Her eyes were open, watching my expression, needing to know I still found her desirable, wanted to be touched by her, no matter what had happened to her. I stopped struggling. She slid her hand into my damp underwear. I caught my breath. Her fingers began an insistent rubbing. I tried to hold her eyes but I couldn't.

My head tipped back and my eyes closed, my breathing nothing more than staccato catches... Then I was somewhere else: a place of white noise and blood-red light, where the body I inhabit every day was replaced by a single nerve ending, pure sensation that began and ended with Tori's fingers. A throbbing pulse built and built until it reached a crescendo and carried me away. Tori had to shift her hands quickly to hold me up as my knees buckled. I came, and came back to myself, drenched. She propped me against the door, kissed me, then licked her sticky fingers, zipping up my fly as an afterthought.

"You looked as if you needed that, and I... I needed to know I still could."

"Glad to be of service." My voice was a hoarse croak.

She tried out a smile. It didn't touch her eyes. "Are you OK to stand by yourself?"

"I think so."

"Good, then if you don't mind, I'll take that bath. Perhaps you could find the gear I left here last time? Much as I like your clothes, they do smell of petrol fumes."

"Point. They're heading for the laundry. I keep meaning to put them in a plastic bag but I never get round to it. Go ahead; I'll bring your stuff."

"I was rather hoping you'd keep me company."

"Are you sure?"

"Randall, *you* didn't hurt me. I don't think you're capable of hurting women that way. Right now the idea of soaking in a bath full of bubbles with your arms around me has a particularly strong appeal."

30

Shit, what can you say to that? I went for the safe approach.

"OK, I'll be there. Go and get started. I'll join you as soon as I've found your clothes."

I only had a shower cubicle, toilet and wash basin in my bathroom, because of the size of my apartment. A couple of years ago I'd read an article on space-saving designs and the place now had an almost unique feature. The bedroom area was on a raised platform with a false floor. The double bed slid sideways on runners giving access to a sunken bath. Tori was in love with the idea. She thought it was great that she could spread the bed with a pile of bath towels so that we could go straight from the fun in the water to fun on land without having to get dry in between.

By the time I arrived with her clothes, the bed was awash in the deep white pile of bath towels. Candles added an intimate light to the room. The scent of some aromatherapy bath oil complemented the aroma of the beeswax church candles. I felt the tension melt out of me. I was disarming the smoke detector when Tori came out of the bathroom wearing one of my robes, carrying a pack of sanitary towels. Her eyes were dark holes in her face.

"You're still bleeding?"

She nodded unhappily. I set her clothes down out of the way, hugging her again.

"Do you really want me in the bath with you while I'm like this?" she whispered.

"Yes," I told her firmly. "'Granny' recedes in water. If it's more than your period brought on early, we need to know. You'll need to see a doctor."

She whimpered and curled into my shoulder.

I stroked her back. "We'll give it a day or so. See what

happens. If it doesn't stop and it doesn't turn into a conventional period, I promise I'll come with you."

"I'm sorry to be such a child about this," she sniffed, close to tears again.

"You're not! In your place, I'm not sure I'd be dealing with this half so well."

"You'd never get into this position in the first place."

"I've been close! Cecily…"

She looked up. "What?"

I shivered. "It's not something I like to remember."

"Please. It would help me to know that I'm not the only one. If it's even happened to someone as capable as you…"

Shit. Well, if it would show her I understood what she was going through. "OK. Get in the bath. I promise then I'll tell you anything you want to know."

Warm water lapped around us. I sat with my back against the enamel, she between my legs, facing the taps. I worked my fingers into the tension knots in her neck and shoulders. She allowed this quiet pursuit for a time, then leaned back. I was forced to stop. Crushing my breasts pleasantly between us she said, "So tell me."

Tori has an interesting way of sugaring the pill, I'll give her that. I slipped my arms around her, cupping her breasts, stroking the buds of her nipples with my thumbs to temper the bitterness of my memories.

I met Cecily two years ago as she came barrelling out of court number one at the Old Bailey. She was working for the Crown Prosecution Service, celebrating her first case and her first win, having successfully nailed my former client to the wall. (I didn't know he was a gangland king pin when I'd taken the job. Story of my life.) She had just thrown her wig into the air with an unseemly whoop as the doors closed behind her. I caught the wig and her simultaneously. I set her back on her feet, took one look at her and knew.

My suspicions were confirmed when she allowed her hand to linger just a moment too long on mine as she reclaimed her wig. Then she openly checked me out. I was flattered.

"My chambers, half an hour."

"Yes, ma'am," I replied as she sauntered off, inordinately pleased with herself. Perhaps I should have taken the hint then, but damn it, I had just gone from being her prey in the witness box to being the prey of a sexually aggressive dyke in the middle of a bastion of straight law. It was one hell of a turn-on. I could not refuse.

It took me forty minutes to find her office. The building was a labyrinth I was unfamiliar with. I should just have followed her after she'd propositioned me. But I didn't want to seem too eager.

"You're late," she snapped when I knocked and let myself in.

"So sue me."

"I just might!"

She stalked around me, tracing appreciative fingers across my shoulders.

"And there I was thinking it was padding. I'm impressed."

She dropped her gown. She wore nothing but her long blonde hair.

"I'm impressed, too."

"Then perhaps you should show me how much."

I did.

"We never really had a relationship as such. She'd just call me up whenever she wanted sex. Anytime. Middle of the night. Four in the afternoon. First thing in the morning. Lunch time. I'd never had sex in so many strange places nor so publicly – you know I'm not an exhibitionist."

"It must have been very exciting."

"It was at first," I agreed. "But it wasn't satisfying. Don't think you have to compete with her memory." I hugged her to emphasis my point. Cecily's bizarre demands, unpredictability and desire for increasingly rougher sex had become too much. "It came to a head when she asked me to wear a strap-on and bugger her. I refused…"

"No."

"What do you mean, no?"

"No. I won't do it. Which part of 'no' don't you understand?"

Her slap caught me by surprise.

"Do it!"

"No!"

Another slap.

"DO IT!"

"NO!"

I caught her hand before the third slap could land. Her face was flushed, her breathing short, excited. She swooped forward, kissed me aggressively, passionately. Lulled into a false sense of security, I let go of her and went with it. The next thing I knew, my head was bouncing off the floor as she swept my feet out from under me. She rode me down, crashing to her knees astride me. I ached everywhere.

"What the fu..?"

She kissed me again, terminating the kiss with her teeth in my lip. I swore, and she reared back laughing. I bucked her off and got to my feet with every intention of leaving.

Then her arms fastened around my knees. Her teeth fastened on my fly…

"That was a mistake." I should have shrugged her off and left. Adrenalin rush after violence is a high easily turned into an aphrodisiac. "We had the most incredible sex, even though it wasn't what she'd wanted, so I was stupid enough to forget about it. She got more and more violent with me when I wouldn't hurt her. She'd never shown signs of this before or I'd never have got involved with her. Eventually I was walking around with cuts and bruises and bites in places I'd never dreamt of. It was starting to affect my performance in my job. I couldn't afford the distraction, the wounds, the tiredness. It sent the wrong message to the clients. So I finished it. I told her I couldn't see her any more. I don't think I've ever seen anyone get so angry. She threw things, she screamed, she ranted. I was glad we were at her place. I fled."

Tori made a noise of discomfort which seemed to be at my narrative rather than her own hurts. Either that or it was something to do with her own memories of Cecily? I pretended not to hear. I'd promised myself I wouldn't pry. If she wanted to tell me, she would. Until then… I went on.

"I hadn't been seeing anyone for some time. Months had gone by, I'd been too busy to miss her and too busy to want anybody else. Christmas was coming. She just turned up on my doorstep on Christmas Eve, looking like a million dollars. She gave me a dazzling smile, then handed me a present. I hadn't bought her anything. I hadn't anything better to do, so I invited her out to dinner as a way of repaying her for the gift. She accepted. She waited while I showered and changed. When she saw the suit and shirt she urged me to open the present. It was a silk tie. She knows how I feel about silk. It was a great match for the outfit so I agreed to wear it."

Tori shivered. "God, I can imagine it. I never realised she was that calculating."

"Neither did I. Believe me, I've called myself every kind of fool since that day! She stood behind me and put it on for me, while I watched her in the mirror. She began to tighten the knot beyond the bounds of reason, but I was sandwiched between her and the bureau, so I had nowhere to throw her. It all happened so fast." I shook my head to try and dislodge the immediacy of the memories. "I had a different bed then. I came round to find the bitch had used handcuffs and fastened my wrists to the aluminium bars of the headboard. The tie was still around my neck. And she had fastened my ankles to the footboard with plumbers' tape!"

My turn to shiver. "She always carried this huge bag, filled with all kinds of junk – and not a few sex toys – as soon as she saw I was conscious, she took out this studded paddle, like an oblong ping-pong bat, then she beat every inch of me below the neck."

"Jesus! I didn't realise it was that bad! How did you stop her? Get free?"

"They were my handcuffs. I knew how to get out of them without the keys. As soon as she saw my hands were free she ran. I didn't go after her. I hurt too damn much, but if I hadn't… That was the first time I ever wanted to hurt a woman, Tori. If I could have got my hands on her then!"

"I don't blame you! I'd have done the same!"

I wondered about that. Tori always seemed such a gentle person. I couldn't imagine her hurting someone, even someone who so richly deserved it.

She twisted round a little bit, her expression thoughtful. "What?"

"Handcuffs, Randall?"

I blushed, glad she couldn't really see me.

"It's not what you think! Or at least, it wasn't to begin with. After I got qualified, I carried wrist binders around with me whenever the job looked as it might entail actually catching bad guys as well as protecting the Principal. Later I discovered that seldom happens. There are easier ways to hold on to a felon. Having someone smash me in the nose with the things sort of left me disenchanted."

Tori winced.

"Yes, well… Cecily came across them in the bottom of a drawer when she looking for something else, during one of her visits. They became part of our sex games. After I passed out, she must have gone looking for them. I got rid of them after that along with the bed."

"Of course." Was it my imagination, or did she sound a bit wistful? I definitely wasn't going there! Once was enough for me.

"I still don't know how she got me on to the bed. Dragged me, I suppose."

It would have explained my other wounds. I'm not light, even if most of my mass is muscle. But a corpse or unconscious body is a dead weight, pardon the pun. Cecily wasn't that strong. Maybe anger gave her strength? She certainly seemed pissed off at the time.

"That explains a lot." Tori mused, trailing soap bubbles over her exposed breasts in a way that almost took my mind off her words.

"Explains what?"

"Nothing."

And with that I had to be content. Clearly this was one of those things she wasn't ready to talk about yet.

Tori swivelled round in my arms, forcing me to move forwards so that she had somewhere to put her legs. We sat face to face like interlocking Kappa icons.

"What about Ashley? He seems like such a nice guy. I can't think what he sees in her. The only thing they seem to have in common is their job."

"I knew she swung both ways when I started seeing her; that's one reason why I never became emotionally engaged, never committed myself to a relationship with her. And she didn't seem to want that from me. It wasn't until we'd finished that I realised she thought what we had was a relationship."

"Perhaps she and Ash have good sex?" Tori suggested.

"Perhaps. Bondage and the law seem to go hand in hand. You can never tell what anyone likes in bed from outward appearances."

"That's true. Look at you. You're pretty scary but you're gentle as a lamb in bed."

"I'm not sure if that's a compliment or an insult!"

"Believe me, it's a compliment."

I hugged her.

"What happened to you with Cecily sounds worse than what happened to me today."

I shook my head.

"Violence from her was something I'd come to expect. What she did didn't really surprise me. Even though it was physically painful, it was her betrayal and the humiliation that stung the most. What was done to you goes beyond that. It violates your right to decide who you share intimacy with. It makes a mockery of the joy and pleasure of that intimacy. Whoever did this was striking at you personally. It wasn't a random act of violence. It wasn't the usual power thing that prompts rape. It wasn't conventional. They wanted *you* to suffer, not just any woman. You."

I held her once more. For some time we just cradled one another. The bath water began to cool. I didn't want to send the wrong message, so I whispered in her ear, "Warm water, or a sea of towels?"

I felt her smile against my shoulder. She disentangled herself to lean back and pull out the plug. I got to my feet and offered her a hand to steady her. She stood up with my assistance, but instead of getting out she stepped in close, pressing the full length of herself against me. I swallowed hard. Lots of responses to this overture went through my mind. 'Do you think we should?' Or, 'Do think you can?' Or, 'What about what just happened to you?' Any or all of them could be wrong. But if she had made a decision to do this, shouldn't I respect that decision? If I just took it slow, let her show me how far she was prepared to go…

As the last of the bubbles drained away around our ankles, I smoothed my hands down her back, scooping up foam and smearing it gently over her pear-shaped behind. She sighed and leaned into me, licking a warm trail from a tendon in my neck to my collar bone. Her hands spread to encompass my ribs, fingers kneading me in a light sensuous massage, slipping over the wetness, using it to her advantage. Our breasts pressed together, rubbing against one another in increasingly determined movements, until I finally picked her up and transferred her to the bed. When I went to my knees before her, still in the bath myself, her eyes widened in alarm.

"Randall, I'm…"

"I know. You're bleeding. It isn't much. This is the only way I can think of to give you what you want that won't hurt."

"Oh God," she whispered, tears springing to her eyes. "I don't know what I did to deserve you. Get up here and hold me."

I know better that to resist a command like that.

In the end we didn't do anything. She put on a looped sanitary towel which would have made things difficult even if she wasn't hurting. We just held one another and touched one another and kissed, before we kicked the towels off the bed into the bath, pulled the quilt over ourselves and went to sleep. At least Tori did. I have too much responsibility in my soul to fall asleep with candles burning. And since I'd been with Tori, I couldn't leave the place in a tip. Old habits of tidiness had kicked in.

When I was sure she was asleep, so that I wouldn't be missed, I slipped out of bed and did all the sensible, practical things that make my girlfriends say I have no spontaneity. I got into sweat pants and a T-shirt while I puttered, then put on a halogen anglepoise, blew out the candles, put batteries back in the smoke alarm, picked up towels. My head was too full of the events of the day to settle.

After my KP detail, I went into the other room to check my e-mail, got back to the people who needed replies, mailed off a copy of a report to a client, dumped the junk mail and made myself something to eat. I'm not usually a quiet person, but that night I made an extra effort for her sake. And she didn't stir.

I sat with a pen and paper, making a list of things I needed to do (I'm a compulsive list maker), picking at a sandwich and glass of fruit juice on a table beside me.

I couldn't recall the last time I'd eaten. I have to eat something about every three hours or my brain seems to slow down. Dean can't understand how I'm not enormous with all the crap I eat. My nervous energy and my physical regimen seem to keep the weight off. I watched Tori toss and turn in her sleep, through the doorway, as I worked and hoped she wasn't dreaming of her experience.

My insomnia deteriorated into doodled sketches in the margins. Imaginary portraits of Tori's attacker dying messily at my hands. I hadn't been able to save her from the pain in real life. I was just as helpless to save her from reliving the experience in her dreams. Physically close by, I was still too far away to help. I was filled with guilt and frustration.

"We might as well have gone to my place and given you the kitchen chair," she said, jolting me out of my misery. I wondered how long she had been watching me.

I set down the notepad and pen next to my empty plate then sat, arms on my thighs, hands dangling between my legs, as she rolled carefully on to one side the better to regard me.

"This is more comfortable than a kitchen chair."

"Not as comfortable as the bed."

"I was planning on coming back to join you."

"When?"

"Eventually." She looked at me. "I just needed to work a few things out."

"Such as?"

"How I'm going to be sure who did this to you, make them suffer."

"You don't have to do this."

"Yes," I told her, "I do. To make sure they can't do it to anybody else. To stop me feeling so bloody helpless.

To prove that you deserve my help."

She ducked her head into the bedclothes. "My avenging angel."

"Damn right!"

"Will you come back to bed and hold me, until I fall asleep?"

I flipped out the desk light, went straight back into the bedroom, turned up the duvet and slid in behind her. Wrapping my arms around her, I kissed the back of her neck.

"Anything else I can do for you?"

She drew one of my hands across her stomach and down. "Please…"

"Tori…"

"I want this!"

"If you're sure…"

For answer, she unfastened the sanitary towel and placed my hand on her smooth mound. I kissed the back of her neck again, slowly, in a long line of descent that coincided with my fingers. She opened her legs to make it easier for me and I let her guide me with her comments and her body's responses. I don't think I hurt her, but I'm not sure that she cared. She just needed affirmation that she was still attractive, that not all sex was about power, or cruelty, or helplessness.

I let her use me to prove it to herself because I got as much out of putting my fingers inside her as she did. But it was frustrating when she went straight to sleep afterwards. I lay there as long as I could before I had to go to the bathroom and satisfy myself. After that I was in no mood to continue making plans. I got undressed, turned off the light then slipped back into bed beside her, following her down into dreams.

4

Tori had booked three days off work before all this hit the fan. As part of her commitment not to let it ruin her life, she was determined to go back when the three days were up.

She hadn't been visibly bruised or scarred anywhere on her body that would prevent her doing her job, even if she did ache. I knew better than to try and talk her out of it. Perhaps she would be in a fit state to dance in another three days? Perhaps she would find that taking her clothes off in public was something she was no longer able to do? In either case, it was a decision she would come to alone. I'd stand by her whatever she chose. I'd meant what I said when I told her I would never make her do anything. The last thing she needed was overprotection.

It was a new experience for both of us, and Tori's desire not to have anyone tiptoe round the subject was a great help. As part of her determination not to let it turn her into a victim, and partly in order to make herself feel better, she resolved to continue with her usual routines as nearly as her still painful condition would allow. Since Dean had not been in touch to do more than ask after my lover, it seemed I had no client. Tori hadn't felt like being alone, but she didn't want to stay at home with me holding her hand either, so I found myself tagging along with her to her daily appointments.

Few people realise what it takes to keep a dancer looking the part. I know I didn't until I accompanied her. To start with we went swimming. Not just fooling about in the shallow end doing handstands and the occasional width.

I thought I was fit until I had to keep up with her. Even aching, she cut through the water like a seal. I gave up and watched after the sixth length. She did twelve laps and stepped out of the water glowing, and looking better than she had since I'd encountered her at her parents. I was too happy to see her well to feel jealous.

We followed that with a visit to one of those cute ladies' gyms: you know the sort, all Lycra bicycle shorts and cropped tops. While Tori did her step workout and aerobics for an hour and a half in a skin tight, hot pink leotard, I lifted weights in a baggy T-shirt and old track pants with worn out knees. Instructors never like it when a woman can bench press a Volvo. I was about as popular as an Ebola carrier in an intensive care ward.

When I went to take a shower, the changing rooms cleared except for Tori. The 'dyke alert' must have gone out as a result of my performance. (And she wondered why I don't normally go to a women's gym!) Still, it gave us some quality time in the shower. Tori seemed to have stopped bleeding and was anxious to continue pushing the bad memories out, replacing them with something new. So the visit wasn't a complete waste.

A light, nutritious (yuck!) lunch followed. Tori usually eats what I think of as proper food when she's with me. But this wasn't a dinner date. Perhaps I was seeing the real her for the first time? I haven't seen that much green stuff on a plate since Dean's last lunch. It occurred to me that the two of them have more in common than I cared to admit. Was I dating the female equivalent of my working partner? Too Freudian for me!

By far the worst was the waxing session after lunch. Tori's mixed parentage meant she didn't need a sunbed to give her the dancer's obligatory fake tan, and her body was so nearly hair free that it was smooth as silk. I suppose I never gave much thought to how it got to be that way; I just enjoyed the benefits like a chauvinist, relying on my lover to always be beautiful and perfect for me. But unlike most men, I've now had a glimpse of the pain that goes into keeping it that way. I watched Tori strip to pretty (and revealing) underwear from a stool she insisted I occupy in a corner of her cubicle. I watched her lie on a towel-covered vinyl couch while a nosy, too chatty beauty parlour assistant heated goo in a pan, applied it to Tori's legs, allowed it to set, then ripped it off! I thought my stomach was coming out with her hair! I couldn't watch. I had to wait outside. When they brought in the electrolysis equipment to zap her more persistent pubic hair, I had to go and sit in the car.

Straight women and femmes have my undying admiration. Periods, pregnancy and beauty treatments: you are the stronger sex. Never let anyone tell you otherwise! I don't even have pierced ears!

Tori was grinning ear to ear when she came out. I tried to hate her, but visions of what I'd just seen kept coming back to haunt me and I couldn't.

I don't know whether she deliberately arranged it that way, or if it was for my benefit, but the rest of the afternoon was filled with restful visits to a hairdresser and manicurist.

No stylist would touch my short barbered locks. My idea of hairdressing is to wait until the stuff is falling into my eyes, march in off the street and demand a dry cut, now, and if they can't do it, leave.

I've also been known to take scissors to it myself. So I just sat quietly said yes and no at appropriate times during the conversation and waited while my lover had the full monty on her long auburn tresses.

Later Tori tried to get me into the spirit of things by ordering me a manicure. I accepted without too much of a fight. Considering the uses I'm usually required to put them to in my sexual practices, short, carefully rounded fingernails are a must. The manicurist tutted at the length, but dutifully washed, filed, buffed and hand-creamed my mitts. I drew the line at polish, much to her dismay. She was sensible enough not to talk about nail extensions or gold and silver little fingernails. I don't have to do anything; people can just tell I'm a lesbian and leave me alone. Tori isn't like that. She doesn't look the part. I'd have been afraid I'd blown her cover that afternoon, if she had been the least bit troubled about being out. She's not. Watching them sculpt her talons made me alternately flush with desire and wince in pain, thinking of the uses she puts them to on me. In her current mood I could imagine they'd be getting a workout sooner than I'd like.

I'll digress at this point to fill in some salient details. By now I'm sure my tantalising hints have you wondering just what my darling really looks like. And the ape she's allowing to bask in her presence.

Victoria Kingston is twenty-five years old, a coffee-skinned, brown-eyed minx. Her waist-length curly hair is natural auburn as a result of her mixed parentage. She's a statuesque five foot nine in heels, weighs about a hundred and fourteen pounds, has clear skin, a 36-24-32 figure and a winning personality. Everybody loves her. Nobody can understand what the hell she's doing with me. Most of the time that includes me.

And yours truly? I weigh in at about a hundred and thirty pounds, most of it muscle, and top out at five foot four which gives my clients pause. (Remember that scene in *The Bodyguard*? Kevin Costner amply demonstrates size and weight are not what make us good at the job.) I'm sure my vital statistics don't interest you. I'll only say I'm thirty-something, tan-free, white, have short dark brown wavy hair and such broad shoulders I look like an American football player in full kit. So no shoulder pads in my suits! Unlike the sun in my sky, I don't have a winning personality. I've been accused of taking life and myself too seriously. That's probably true. I have frown lines rather than crows' feet and way too much silver in my hair. Probably because of the job. Not because of my girlfriend.

"Please can we go back to my flat?"

She was stroking my thigh while I drove as a way of persuading me. If she didn't stop, the point would be moot, because we'd never arrive.

"Randall, I need more clothes than this if I'm going to stay on at yours."

"And if we find out nobody has tried to get in, you won't want to come back." I put her hand firmly on her own knee when we reached a convenient set of traffic lights.

"You could always stay at mine."

"We've been through this."

"I'm not made of glass!"

Shit! What could I say to that?

"All right."

I indicated, spun the wheel and pointed the bonnet toward her home.

I didn't really want her flat to have been touched, but it would have made things easier if we could have arrived to find the lock plate gouged. I wanted to protect her, but I couldn't do it if she wouldn't let me. She was my lover, not my client.

In the event, I needn't have worried – or perhaps I should have worried more. While the door seemed shut firmly enough, the rest of the flat showed a more violent face.

Tori stood in the doorway and trembled. All the work she had put in on getting her life back under control was ruined by the sight that met us when she opened the living room door.

The soft furnishings had been slashed. Everything that could be ripped had been ripped. Anything that could be broken was broken. How her neighbours hadn't complained was beyond me.

Maybe they had? And the police had found nobody here when they arrived. Or perhaps the perpetrator had brazened it out when the law turned up on the doorstep? These were questions for another day.

I bundled Tori back into the car and drove her to my place, then called Dean and Craig. It was my good fortune that Craig was working the late shift and Dean had closed the office for the day. They both agreed to come over.

It took a while to calm her down. The boys arrived conveniently as I'd got her settled. I left Craig to keep her company. He is a nurse after all; he should know about hysteria. Then Dean and I drove back to her flat in his Range Rover.

"Bloody hell! There's not much we can salvage here."

"I know. Let's just do what we can to clean the place up before she sets foot in it again. Empty is better than trashed."

He was in perfect agreement. The two of us put our backs into it and had everything liveable in about three hours. I was reluctant to leave Tori longer than that. There wasn't really anything else we could do. His car had piles of bin bags with the things we couldn't save in the back and the few clothes still wearable in a hold-all in the front. The bastards had cut the wires on her electrical appliances. Her tropical fish were dead, her freezer had defrosted, the food was starting to go off and the floor was flooded. Nothing from telephones to CDs had escaped the rampage.

"You know, whoever it was did this before she was raped."

"That had occurred to me, but I wanted your opinion."

He sat down at the scratched but otherwise whole table on the remaining hard-backed chair.

"Is that why you left Craig looking after Tori instead of me?"

Time for some brutal honesty. "Not entirely. I meant what I said, about your helping me to catch the person that did this. But I still wasn't sure how you felt about Tori after the dinner party fiasco. I didn't think she needed to wonder about whether you blamed her, at a time like this."

"Fuck! You don't believe in pulling your punches, do you?"

"No." I looked at him.

Dean ground his teeth then grimaced back.

"I'm sorry. I overreacted."

"OK."

"OK? That's it?"

"As far as I'm concerned, yes. You're my friend. I can see you're sincere. I'm not a queen. I won't make you pay for the next twenty years. Life's too short."

This business had brought that home to us all. I could see him wondering how he would feel if something like this had happened to Craig.

"You're right. We should get together on this. Find out who's responsible."

"Tori doesn't know who it was. She thought at first it might be someone she knew. Maybe an ex."

"It was a personal attack I grant you, but... I don't know. It feels wrong, Randall. It really might be something to do with the club."

I was about to lay into him for his prejudices when he held up a conciliatory hand. "It needs looking into. If I'm right this won't be an isolated incident. We should find out if any of the other girls have been victims of similar attacks, anything from this -" he waved a hand around us "- to what happened to Tori. Violence always accompanies the sex industry. It could be our starting point."

"And the ex-girlfriends?"

"I'll look into that. You haven't got enough perspective. You'll want to go wading in full of righteous indignation and beat the crap out of them. Getting bound over or imprisoned for assault won't do Tori any good, no matter how noble a gesture it might be."

I turned my back on him full of frustration.

"You know I'm right. Let's do this properly and get the bastard in a way they can't get out of. Once we know we've got the right one, I'll happily stand back and let you kick skittles of shit out of them and swear you were with me at the time. But let's make sure we get the right one first, OK?" He laid a kind hand on my shoulder.

I really wanted to hit something, but Dean's voice of sweet reason routine had short-circuited me. He was right. But that didn't make it any easier when all I wanted was a target. Which is when I decided what I was going to do tomorrow.

I'd followed Tori to her appointments. She was going to have to do the same for me. Tomorrow we'd go to my gym. Apart from shooting, there is no finer way to get the urge to kill somebody out of your system.

I rolled my neck and settled the Kevlar vest more comfortably into place as the instructor squared up to me on the mat. It hadn't been easy to persuade Tori to come. But what she had seen in her flat convinced her that the violence wasn't over. I'd shamelessly used that to my advantage. The prospect of sitting on her hands alone, or risking the streets without me, convinced her a trip to my world wasn't the worst thing that could happen.

Unlike your usual gym, this one has no exercise equipment, no weights to lift, no aerobics classes, step or otherwise. What it did have was a bunch of very determined people wearing their workday clothes – which in our case meant Kevlar vests and suits – and the occasional padded mat.

It is important that a bodyguard be able to take a certain amount of punishment as well as dish it out. So along with martial arts classes, this place employs a selection of pugilists to beat the shit out of us. I know what you're going to say: she lets herself get hit but she can't watch somebody have her legs waxed? It's different somehow. Believe me.

"Ready?" my opponent inquired.

"Ready."

For the next hour I endured a gruelling regimen that made Tori wince, grimace, gasp and swear, before she finally clapped her hand over her mouth and endured in silence.

I felt better about running out of her waxing session at the end of it.

"Was that really necessary?" she asked afterwards in the changing rooms.

"Yes. I'll be less likely to fold if someone takes a punch at somebody I'm guarding. If someone does floor me I can get back up. It takes the fear out of falling, means you can do it properly." I peeled out of my body armour and sodden T-shirt.

"It all looked very painful," she said doubtfully, relieving me of my towel to rub my back dry before I got into a fresh T-shirt.

"Not as much as you'd think. It hurts the guy smacking the Kevlar more than me."

"What's next?"

"Now I get to fight back."

"I like the sound of that much better."

I grinned. "Don't be so sure. He won't just stand still and let me hit him."

"I knew there had to be a catch."

"Always." I kissed her and strapped the Kevlar back on.

"Isn't that an unfair advantage?" she asked as we walked through to the next room.

"Only if the other guy isn't wearing any."

They all were and they were all men. About a dozen or so had already collected in the room; a few other stragglers drifted in behind me, falling into conversation about techniques, shadow-boxing with themselves, half-heartedly sparring or checking out one another's moves.

"Brought some fresh flesh this week?"

I gave the speaker what Dean calls The Look.

"She's my Principal." Tori, to her credit, did no more than blink.

"You know the rules, no one but fighters," someone else complained.

"I have nowhere else to stash her. Where could be safer than a room full of bouncers and bodyguards? She'll keep clear."

I settled her against a wall, on one of those plastic and stainless steel stacker chairs you see everywhere from village hall meetings to doctors' waiting rooms, amid a chorus of complaints and cat calls. And one moan that he'd planned to use the chair to hit his opponent with. I ignored them all.

"Does that mean I'm your client?"

"Yes, unless you want to fight one of these idiots."

"No! I sort of like the idea of being your client." She touched my face. I swallowed hard and firmly put her hand back into her lap. "What? There's a no touching rule?"

"In a way. It is considered very unprofessional to get involved with your Principal."

"What if you were already involved before they became your client?"

"Doesn't happen. You'd be advised to get someone uninvolved to guard you."

"Why?"

"Too close to the situation. An involved bodyguard might overreact." As I had last night.

Someone yelled my name. "Be right there!" I called back. "Can we talk about this later?"

"Of course. I thought I knew what you did, but I'm beginning to see that I knew very little. Be careful, please?"

"For you."

I went to join the others.

"McGonnigal, you've drawn Spink."

Leon Spink is a huge black guy. He was beginning to build a gut, which meant he was less in demand for clients that require running around, but more for those that require standing around looking impressive as part of the job description.

There isn't any particular enmity between us; let's just say that he's not a big believer in women as bodyguards. He gave me this tombstone grin, pearly white perfect teeth in the ebony of his face, cracked his knuckles and said, "I'm going to enjoy this."

I knew I wouldn't. But Tori's presence meant I was going to make a damn good showing. Nobody was going to wipe the floor with me in front of my girlfriend, I promised myself that.

Everyone paired off and began the circling and talking to psyche out their opponents.

"I'm going to show you why women shouldn't be in Personal Protection, little girl."

The mammoth body began a lumbering run towards me. His arms spread wide to gather me into a bear hug that would bruise ribs even through the Kevlar and break any limbs that got in his way. There was nowhere I could run without looking like a coward, and precious few spots on his body that were not protected by something. He had no neck to speak of; his arms and legs were rolls of fat and muscle; he wore a box to protect his cock and balls; and the Kevlar vest sandwiched his torso.

As the inexorable juggernaut barrelled towards me, I did the only thing I could think of. At the last moment I dropped into a squat, then lashed out with a foot to his right kneecap.

A sickening snapping noise stilled all movement in the gym. Leon Spink shrieked, lurched, then fell backwards, crashing to the floor. I stood. As quickly as that it was all over.

All bodyguards know elementary medicine. Nobody needed to examine Spink to know I'd broken his patella.

He'd be out of action, and work, for some time. With the weight he was carrying, he might never be free of pain, even if I hadn't permanently weakened him. I didn't like what I'd been forced to do, but what choice had there been? He wouldn't have stopped till he'd proved his point and I couldn't afford to be hospitalised, now of all times. I'd acted out of instinct and self-preservation. It was what I was trained for.

The real medic we had on hand immobilised his leg and called for an ambulance. Since I'd been responsible I got changed, then sat with him till it arrived. Tori stayed in the background on her chair. Spink did his fair share of cursing and moaning about his fate to the air, then addressed me directly.

"You're good."

"Thanks."

"Been lookin' for an excuse to get out. My old lady thought it was time to move on. Looks like you've given me what she wanted."

I wasn't sure how to answer that. It was sort of a back-handed compliment.

"Someone will need to take my place till they can find a replacement in my current job. I'll phone and recommend you."

"Leon, I can't…"

His laughter interrupted me. "Sure you can. It won't interfere with your client. Might even be helpful to you. I'm bouncin'. At your lady friend's club."

I was so carried away with this gift from the gods which had fallen so conveniently into my lap that I didn't notice how quiet Tori was until we reached my apartment.

"So that's what you do," she said quietly as I turned off

the engine. "You hurt people."

"I protect people."

"That wasn't how it looked to me."

"Would you have preferred I just let him wipe the floor with me? He would have."

"Of course not, but…"

"There are no buts, Tori. I do what I have to, we all do. It's my job."

She turned her face away, looked out of the window.

"I'd never hurt you, you know that, don't you?"

She was quiet for much too long.

"Tori?"

She let herself out of the car. I scrambled to follow.

"Tori, you don't think..?"

She turned at the door to confront me. "I don't know what to think. It's not what I expected. You're not what I expected. I know you sometimes carry a gun, that you've promised to get whoever was responsible for what happened to me. But you didn't think. You just did it. You didn't know that man beyond casual acquaintance, but you're not even sorry. I'm not sure I want anything to do with that level of violence!"

I didn't know what to say.

I've been through this scene too many times. It always ends the same, with me alone. I didn't want to lose Tori, but I can't change what I am. I don't know how to do anything else. Even if I stopped, the training would always be there, waiting, like a sleeping tiger.

I hadn't intended to show off or frighten her. Just get the frustration out of my system. Show her she was safe, that I could protect her as well as any man.

"Would it help if I said I'm sorry?"

"No. You wouldn't mean it and you still wouldn't feel

remorse. You've just spent the entire journey gloating over your triumph. That that man's injury has opened up the possibility for you to solve the case and win a battle against injustice."

"I wasn't gloating! And what's so wrong with wanting to solve the crime? It's your injustice, Tori. A chance to…"

She sighed. "You'd feel just the same if it was some nameless, faceless client."

"No, I wouldn't. I'd have no personal stake in that."

"Can you honestly tell me you don't feel more strongly about exorcising your frustration than about how I feel?"

"Yes!"

She didn't look convinced. I tried again.

"I've never experienced what you have – I can only imagine the pain and terror you went through. My sympathy with your feelings is more important than making myself feel better." I took her hands and looked into her eyes, tried to communicate that to her by touch if she couldn't see it in my face. "You're important to me. More important than getting the culprit. More important than my inadequacy. More important than my frustration."

"And if I asked you to stop, not to go after them?"

"Is that really want you want?"

"Just answer the question, Randall."

"Two days ago you asked me if I'd kill them for you!"

"Would you stop?"

I hesitated too long, and she knew me too well. She let go of my hands and stepped away. "Justice means more to you than people, Randall. Getting the villain means more to you than to me. You've got the bit between your teeth. You won't let go."

"Why is that a problem?"

"You really don't see it, do you?"

"No, I don't. I don't want to lose you. Help me understand, Tori."

"I'm not sure you can. I'd like you to call me a cab. I'd like to go home now."

"You can't! Your flat is..."

"I'll live with it."

"It isn't safe!"

"Neither are you!"

"Please don't go."

She looked at me sadly, then came forward and touched my face.

Over her shoulder I saw Cecily in the doorway enjoying our little drama. Then Tori was speaking. Her voice was quiet, her words soft. I almost missed them over the pounding of my heart and the voice screaming in my head, 'You're losing her.'

"That afternoon I spoke in anger, in fear, I was terrified, abused, I didn't know what I was saying. When I asked you if you'd kill them for me I meant it. Then. I don't mean it now. I want to put it behind me and forget. I don't want everybody to know. I don't want people pointing the finger saying, 'There goes the rape victim.' I want to be known for what I can do, what I am, not what somebody tried to make me. I don't want to be the cause of more violence. I want to get on with living my life, forget about what happened, be a dancer, be happy, make lots of money and have you love me."

"You still want me?" I wasn't sure I'd heard right.

"Yes. I want you. I just don't want to be part of your world. The violence scares me. I can't stop you doing this. Just don't make it your life's work. I don't want you to hunt down this deviant to the exclusion of everything else. I want a romantic relationship with you, not a client/bodyguard relationship."

"Don't you think you're worth fighting for?"

"Not in the way you mean."

Cecily chose that moment to interrupt. From where she was standing I suppose she couldn't tell the crisis was over.

"Lovers' spat?"

Tori's expression switched from aroused to ugly. She lunged for the door. Whatever Cecily saw in her face made her back off so fast she slammed into the wall in her hurry to get inside. I grabbed my lover and swung her into a tight embrace.

"Whoa! What happened to not wanting to be a part of my world because the violence scares you? That's quite a U-turn there, babe."

"I…" She blushed furiously with embarrassment. "After what you told me last night I just… Oh, hell. This is how you feel, isn't it?"

I didn't need to say anything, and I wasn't going to rub it in.

"You've got that 'I want to fuck you senseless' look on your face."

"I have?" I asked, ingenuously.

She sighed. But she looked pleased. I kissed her, she tried to hold back for form's sake, but eventually she had to return the kiss. I put my arms around her. Her hands slipped under my battered jacket and started stroking my ribs. I steered her towards the door.

"I suppose that means I won't be going anywhere for a while."

"God, I hope not," I breathed into her ear.

5

"I always forget how hot you look in a tux. Until I see you in one again. Promise me you'll leave it on when we get home? I've always wanted to fuck somebody wearing a tux."

How the hell was I going to concentrate on the job if she kept saying things like this? I was going to have to start carrying spare underwear about too, if she didn't keep her hands to herself when I was driving.

She gave a delightfully ribald laugh then left me alone to try and gather my scattered wits and get us to her club in one piece.

Lap dancing is a growth industry. Since Peter Stringfellow converted Stringfellow's night-club in London into a lap dancing bar they've been springing up like wildfire.

After initial protests had died away, this place was fast to follow. In a town that gets much of its revenue from tourists, anything which will bring in more punters gets first priority for development. Sun, sea, sand and silly hats, a trip to the Tower, the Sea Life Centre to see the sharks, Madame Tussaud's to see the waxworks, the Pleasure Beach to ride The Big One and doughnuts on the Prom with the kids by day. A nice meal in one of the restaurants in the evening and a walk through the Illuminations, if it's the right time of year. Then while a sitter watches the kids, a couple of jars in the nearest watering hole and a boogie at a night-club. Then round off the night by slipping away from the dozing wife to a lap dancing club to watch pretty girls get their kits off. What more could anyone ask?

Not including the sole male lap dancing venue, there

were, at last count, five clubs. All of them were former night-spots, some in the quieter South Shore area, one on the Promenade itself, and some right in the town centre. They range from places businessmen are not afraid to be seen to the downright seedy.

Tori's place of business is unimaginatively called the Bird Of Paradise. One of the upmarket places, it can be found up a side street between a hairdresser and a furniture shop on the fringe of the town centre. It's not a million miles away from our office – another bone of contention between Dean and me. He thinks such places lower the tone.

Because this is a lap dancing club, nobody under twenty-one gets through the door – they check ID – and usually only members, unless they know you, or the business you belong to. Though of course there are plenty of short term memberships available to the tourists, which was going to make my job harder. Everyone has to sign in, whether they're members or not. The security protocols might sound stringent, but they have to think about the licence and protecting the girls. And it's most definitely in that order.

The club entrance is a candy pink and white striped pavilion, covering a flight of external stairs and the double doors with their attendant security and doorman, then a second flight of steps inside. These lead through more doors on to a raised catwalk of plush carpet, with ornamental wrought iron and sandblasted glass panels for a railing, like a 1920s cruise liner. Two bars, one to either branch of the arms, are adorned with topless bar staff and pretty girls draped in feathers and not much else. The balcony runs the entire length of the club.

Here and there are slim tables, just big enough for a

couple of glasses and a bottle – which will cost you an arm and a leg. The walkway sweeps down two curving stairways that debouch on either side of a stage with a fireman's pole as its central feature.

More tables, a little bigger, for groups and those not afraid of being seen in such a place, dot the open floor space of the mezzanine together with another bar. Two star-marked doorways underneath the stairs denote the private rooms where you can pay the girl of your choice to all but masturbate you to a climax, while you can't lay a finger on her in return.

Two similar doors at the back of the room lead into the amenities. His and hers. The men's toilet is usually full of punters and the women are only ever the staff.

Other penguin-suited bouncers circulated amongst the clientele and the girls as I escorted Tori into the club proper. A few of them nodded to Tori; me they looked up and down speculatively, wondering whether I was part of the Blackpool bouncers' mafia: competition or an ally. I hoped it wasn't going to degenerate into a pissing contest. The business with Spink had put enough of a crimp in my relationship with Tori, and I wasn't anxious to add to my troubles.

Aside from that, we didn't get many looks. Or rather Tori didn't. She deliberately dresses down to enter and leave so she can do it without hassle.

I don't know whether I got more looks from the clientele or the girls. Both of them were curious about a woman in drag. I could tell the men wondered whether I was part of the act, while the women were wondering what was under the suit and who was getting it. I hadn't been back here since the first night I'd met Tori, I'd always waited outside to pick her up, so it was doubtful they'd remember me –

I'm not the only woman who comes here to watch – or know I was dating one of their dancers.

I gave her a hand up on to the stage. She blew me a kiss before disappearing through the curtain. I shook my head, twitched my pants to realign the creases and rearrange my underwear, then went to report to the management.

"Spink says good things about you."

I said nothing, just waited for the punch line.

"You don't look big enough to do any real damage."

"Did Leon tell you how he came to be in the hospital?"

My questioner looked uncomfortable. Good, Spink had told him. Now I wouldn't be forced to prove myself by breaking someone else's bones.

"I can do the job. If you think I won't be impressive enough standing at the doors, fine. It's bloody cold out there. I'll be happier circulating seeing nobody does anything they shouldn't to the ladies. They might be more inclined to listen to diplomacy from me than some of the neanderthals you employ."

I knew some of the other staff and didn't think much of them. They were brawlers. The whole point was not to get into a fight in the first place – something my employer obviously knew too. Relief fell across his face like a curtain.

"That would be good. I told the others you'd be coming. Most of them seemed to know your name. This is not your usual line of work. I was told you're a bodyguard."

"Yes."

"You're not working for anybody specific at the moment?"

"I can't discuss that. Let's just say there'll be no conflict of interest. Once someone else fills this position I'll go back to doing what I do best."

"I can only pay you the going rate for a bouncer."

"I wouldn't expect anything else."

He looked relieved. "I suppose this will be a bit of breather for you, not having to dodge bullets and what-not."

I thought about my last two assignments and nodded. "Yes. It will."

"Erm, yes, well, if you wouldn't mind, circulate on the balcony level for an hour or so, then make your way down to the mezzanine. If one of the lads taps you and says, 'Star 1' they'll want you in the left hand room. 'Star 2' is the right. Someone has to be there when the girls go for a private dance. Some of the gents think they'll be able to get their hands on them then and need a bit of presence to persuade them otherwise. Will that be a problem for you?"

"No."

"You sure? You're a woman. I mean..."

I squashed my irritation. You wouldn't believe the amount of times I've heard that line. It doesn't pay to get angry. Just project competence and nip it in the bud right away.

"This is a job. My personal opinions and my politics don't enter into it. Anything else?"

He looked at me for a moment, then decided to give me the benefit of the doubt. "If somebody yells, 'Heads up', that means all hands to the main doors. Sometimes a crowd of drunken blokes'll try their luck and we don't allow that."

"Glad to hear it."

"One of the girls calls, 'Help,' or the other bouncers, 'Help here,' that means they can't handle the situation. If you're nearby, you pile in, break up whatever's going on."

"OK. What about the police?"

"We are a legitimate business enterprise. No sex for money goes on in this establishment. From time to time, the law drops by, but they're plain clothes and they don't usually cause any trouble. Their Chief Super is a member. We don't get raided when he's in. And he's in tonight. Front and centre on the mezzanine."

Interesting. This was the kind of information that might be useful to Dean some day.

"One more thing. A couple of the lads have been approached by the girls to look the other way in the Star rooms so they can have full sex. It's not to happen! They might try to bribe you, but stick to your guns. It's my licence if this place gets a reputation as a knocking shop. If the girls are stupid enough to make arrangements outside of club hours with the punters, that's their business. I'm not having them screwing the public on my premises. There is a bonus for anyone who reports it to me."

"I understand."

"On your way, then. It's pay in the hand at the end of the night. Your tax affairs are your own lookout. And if you're crap, you're out."

"I won't be."

The night began quietly enough. The bouncers and I sniffed one another like wary dogs staking out territory. Muzak gave way to the first dancer. More clients arrived, occupying balconies and tables, making a stroll along the catwalk an obstacle course negotiated with care and diplomacy. The feather-clad girls draped themselves around me and I draped them round something, or quite often someone, else. One of the bar staff got fresh with me, but I thought of Tori and wasn't tempted. Much. The noise level rose. More clients arrived. Then I broke up my first fight.

I was about to descend to the mezzanine when two guys went for one another. The woman milking both of them leapt clear with a cry of "Help here!" I was closest.

I didn't see who'd started the affray, but the glitter of what might have been a knife and a broken bottle made me wade in impartially. I grabbed each combatant by the back of the neck and smacked their heads into the table. Both went limp and stopped struggling. I continued to press their heads to the melamine.

"Are we finished, gentlemen, or do I have to ask you to leave?"

Affirmative grunts came from the faces being ground into their spilled drinks.

"Good." I relieved them of the weapons they'd been about to make use of, then let them up. Bouncers converged from all sides. The cavalry. Too late.

"Fuck! Wasn't that a bit much?" the first man on the scene grumbled.

"Yeah, you could have broken their noses and then…"

I interrupted the second to hand over the flick knife and smashed bottle the bravos had been about to fight with, and said sweetly, "I don't know, gentlemen. Why don't you decide?"

Halfway down the stairs a third man caught up with me.

"You went up against them barehanded, knowing they had weapons?"

"It was that or a bloodbath on the balcony. Which would your boss have preferred?"

"Didn't you..? I mean, weren't you worried that you might have been..?"

He really was very young. I stepped aside to allow a couple to pass me. He joined me against the banister.

"This is what we do. You'd be a fool if acting to stop a situation like that doesn't scare you shitless. But you practise and you work until you know what to do. Then you do it. If the thought of being cut makes you freeze you should get out of the job. Now."

"How do you learn? Will you teach me?"

I hadn't a clue who he was, but he seemed in earnest. I let him follow me the rest of the way down the stairs, snagged a napkin from a table and requested a pen from one of the bar staff. I wrote out the address of my gym and gave it to him.

"If you're serious, go in the morning and tell them I sent you. Tell them what you do for a living and why you want their help. Somebody will take care of you and show you what you need to know to get started. Other than that all you can do is watch and learn."

"Thanks!" He was like a dog with two tails. "I really appreciate this!"

I let him bound around enthusiastically for a while then shooed him away so I could get back to work. I wondered if I was ever like that.

I'd arrived in time for Tori's first number. If you've never seen what goes on in a lap dancing club, nothing can prepare you. Most people have watched *Showgirls* (good) or *Striptease* (not so good), or seen one of the handful of documentaries Channel 4 or Channel 5 have been brave enough to show. (*Divas* comes to mind.) So it won't shock you when I tell you that Tori strutted out on to the horseshoe-shaped stage and very artistically took her clothes off to something slutty by The Artist Formerly Known As Prince, and slithered suggestively up and down the fireman's pole.

Since this place used to be a strip club, (and yes, there is a difference) there were no seats next to the stage. The girls have been pulled off by over-enthusiastic clients in the past, so the whole tucking the money into their g-strings bit doesn't happen on stage any more. Instead, girls not currently dancing wander around with tip buckets. If the clients like what they see, they tip well; if they don't, they tip badly or not at all.

It helps that someone had the bright idea of making the tip buckets those artificial vaginas they sell in sex toy catalogues. It's not in good taste, I grant you, but it is safer than the way things used to be. Now they can't get their grubby little mitts on the real thing, punters happily push their fingers into these with a donation, drool over the performer (or the girl carrying it) imagining where they'd like to be sticking their cash. And quite frequently telling them all about it in fairly graphic terms. If I hadn't known it was part of the job, I'd have punched some of these creeps' lights out. The girls put up with a hell of a lot. I couldn't do it.

I contrived to be in a position where I could keep an eye on the audience and watch the act at the same time. I don't know how, over the stage lights, but Tori must have seen me. She directed every lewd gesture and lascivious move in my direction. When she threw back her head, wet a finger and trailed it down the length of her body, I was just as unable to look away as every man in the room.

She has a presence on stage that grabs attention and hypnotises everyone. The applause when she finished and gathered up her clothes and an armful of these bulging pseudo-pussies was tremendous.

"What I wouldn't give to fuck her brains out!" one ecstatic voyeur moaned.

Never in my life have I taken such great pleasure in

whistling jauntily and grinning ear to ear as I walked past someone. I think he got the picture.

Tori had not long left the stage when someone tapped me on the shoulder and said, "Star 2."

Obligingly I took myself off to the private booth on the right of the stage.

An Asian girl met me there with her inebriated client. He paid a cashier outside, then the door was unlocked and we went in. It was a small plush room. There was a single sturdy recliner under muted spotlights for the client, a micro stereo, a collection of CDs for the girl to dance to, and in the shadows behind the door, a tall bar stool for me.

I made myself as comfortable as my damp underwear allowed, then watched as the girl cued up the CD in this soundproof booth and commenced gyrating. The music she chose wasn't a million miles from what Tori had stripped to. And whenever her back was to the client her eyes were on me. I ran a finger round a suddenly tight collar.

When it was over, the client staggered out past me, while the girl clothed herself in the revealing dress they walk the club floor in when they're not dancing. I made to leave, but she was a fast mover. Her hand was on my shoulder. Breathy words tickled my ear. "Did you enjoy that?"

"More than he did, I suspect."

Her other arm twined around my waist, fingers heading for my crotch. I clamped a hand about her wrist.

"Tori's a very lucky girl."

Her tongue traced the outer edge of my ear. I snatched my head away, ashamed to find that I didn't want to. The mind may be true, but the body just wants what it wants. It doesn't care who's doing the job. Names don't matter to the libido.

I opened the door and her hands fell from me. The sounds of the outside room washed over me. Her chuckle followed me even over the sound of the booming music as I fled to the bathroom.

The slap rang out like a gunshot in the tiled facility.

"I didn't do anything!"

Tori wiped off my earlobe and exhibited a lipstick-smeared finger. "Then what's this?"

Damning is what it was, but I couldn't say that. She didn't give me time to say anything. She slammed out of the bathroom leaving me with a smarting cheek, a dripping face, a towel in my hands and an audience of other interested dancers. This gig was not turning out at all the way I'd planned.

"Here, allow me." The girl whose assistance I'd come to on the balcony claimed the towel from my hands and patted my face dry. One of the others took over cleaning the rest of the lipstick off my ear.

I was surrounded by an ocean of beauty, smothered by soft touches and softer hands. This would be a fantasy of several people of my acquaintance. I didn't want any of them! I tried to push through them gently, politely. That wasn't easy when the ladies were determined and there was so much bare flesh on display. I mean, where do you put your hands? I finally stuffed them in my pants pockets and let them get on with it. It seemed by far the quickest way to get it over with and provoke no one.

The story of my disarming the two hotheads had done the rounds quickly. Among the girls, I was the hero of the hour. Getting away wasn't going to be easy.

Another idiot customer provided me with an escape. He barged into the bathroom with hands outstretched to grab. The massed girls cried out and backed away. I moved between them and forced the idiot's arm up his back and frog-marched him out. It wouldn't do my reputation any harm, but it would make my life difficult if I got cornered by the ladies again. By the time I'd escorted him off the premises, there was no sign of Tori. Miserably, I went back to work.

Unfortunately, after that I was in great demand to sit in the Star rooms. I have never spent so many hours squirming in my life. Even the girls who were straight directed their attentions to me when they weren't facing the clients. (Teasing me or repaying me? I didn't know.) They knew that since I had to see that the men behaved themselves, I couldn't look away. If I had been unattached, I would have enjoyed it. As it was, their attentions were a torment.

It got worse.

Tori insisted I sit in on a private dance with a client. Unlike every other woman that night, she ignored me and directed her entire attention to the still sober man in the chair. Without contact, she did almost everything she would have done had we been in bed together and looked as if she was enjoying every minute of it, to punish me for my imagined transgression. Thank God the man never tried to touch her. By the end of the session, which seemed to go on forever, all I wanted to do was kill him.

He passed me wearing the same look I had given the man that had said he'd have given anything to fuck her. It's true: what goes around comes around. Remind me never to do smug.

She snapped off the stereo and started to get dressed. I couldn't look at her. When she had her clothes on she came over to me and tipped up my face.

"That really hurt you?" She seemed surprised. "Maybe I

71

don't know you as well as I thought I did."

Damn straight, she didn't! "I didn't do anything, Tori. I've never cheated on anyone in my life. I may be a lot of things, but a two-timer? Never! You saw what you wanted to see. You wouldn't let me explain."

I tried to get off the stool and leave. I didn't want her to see my hurt.

She wouldn't let me. She pushed me back into my seat and straddled me.

"I'm sorry. This whole business has got me turned around, mixed up and confused."

She was confused? What about me? I didn't know whether I was coming or going!

"Neither of us is thinking straight, Randall. Let me make it up to you…"

Her hands started doing things they shouldn't in a public place. Hyped up as my body was, there was no way I wouldn't lose it completely if she carried on like this. But if I told her to stop, would she accuse me of wanting someone else? Jesus, this was too much for me!

The door cracked open allowing in a blast of the music outside. Tori moved away, and the cashier asked, "Tori? You finished? Somebody wants the room."

"Be right out, Hank."

Hank gave me a speculative look, then closed the door again.

I used the pause to stand, rearrange my clothes, try and regain some perspective. When Tori came at me again, I kept some distance between us.

It was her turn to look hurt.

"Randall…"

"I have a job to do. If I don't get out there and do it I'll get fired. I've never been fired. It would reflect badly on my professional reputation. It won't look good for Dean's business, either. I haven't got time to play games with you. I'm not made of stone. I can't watch you make love to somebody else and feel nothing! Any more than I can stop my body's reaction when other girls direct their dancing at me. It doesn't mean I want them. Even if they do try it on with me."

I put my hand on the door knob. "Think about that. And when you've thought about it, get back to me. I don't want this business, any of this business, to come between us. I love you."

And I let myself out.

I was shaking when I stepped outside. I don't like scenes, but I could not handle Tori blowing hot and cold on top of everything else.

Let somebody else sit in the Star rooms and get hot and bothered; I took myself back up to the balcony. I needed physical as well as mental distance from my problems. It really was a bad idea to get involved with your clients.

Somehow we all got through the remainder of the night. I didn't see anyone who was a definite candidate for Tori's rape. The customers went home. The girls went to get changed. The lights came all the way up. The cleaners got to work. The bouncers got paid.

I queued with the other suits outside the manager's office to get my cut. I didn't see my fan boy and no one spoke to me. They were still deciding whether I was the enemy or not.

"I see Lisa still isn't back," said the cretin I'd given the knife to. Lisa Moran was one of the dancers; Tori had mentioned her, a student on her gap year.

"Yeah, third night in a row. Dyke bitch, she's going to get her ass fired," said another guy.

I didn't say anything. Working here was going to be hard enough without picking a fight with my co-workers. But I took careful note of who had shown his colours, then made a point of changing the subject, introduced myself and set about putting faces to names. Among them were Villiers and Grey, the heroes from the balcony, and Vic, aka the prick. How appropriate.

When I reached the desk I noticed my pile of bills seemed higher than the others.

"What's this?" I asked.

"Bonus."

"For what?"

"Making sure there wasn't a bloodbath on the balcony."

I wondered why the youngster (at least I assumed it was him) had felt motivated to report my own words verbatim. I handed the extra back.

"I was just doing my job."

He licked his lips, looked uncomfortable, but accepted the money. A ripple of conversation started behind me. Crap. They'd think I was brown-nosing the boss. Oh well, too late now. As I turned to leave he said, "Can you wait? I'd like to talk to you about young Brian."

I frowned. The name meant nothing to me.

"The one who asked you to teach him? He's my son."

Ah; now it was crystal. But I had Tori to pick up. I hoped.

"Of course. I have some arrangements to make. I'll come back."

Tori was sitting on the edge of the stage, wearing her street clothes, swinging her legs so that her heels drummed on the hollow wood. She looked up at my approach.

I slowed. I admit I was hesitant.

She pushed herself off and stood before me toe to toe. For a moment, I thought she was going to slap me and walk away. The sharp pain I felt in my chest at the thought of that wasn't wholly physical. My mind began to scrabble about, hunting for things I could say to make her stay. But it was late. I was tired. Everything I came up with sounded hopeless.

When she slipped her arms around my waist beneath my jacket, laid her head on my shoulder and whispered, "I'm sorry," into my neck I almost wept with relief.

I closed my eyes, put my arms around her and held on tight.

"Will you take me home?"

"As long as you mean to my place."

She sighed. "Randall… "

"I promise I'll look at your locks tomorrow. Once I'm happy with your security I'll take you home, if you're so anxious to be rid of me."

Her hands began stroking my ribs. "Not that eager," she said giving me a look that boded well for what remained of the night. "Remember what I said about women in a tux?"

I swallowed and nodded. She smiled. My knees began to weaken in anticipation. "Tor…" I coughed and started again and her grin got wider. "Tori, your boss wants a word with me about his son."

She looked thoughtful. I wondered if this had anything to do with her. What she actually said was, "Young Brian? I thought I saw you talking to him earlier. What does B Senior want?"

"I don't know. It might be to do with that business on the balcony."

She grimaced. "I heard. A knife and a broken bottle! What a way to start a job!"

"I've had worse. At least neither of the fools knew what to do with them. What I'm getting at is, this might take a while."

"I'll go and have a natter with some of the girls. They are not all anxious to go home. They don't all have such understanding partners to go home to."

I've been there. She kissed the tip of my chin and vaulted back on to the stage. "Go on," she said with a smile. "You know where to find me when you're finished."

Brian Senior, as Tori had called him, was busy filling out what my elementary knowledge of accounts told me was a day book when I presented myself at the open door of his office. He set his pen down in that prissy way compulsive tidiness addicts have, closed the book, then aligned it perfectly on his desk before gesturing me to a seat. "And close the door," he said as an afterthought.

He ground out the stub of a slim cigar in an already crowded ashtray. "Brian says you've given him an address."

"Yes."

This wasn't why I was here, but I wasn't going to help him. We'd get to the real reason he wanted to speak to me a lot faster if I didn't encourage padding. Dean's the subtle one; I go straight for the throat.

"What does this place do?"

"It's a gym."

"They train you to fight?"

"They can train people to fight. They teach martial arts, boxing and self-defence."

"That why you go there?"

"No."

"They train bodyguards?"

"There is no training for that."

That's not entirely true. Police and ex-military men run courses on bomb disposal and self-defence, for officers who guard political officials. And there are private courses.

I've done both. They can impart the mechanics, but no one can train you to stand in the line of fire for a stranger. You've either got it or you haven't.

Brian Senior knew what I meant. "You think it will help him?"

"It will keep him alive and in one piece and make him reconsider his career choice."

"Best way I suppose. Kill or cure."

I wondered what Brian Junior thought, but I wasn't about to ask his father. If we'd exhausted the subject of his son, we could get down to the business at hand.

"You still work for that PI?"

"With, not for. Yes, I do."

"Ah."

"Do you need help or advice?"

"Do both cost me?"

"Help does. Advice is free. I might advise you to get help, depending on the problem."

"The girls. There have been… difficulties."

"Difficulties?"

"Some of the girls have been followed. One of the girls seems to be missing. At least, nobody's heard from her in a few days."

Lisa of the malicious gossip?

"And some have been attacked."

"How many?"

"Definitely three, maybe four."

Five, I thought. Dean was going to be insufferable if they were connected.

"Most have boyfriends, some are married. Their blokes usually pick them up. Some of the girls, ones that live nearby, have said they've heard footsteps following them, or laughter. One had her house broken into, though that might not be related. One girl got knocked down and beaten after getting out of her taxi! Another one got raped. No one saw their attackers."

"Have they reported it?"

"No."

I gave him The Look. He squirmed, then tried for defensive. "Look, the law don't take it seriously when exotic dancers get assaulted. Even if they catch the bastard that did it, when they get him to court he pleads enticement. Mitigating circumstances. Provocation. The buggers always get off! We might have the Chief Super as a member, but he's about as much use as a chocolate fireguard when it comes to getting a conviction against what even he sees as offences against sex industry workers. The girls might as well be prossies for all the police care."

"So you haven't spoken to him?"

"Nobody speaks to him! Except the girl he's paying to sit in his lap or serve his bloody single malt."

"Why me? Why now?"

"The lads saw what you did tonight and word's got round. They respect you. The girls have seen you in action first hand. They like you. They think they can trust you."

I wish people wouldn't look so surprised when they say that!

"When they found out what you do for a living, they asked me to speak to you."

"Are any of them willing to speak to me personally? Tell me in detail what happened?"

He looked uncomfortable again. "They might be."

"Has anything been attempted to put a stop to this? Find out who's behind it?"

"Things like this do happen from time to time; they usually take care of themselves." I glared at him. "Some of the lads have taken to seeing a few of the girls home."

"And that's it?"

"Some of the girls live too far out of the way."

And some of the girls wouldn't want the added hassle of getting rid of a bouncer who thought he should be 'paid' for his services.

"So how did you get involved? It certainly isn't out of the goodness of your heart. And why haven't any of them approached someone privately to get help?"

Now he was really squirming. Understanding dawned. "Do you have a clause written into their contracts forbidding legal interference?"

"Everybody does! How else would clubs like this run? If all the girls screamed about harassment, I'd have no staff and no money before you could snap your fingers!"

"So what's changed?"

He tried to bluster. I stood up and slammed my palms on the table.

"Cut the crap! Why are you asking for help now?"

"Because they've threatened to leave if I don't!" he roared. "And your bloody girlfriend's the ringleader!"

I blinked then sat down.

I hadn't expected that. Had Tori known about the others, but been hampered by the clause which would get them fired? Had her own experience forced the issue? Remembering her plaintive words of the day before, I couldn't see it.

More likely she'd mentioned something, inadvertently, to one of the other dancers, which had opened the floodgates to other revelations. Four of them. I winced.

Seeing she was not alone, and that the perpetrator wasn't showing any signs of stopping, perhaps she'd had a change of heart? Decided to enlist my help on behalf of everyone? Lately I was encountering the changeable nature of women more and more. I see why it makes men crazy. Until now I never realised how much I thought like a man.

Brian Senior was looking at me expectantly. I was damned if I was going to apologise for Tori. Not when she was finally doing the right thing. But something needed to be done, right away, to protect the girls.

"There are a couple of things they can do, cheaply, in the short term. But if they want this menace gone, that will require proper detective work and real money."

His turn to wince.

"It's your problem in so much as you'll lose your dancers if it doesn't stop. See if they're willing to talk to me. Then I'll have some idea what needs doing and be able to give them an estimate of what it will cost. If they club together the fee won't be insurmountable. We don't charge the earth. I'll be in tomorrow. You can tell me their decision then."

I stood again. "Even if you don't decide to employ me for more than my brawn, I'll give you the name of a bonded cab company. The drivers are built like Mack Trucks."

His eyes lit up at the sound of that.

"Before you get your hopes up – while they're happy to check out the house and escort the girl safely inside, if they do have to fight their fee goes up. If they get injured, the client has to pay their private hospital bills. If they have to perform the same service for the same client twice and get injured again, they terminate the contract. They're not bodyguards. They don't get paid enough to take serious damage. They're just a few blokes who don't mind helping people in trouble."

He looked thoughtful. "I'll mention it to the girls."

"You do that."

The air in the club was redolent of stale cigarette smoke, disinfectant and air freshener. With the lights out, cleaners and clients gone, bouncers and bar staff absent, dancers and music stilled, it was a different place. I picked my way across the dimly lit mezzanine between tables with upturned chairs on top, and scrambled on to the stage with less agility than Tori.

It was getting on for three-thirty in the morning. The cooling atmosphere made my bones ache. I rolled my neck and heard it pop as I pushed through a tinsel strip curtain to reach the dressing room backstage. Nothing made me want to take a twirl on the boards.

I rapped twice on the plain wood door. It opened under my hand almost before my second knock was complete. The wary expression on the opener's face melted into welcome on seeing me. I wondered what or who she had been expecting that had her so worried. The Asian girl who'd got me into so much trouble smiled and stepped aside to allow my entry. I wasn't sure if I should.

Tori took my hand and drew me into the cramped dressing room. With only the five of us it was a squeeze. God knew what it was like when they were all there. Cigarette smoke didn't help. Reading my mind, the girl from the balcony said, "We don't all use it at once. Some of us change in the toilets, it's quicker."

"It just seems so..." I struggled for a word – "tawdry, for what you do."

A raven-haired Cher wannabe blew a plume of smoke from her pouty lips, regarding me over her cigarette. Her look was frankly sexual. Though I felt the heat creep up my collar, my skin crawled. There was something wrong with this picture and I didn't know what it was.

"I like her, Tori," she said. "Throw her my way when you've finished with her."

"Stop it, Sammi. This one's mine."

Tori kissed me possessively – open-mouthed – to prove her point.

Catcalls and wolf whistles brought me back from dreamland as Tori let me go. My breath was slow coming back. I set aside contemplation of Sammi's subtle wrongness. Tori grinned wickedly and mouthed *later*. My internal barometer rocketed another ten degrees.

She turned to her comrades brightly and said, "We have to be going."

I found myself looking at a room full of very nervous women. It didn't take a detective to know I'd found the other victims. Even the promise of sex with Tori could not make me leave ladies in need like that. Chivalry wouldn't let me walk away.

"Can I give anyone a lift home?"

Sammi and the Asian girl, Liu, fell all over me with gratitude. The girl from the balcony looked less happy. "I live in Garstang. I can't ask you to go all that way at this time of the morning, not after you've dropped Liu in Ansdell and Sammi in Bispham."

She had a point. But I couldn't just leave her. "Is there a phone I could use?"

Four mobiles were thrust at me. I accepted one from the lady from Garstang and stabbed a ten digit number into the keypad. There was a moment of silence, then the call connected. It was answered after the first ring.

"White Knights?"

"Hi, Virg. Are you busy?"

"We can always find time to help a lady in need. Who,

82

when and where?"

"I need a Knight to the Bird Of Paradise ASAP. One pickup. Destination Garstang. The full monty: escort, check out, check in, possible eject."

"Nil problemo. Alan's in that neck of the woods. ETA ten minutes. Do you?"

"Perfect. You're a prince. Thanks."

"Anytime. Always a pleasure doing business with you, Sensei."

I laughed as he cut the connection.

I explained about the White Knights enterprise as we made our way upstairs. It was set up three years ago by a group of ex-bodyguards. The eclectic group were brothers and – probably not coincidentally – shared first names with the Tracy boys of the Thunderbirds series. After toying with the idea behind International Rescue, they came up with a non-copyright logo that expressed the same sympathies.

They were good. Dean and I had used their service many times. They were reliable, never overcharged and were well able to take care of themselves. I knew. I'd mentored their karate class myself. Hence the nickname, Sensei.

Joy, the lady from Garstang, was wary of accepting any of this at face value – until Alan pulled up in his armour-plated limo. Then Liu begged to stay the night with her, cadged a ride and everything was settled.

We made our way to my car and watched them pull away. Brian Senior locked up behind us. He bade us a muffled good night from the depths of his high-collared ski jacket, then stomped across the car park to his BMW. He didn't look happy to see me unlocking a Porsche. I wasn't about to tell him it's not genuine. It's a kit car received in payment for my first professional job.

I'd just got Tori installed in the front passenger seat and tipped up the driver's seat to let Sammi climb into the back, when something sparkled through the air towards us.

Tori shrieked. Sammi's eyes opened wide in terror. Training kicked in. I stepped into the object's path and snatched it out of the air. A flick knife.

Tori began climbing out of the car to come to me, but I barked, "Stay there!"

She shut the door with alacrity. I practically shoved Sammi into the back, dropped the seat behind her and hit the headlights. It would ruin the night vision of anyone planning to aim anything else, and might show me my attacker – whose identity the weapon had more or less given away.

Either the guy from the balcony had got his knife back, his friend had an exact duplicate, or the bouncer I'd embarrassed had decided to pay me back for the insult. I didn't think it was the clientele.

I couldn't see anyone. The sound of Brian Senior's engine as he turned it over, oblivious to our little drama, drowned out any sound of running feet. I swore and climbed into the car.

I tossed the knife into the glove compartment in front of a white-faced Tori, then jammed the keys into the ignition and started the car.

"Bispham?"

"Yes. Red Bank Road. The promenade end, near the shops."

I nodded and we got under way.

We were ghosting along a deserted promenade when Tori found her voice. "You're bleeding."

"What?"

"You're bleeding."

I'd been so angry I hadn't noticed the cut. It wasn't deep, but it was insistent. I took my injured hand from the wheel and fumbled towards a pocket. Tori pulled out a handkerchief before I could ruin the suit and carefully bound it up while I drove one-handed. Power steering is a wonderful thing.

"Thanks."

"You're welcome."

"That was the most amazing thing I've ever seen!"

Sammi's voice almost sent me through the ceiling. I'd forgotten she was there.

"Sorry." She didn't sound in any way contrite. She and Liu were two of a kind.

I suddenly found my job and my prowess being promoted ardently by an unpaid advertiser. Tori twittered excruciatingly all the way to Bispham, allowing neither of us to get a word in edgeways.

I was confused all over again. She sounded like my greatest fan. This from the girl who didn't want anything to do with my violent world? She was making me out to be James Bond or something! Maybe it was the tux? I really don't understand women.

Outside Sammi's bed-sit I locked Tori in the car until I'd checked the place to my satisfaction. Sammi's security was pretty tight. I just made it back to the car without being groped - is nobody straight any more? - escaping with only a grateful lipstick smear. Tori cut me off in mid-explanation, with more understanding than the last time.

"She thinks you saved her life. Of course she kissed you! Anyway, you were visible at all the windows while you were checking the inside. And you weren't absent long enough to take advantage of her, even if she wasn't a trans. I know how you feel about that."

That explained the wrongness I'd been sensing. I knew her legs were too damn perfect! And no matter how well the transition goes, you can't change pheromones. She still smelled male to me.

"Er, thanks, I think."

"Can we go home now? I'm really tired. I need a shower before I can even think about going to sleep. I stink of secondhand cigarette smoke and other people's booze."

"Of course." I started the car. I was anxious to grill her about her change of heart and this might be the perfect time.

"And I'd like to take a look at your hand in better light."

"It's nothing, really."

"It should still be cleaned properly, you don't want it to infect."

"Whatever you say, nurse!"

She drilled me in the ribs with one taloned finger. I grunted with mock pain.

"And I'd like to fuck your brains out while you still have that tux on."

I nearly swerved into a lamppost. She chuckled wickedly.

"Home, Parker!"

"Yus, milady!"

I managed to get us home in one piece.

She took a look at my cut.

I did not manage to find out why she'd changed her mind about investigating the rape.

We eventually got around to that shower.

And sex in a tux is something else!

6

"Randall, you've got to come!"

"I'm in the shower, babe."

"Randall, please! I need you."

I wish I could say she was calling me because she wanted sex! It wasn't that. The tone of her voice through the door sounded scared. After what she'd been through, I wasn't about to refuse any reasonable request. So I switched off the water, swathed myself in a bath towel and shot the bolt.

Tori grabbed my arm and dragged me into the lounge, pointing at the news programme showing on the television. I just had time to notice that her face was drawn and pale before what the reporter was saying penetrated and I gave all my attention to the screen.

"…early this morning. The mutilated body of Lisa Valerie Moran was found bound and gagged on the floor of her rented flat in Waterloo Road, Blackpool. She was discovered by her landlady, Eileen Stokes, after neighbours reported an unpleasant odour coming from the flat.

"Miss Moran, twenty-three and a student at the London School of Economics, was here on a working holiday. She had been living in Blackpool for five months and had few friends outside of work and no family in the area, so her disappearance went largely unnoticed.

"She had been absent from her vacation job, as an exotic dancer at the Bird Of Paradise Club, for several days, causing concern amongst her colleagues, who said she had previously been a punctual and regular attendee.

"Mrs Stokes, Miss Moran's parents – Mr and Mrs Steven

Moran – and her employer Mr Brian Jones, proprietor of the Bird Of Paradise, are currently assisting the police in building a more complete picture of Miss Moran's life. The police will be speaking to her fellow workers and anyone else who thinks they might have useful information. They have no suspects at this time…"

Not getting an argument about why she should stay at my place should have made me feel better. It didn't, not when the price of Tori's compliance was another girl's life and fear for her own. Holding her while she shook and fell apart, undoing all the work she'd put in two days before, left me feeling frustrated and useless. I didn't care what it took we had to find out who was responsible.

I'd have to fill Dean in about this new development, as well as Brian Senior's revelations of the night before. Especially if the ladies from the Paradise did decide to employ us. This was the kind of complication that could put us all in jeopardy, and not something that should be discussed over the phone. Especially not with my distraught girlfriend in earshot.

I calmed her down. I was just wondering where to go from here when she said, "Would you mind if I invited the girls over? I'm sure they'll want to talk about this. If the police do come looking for us, it would be better if we were all in one place, don't you think?"

Actually, I didn't. The local constabulary might not be Scotland Yard, but even they would wonder if it wasn't an attempt by the perpetrator to set their story straight or establish an alibi. I wasn't going to tell her that. If she hadn't thought of it herself, I wasn't going to suggest anyone she knew might be a murderer as well as a rapist. And her outrage and indignation would be genuine when the detectives who questioned her suggested as much.

So I agreed. I even ferried them over.

I was tempted to stay, surrounded by this ocean of beauty, but I remembered the trouble that had got me into last night. The smell of conflicting perfumes became cloying, and there were too many people in the room. I began to feel claustrophobic. And girl talk? I can't do girl talk. I made my goodbyes and left, secure in the thought that, even if the killer was amongst them, surrounded by so many people Tori would be safe.

As often happened, I ran into Cecily on the landing. I swear she sits behind the door and watches through the spy-eye for me coming and going alone. I mean, where was she when Tori was seeing me off with a passionate thank-you for fetching her friends? And why wasn't the bitch at work?

"An orgy, Randall? I'd never have guessed that milksop Victoria could make you so bold! Or is it just that you were the only man in the room?"

"Go fuck yourself, Cecily."

"I do, Randall, I do, when Ashley's not around to do it for me. You wouldn't believe the number of vibrators I've burned out, the batteries I've exhausted, dreaming of you."

Shit, what do you say to something like that?

She stroked her lacquered talons, lilac today, over the creamy expanse of flesh at her throat, towards the pearl buttons of her shimmering satin shirt.

My eyes followed their progress of their own volition. I forced them back to her face. She was – damn her – smiling. The job, the situation I found myself in, was leaving me in an almost constant state of arousal. Her signature perfume Samsara stole over me making it worse. Cecily read me easily and took advantage of the situation.

"Poor baby! Has Tori sent you away while she plays?

Is that why you're frustrated? You can come and play with me."

"Some of us have to work."

"Some of us get to choose when we work from home."

I straightened my back, turned and walked towards the stairs. Off guard, Cecily was too slow to block my way. Not to be outdone, her voice drifted after me as I descended.

"The strong silent type. I've always liked that about you, Randall."

Coming from her the compliment tasted like ashes. At least I had the satisfaction of slamming the door on her as she had on me the day before. Yet it felt like a hollow victory.

I changed gear with more force than it deserved. I was rewarded with an unpleasant grinding sound, as the car protested at my taking out my own shortcomings on the gearbox.

Fuck it! I had more important things to worry about than my screwed-up desires.

Finding a parking space in this town after midday is impossible. I finally left the Porsche clone in the multi-storey on top of Wilkinson's. I wasn't sanguine about my chances of it being in one piece when I got back, but I didn't have much choice. I hiked back through the drizzling rain to the office.

Rain and the Illuminations. It never fails.

Dean was hard at work, typing a report on my desktop PC while he argued about something completely different over the hands-free phone.

There was nobody was in the tiny waiting room and the appointment diary showed me there were no client consultations for at least the next hour. I stuck a Back In

Ten Minutes sign on the door to discourage potential drop-ins and waited until he was free.

Stabbing the cut-off button, he threw the headset into the waste paper basket with a curse vituperative enough to curl hair, pounded a few more words on to the keyboard, then spun his swivel chair to face me.

"I wasn't expecting you today. They let you out early at the zoo?"

I rescued the headset and hit Save with the mouse in passing.

"Nope. I didn't get home till after four. I thought I'd come down and buy you lunch."

He snorted.

"Aside from the fact that your idea of lunch is Chinese take-away, the only time you ever volunteer to pay is when you need a favour."

"They don't call you a detective for nothing. I'm speech-less at your awesome powers! I cower in the shadow of your wisdom! Teach me, master!"

"Fuck off, Randall! You're not getting round me that easily. Besides I've already eaten. As if you didn't know."

I grinned. The take-out I'd picked up on my way was in the waiting room. I fetched it, and watched Dean grimace as I broke open the disposable plastic chopsticks and opened a carton of stir-fried bean sprouts with noodles. I could see I'd got his attention as well as piqued his curiosity.

Between mouthfuls I filled him in on what had happened last night while the printer chattered out his report in the background. His expression became grimmer as I went on. When I reached the part about this morning's news about the missing (now deceased) dancer, he got up and began to pace.

"Do you think they'll employ us to investigate this officially?"

"I hope so. Tori's having a council of war with the ladies in my living room right now. I'll try and get her name on the contract. If it comes to it, I'll sign it myself."

"Don't be stupid, Randall, you know you can't. Legally, we wouldn't have a leg to stand on. And with this latest wrinkle we'll probably need all the help we can get."

My business partner was no happier with the idea of getting caught up in a murder enquiry than I was. And not because of the possible danger to his own life and limbs. The police really do hate 'amateurs' messing about in (or messing up) investigations, and the local plod has less cause to like us than most.

In summer we'd taken on a case that looked like industrial espionage, only to have it blow up in our faces. Several people died. If I hadn't abseiled off the Tower in a bid to save Dean's neck and draw the murderer out, I might have been in prison myself. Dean had been careful not to take on ugly cases, or step on any of the Constabulary's toes since then.

"Make sure one of the girls signs the contract. And it would be better if it wasn't Tori. Make sure we get a firm commitment from them to pay us. Cash or cheque in advance if you can get it. I know you've got a personal stake in this. Hell! I like Tori, even if I don't agree with what she does for a living. She's good for you! But we can't afford to work for free."

"Message received and understood."

"From what you've told me, the incidents might not be connected. It's seldom that someone vandalises, stalks, makes an attack in so public a fashion, commits murder and then rapes. Unless they wanted to throw someone off the scent. The events can't have been reported in chronological order."

He scrubbed his hand over his close clipped hair and poured himself a tiny cup of his personal addiction: Turkish coffee, strong, sweet and thick.

Dean liked the idea of the hard boiled PI image as propounded by Dire Straits song *Private Investigations.* Unfortunately, he wasn't cut out for it. He couldn't stand whisky and he thought Venetian blinds were passé.

Instead for ambience he relied on the smell of coffee strong enough to stand your spoon up in, bought from a European café across the road and kept in an insulated jug that looked remarkably like an authentic ragweh. (And as it happened, sold by a very cute guy. Dean doesn't fancy him at all, but the idea that he might keeps Craig attentive. A plus I'm sure he thought of in advance.)

He took a small sip, savoured the brew and slowly let it trickle down his throat as he ordered his thoughts. He's not a psychologist, but he is a student of human nature, a careful observer and very good at what he does. I've learned to rely on his instincts.

"The murder must have happened before Tori was raped, not afterwards. For the neighbours to be reporting the smell of decomposition, the body must have been there for some time. We know the girl had definitely been missing for five days?"

I nodded. He had me give him precise details from the TV broadcast again. He scribbled hasty computations on a yellow legal pad, a hold-over from his time as a solicitor.

"She must have dropped out of sight before that. Like the reporter said, with no friends or family to check up on her, that's easily done. It sounds as if she's been dead more than a week. Which places her murder long before Tori's rape – that's if both crimes were committed by the same person."

He tapped the mechanical pencil against his perfect teeth. "And I'm not convinced they were. I'm not saying women are incapable of murder, we both know that isn't true! They're just less likely to kill. And they use subtle things like poison. Found weapons like scissors. Heavy household appliances. Or a weapon that has meaning to the victim. A favourite golfing trophy or paperweight. The victim was bound, gagged and badly mutilated, according to the news report?" I nodded. "Then she would have struggled. If the crime had been committed in her home, someone would have heard something. She lives in a flat. Their walls are paper thin."

"I'd agree with you if I hadn't seen the state of Tori's place. That looked like a bomb had hit it and no one reported hearing anything about that."

He waved that away.

"Smashing or breaking sounds can be muted by determined vandals. Carefully timed. Done when everyone was out. Disguised as furniture moving. Unlike Tori's place, Waterloo Road flats are holiday lets, OAP bed-sits and accommodation for the unemployed. There is someone at home in most of the buildings in that area nearly all the time. It's unlikely she was killed in situ. Someone would have seen or heard something. And the smell of blood would have come through a great deal faster than the smell of a decomposing body."

I bagged the remains of my lunch and bulls-eyed the waste paper basket, appetite gone.

Dean continued, "I'll ask my friends at the Evening Post and Gazette for the low-down. Perhaps they'll be able to shed more light on how she died. Give us a time line.

If Mrs Stokes is the typical Blackpool landlady, rather than being cagey she'll be playing it for all it's worth."

That was probably true. The police would have more trouble shutting her up than getting a statement. Everyone wants their fifteen minutes of fame.

In deference to my digestion, he changed the subject. "How are you managing at the club?"

I considered my answer.

"It's not as straightforward as I first thought. Physically, it's less demanding than I'm used to. Mentally and emotionally, it's something else."

"Rather you than me! I couldn't manage to work in a male strip joint, even if I wasn't going out with one of the dancers. Craig and I would last about five minutes. You have my admiration for your self-control and willpower."

I wondered what he would have said if he could have seen the mess I'd got into last night. Dean's good impression of me means a great deal, so I said nothing.

Which brought me full circle to face my frustration. There was nothing we could do about the dead girl, or the other attacks at the club, until we got the contract signed. On the other hand…

"Look, I know we haven't got the official go-ahead to investigate this, but I was wondering… Even though Tori maintains she can't remember much about what happened to her, she smelled of perfume that wasn't hers and was raped with things other than what nature provided. I know this could mean the guy's impotent, or just wanted to be even more cruel, but do you suppose it might be worth looking at her ex-girlfriends? There were only two and…"

"I thought you might say something like that, so I took the liberty."

He looked back mildly as I stared at him.

"I couldn't have you haring about ripping their arms and legs off before we knew if they were involved. This is your girlfriend we're talking about! You haven't got enough perspective. I saw you at her flat the other night, remember?"

I had to fight the urge to hit something again, which I suppose proved Dean's point. I swallowed my chagrin that he'd taken this away from me and asked, "And?"

"They couldn't have done it. One's out of the country till Friday. On holiday with her parents, on a cruise for the last three weeks. The other has moved away, and I have it on good authority that she's been in hospital with multiple broken bones since the day before Tori's attack. Climbing accident. She fell off the side of a mountain. I've checked everything as thoroughly as I can. There's no way, Randall. I'm sorry."

"I'll try and talk to Tori. See if she remembers anything that might help. If I can think of a way to do it without upsetting her."

"Don't be too hard on her, Randall. That kind of experience is something you want to block out. You can't blame her if she just wants to put it behind her and get on with her life."

She'd said as much to me the other day.

Dean sipped his coffee, stacked his report and watched with thinly disguised amusement as I sat spinning my wheels. He knows I'm not much for hanging about doing nothing. Finally I asked him whether there was any business here that needed my attention.

"Your former client phoned and apologised for wasting our time. He's paid us the minimum fee for staying on standby."

That was good to know. Money for nothin'. Just how I liked it.

"The other actual investigations we've got on hand are ticking over without any help from either of us."

In other words, we were at the 'awaiting developments' stage. It sometimes seems to me that ninety percent of the detective game involves sitting around waiting for something to happen.

Just as I thought I'd have to brave the wet streets and squeeze back into my crowded apartment for an hour or two before checking out Tori's flat, he threw me a bone.

"If you can manage to call back for a couple of hours this afternoon, we have a possible Principal who wants to talk Personal Protection with you. It doesn't look like the hours will clash with the ones you're putting in on Spink's behalf."

"You waited to spring that on me till now?"

"Sometimes I like to watch you squirm."

"Cheers! What time?"

"If you could be back here by four?"

"No problem."

He gave me the once over.

My job means I go through a lot of clothes. I have to buy three suits, same style, same colour, so I can mix and match jackets with pants as they get ruined. I never have to worry about wearing last season's fashions. Nothing I have lasts that long. Because I was fixing up Tori's flat, today I was wearing jeans.

"I take it this is a suit and tie job?"

"That might be appropriate. It's the local Liberal Democrat MP."

"Bloody hell! He isn't exactly Mr Popular! I know why he thinks he needs a bodyguard. But his politics don't conflict with mine... All right, I'll be here."

"One more thing. Are they paying you at this club?"

"The going rate for bouncers, yes."

"And what is that, exactly?"

I told him.

"You're worth more than that!"

"Thanks. When I'm doing more to justify it, I'll ask for a raise. For now I think it's important to be 'one of the boys'. The manager knows if they employ us to find the nut or nutters it won't be cheap. I've suggested all the girls involved ante-up towards the fee. He's promised to put it to them tonight. Besides, staying on as a bouncer for long wouldn't be very good for my health."

Bouncers in this town are run by the small-time equivalent of the Mob. Independents get muscled out. Permanently. It was only because I was filling in for Leon Spink that I'd been left alone. Apart from the knife thrower. I hadn't mentioned the incident to Dean. But that bouncer and I were going to have words.

I started collecting up the tools, wire, sensors and alarms I needed to make Tori's apartment secure. "I'll see you this afternoon."

He turned back to his work and I left to make Tori's flat safe.

Before you start thinking 'cowboy,' let me tell you I know what I'm doing when it comes to installing alarms. After Dean took me on as a partner, it quickly became obvious the business wasn't going to support us both all the time. In one of my rare flashes of brilliance, I'd suggested, since I already dealt in Personal Protection – we could stretch a point and expand to protecting homes and offices - with dogs, security guards and bouncers or by electronic means.

In our spare time, we take courses, visit suppliers and manufacturers and encourage them to visit us with samples, and after a City And Guilds in electrical engineering, yours truly can now fit and advise on home protection for our clients. It's proved a lucrative sideline. We've also built up contacts like White Knights, who help us out for knock-down prices as thanks for our referrals.

The rest of day flew by. I hadn't risen until eleven, due to the late night. Being the unofficial taxi for Tori's girl-friends, visiting Dean, changing the locks on the doors and windows in Tori's flat, fitting motion sensors, then the client interview, took me till nearly eight. I just had time for a bite to eat and another shower before it was back to the Paradise.

"Promise me you'll take it easy tomorrow," Tori scolded, flicking imaginary lint from the shoulder of my suit when we reached the top of the stairs.

"As far as I can with two jobs to do, I will. The politico needs me for four hours in the afternoon. I couldn't turn it down. The business needs the money."

She winced. "I'll see if I can persuade the girls to take you on."

"Thanks. I take it you had no luck this afternoon?"

"I wish!" She wrinkled her perfect brow in frustration. "They want to do something but they don't know what to do for the best. They're afraid something terrible is going to happen to them in one breath, then in the next they're sure it has nothing to do with them and they're safe! I'm beginning to see what they mean about democracies. At least in a dictatorship a decision gets made and things get done. How on earth does anything happen in a society where they make decisions by committee?"

I grinned. I'm sure my new client would have a few

things to say about that opinion.

I drove us to work, saw her to the dressing room and managed to avoid any perilous entanglements with the girls on the way back.

Walking the mezzanine, I headed for the balcony. I hadn't been up there long when Brian Junior caught up with me.

"Thank you for giving me that address."

"My pleasure."

"I really think it will help. They've enrolled me in a class on self-defence. They think it will 'suit the requirements of my position best.'"

"It's certainly what I'd have suggested, given that you want to go up against fools with weapons barehanded."

He smiled nervously. "I'm sure my dad will feel better about me doing this job if he thinks that I really know what I'm doing."

"I doubt that. Most parents worry about protecting their kids all their lives, no matter how old you get. But you might be right. It's good that you both still care what happens to one another."

He may not have heard the note of bitterness in my voice, because he took my words at face value. Either that or he chose not to pry.

He was making a polite withdrawal, when a nearby cry of 'Help here' was choked off. The pair of us moved on the disturbance. A mean drunk had his hands around the throat of one of the girls, across a table. I motioned Brian to get into his field of vision and keep him talking. I circled around behind him.

"You don't want to do that," young Brian said soothingly.

"Fuck off! You don't know shit!"

The drunk tightened his grip and the girl moaned in pain.

100

"Come on, mate, you hardly know the lass! I'm sure she's sorry for whatever she's said to upset you. Isn't that right?" He turned his attention to the girl. She tried to nod but could hardly move her head.

"Doesn't matter if she is!" the drunk slurred.

"Why don't you let the girl go and tell me what the problem is? I'll do my best to try and sort it out. I'm sure there is no need for this unpleasantness."

The drunk snarled, his attention all for Brian.

I moved in and hit him at the base of his skull. A combination of the drink and my blow put him out for the count. His hands spasmed and he released the hysterical girl before he slumped across the table.

I checked the girl's throat. She was OK, but she'd have a necklace of bruises for at least a week. I had Brian take her to the Ladies to cry and clean herself up.

When they were gone, I checked Sleeping Beauty. He'd have a headache but he'd live. I hoisted him over a shoulder and carried him outside. The doorman called him a cab, and he came round just before it arrived. I gave him a stiff lecture before sending him home. By the time I returned to the club, the girl had a feather boa around her neck and was sitting on a more considerate fellow's knee. Brian was keeping a close eye on the proceedings.

"Dad can be a bit bolshie if the girls don't seem to be pulling their weight," he said, explaining the speed of her recovery. "I'll watch over her for the rest of the night."

"Nobody will demand your presence elsewhere?"

"No. That's one of the few perks of being the boss's son," he admitted.

"You did a good job out there."

He beamed. "Thanks!"

"I haven't seen your dad around. He still helping the

police with their enquiries?"

Brian winced. "Yes. If you see him, I wouldn't mention it to him. It's a sore point. When he heard what had happened he went off his head! You'd have thought the girl had died just to spite him! 'The last thing we need with everything else going on!'" He shook his head. "That was about the only repeatable thing he said. I suggested he should watch where he aired that opinion, else the boys in blue would be asking him where he was on the night she was killed. He always tries to be seen as a respectable businessman. Now he's got the papers, the police and his bank managers all looking at him as if he was a glorified pimp."

Bang went my chances of getting him to throw his weight behind the suggestion that the girls employ us to look into the incidents.

Another bouncer beckoned further along the balcony.

"Sorry, gotta go."

"Of course. Have a better one."

"God, I hope so!"

The night was troublesome. It seemed that without the influence of a high-ranking police official among them, everybody was taken with the desire to misbehave. I spent more time breaking up fights than patrolling. I actually relished the few occasions I was asked to sit in the Star rooms for the breather it afforded.

By the two a m closing I still hadn't been called into the office for anything more significant than my pay. By then I was too tired and dispirited to pursue the issue of a contract.

Tori, too, was despondent. Either the general mood had rubbed off, or her own situation and Lisa Moran's death was weighing heavily on her mind. I didn't press her for reasons.

All the girls with no one to pick them up called for White Knights to take them home. I was just happy to drive Tori back to my place, shower and fall into bed beside her. Not even the promise of tuxedo sex could keep my eyes open a minute longer.

7

I scrambled on to the low wall surrounding the penultimate level of Blackpool Tower, clipping the rappelling line coiled around my waist to a piece of chicken wire, while he checked the position of his men and made sure there were no witnesses. I hid the line before he looked back.

"You're going to have to do this. I'm not going to make it easy for you. I've got more pride. And I don't think you can't afford the noise of shooting me without a silencer."

I thought for a minute I'd pushed him too far. That he'd call one of his thugs to do the job. But I'd read him right. He wasn't afraid of getting his hands dirty.

Snarling, he ran at me full tilt, palms out to push me off. I grabbed him as he barrelled into me. His momentum carried us both over the edge.

He screamed as he plummeted toward the roof.

Line played out. I spun end over end. Chicken wire stretching in slow motion as I fell…

I woke drenched in sweat, smothering a scream.

Tori slept peacefully on. For a moment I wanted to wake her up, needed someone to hold me after reliving my plunge from the Tower. Then I pulled myself together. Right now she needed me to be strong. And I needed to put that mess behind me.

I climbed carefully out of bed so that I didn't rouse her. It was still early but I was wide awake. Normally I sleep like the dead, don't dream anything that I can remember. When my body-clock has been disturbed, as it had by the hours this job demanded, I have nightmares, and relive some significant moment in my life - like that one – where

I've found myself facing certain death. In my line of work, that happens more than I'd like. As you can imagine, my dreams are fairly colourful.

I stripped out of my T-shirt and Calvins and stepped under a shower as hot as I could stand. Stinging needles of water eased away the last vestiges of the dream. By the time I emerged ten minutes later, I was almost fit company.

I'm not a morning person.

As Tori was still sleeping, I dressed in sweat-pants and a fresh T-shirt and took myself into the lounge/kitchen and swallowed down a multivitamin with orange juice.

I'm not a breakfast person either.

I fished my Walkman and a Bon Jovi tape from a drawer, then slid the exercise bench and bars out from their place beneath the sofa and the weights from the bottom cupboards of the kitchen cabinets. After a few warm-up stretches to *You Give Love A Bad Name*, I settled down to the steady mindlessness of lifting weights.

I was on side two of the tape, lying on my back, on the God-knows-how-many'th repetition, eyes closed, humming tunelessly along with *Living On A Prayer*, concentrating on my breathing, when I felt the air move. I opened my eyes in time to see Tori sweep past in a swirl of silk dressing gown to open the apartment door.

Sammi, Joy, Liu and two others girls whose names I didn't know tumbled inside. After their initial greetings for Tori, their eyes were all for me. They scurried over, cooing about my muscles and the healthy glow of my exertions, running their fingers over my slicked arms as if I was a prize heifer. I dropped the weights quickly enough to dent my cork floor and elicit the usual pounding on the ceiling from my landlord. I fled to the sounds of their laughter.

When I returned in my usual uniform of suit pants and silk shirt, Tori had collapsed the exercise bench, slipped it back under the sofa and rolled the weights across the floor to the cupboards. Putting them away gave me a few moments to force the blush from my skin before I had to face them again.

They were sitting quite primly, as if nothing had happened (maybe Tori had given them grief about it?) along my sofa and every available seat when I returned. I would have sat on the floor, but this felt like an official visit. I stood in a kind of parade rest, a stance you learn to adopt when you're spending any length of time on your feet, and tried to look capable.

"We're sorry to turn up unannounced," Joy began.

"And so early," Liu added.

"But we've made some decisions," from Sammi.

Then they allowed Tori to do the talking.

"Yesterday morning we got in touch with Lisa Moran's parents. We gave them our condolences and asked what was happening to Lisa's body when the authorities released it."

Of course, since it was a suspicious death, there would be an autopsy.

"You can sit by me," Sammi interrupted, revealing a miniscule space on the sofa.

"I'm fine, thanks," I assured her, determined not to get distracted.

"They're taking her home to Cambridge," Tori continued. "She'll be buried or cremated there. We didn't get into details. We're arranging a memorial service for her. It was our thought that you and Dean might want to come; you could sit with the bouncers, take a look at the guests who turn up. By now you know most of the cast in our lives. If someone is out of place or looks as if they're gloating instead of grieving, that might be a good place to start looking, don't you think?"

I did, but I sensed there was more to this impromptu gathering than throwing me that particular bone. I simply nodded and let her speak.

"We'd also like to employ you and Dean to look into what's been happening to us. Officially. We want to sign a contract."

"We've got the money," one of the unnamed girls said, opening a huge handbag. Stuffed full of twenty pound notes.

"Give me a minute and I'll print some contracts up." I went over to my PC and booted it up, gave the printer the appropriate commands and paper. While it got to work, I asked, "What changed your minds?"

"We've been watching you," Joy said. "We trust you. Tori's told us about what you do and… Well, you know about Lisa. We're scared. We don't want it to happen to us."

"I was sorry to hear about Lisa's death. I don't think I ever met her."

"She was new. She started after you came down to watch the last time, but before you became a bouncer at the club." This from Liu.

"You know we can't directly investigate Lisa's death, not without her parents' say-so?"

"I told them that, Randall," Tori replied. "After talking to them I'm sure you won't get it. You might find something out while you're looking into what's been happening to us. If it's the same person doing it."

"That's true. We'll have to hand it over to the police if we do. They don't take kindly to what they think of as amateurs tripping all over their investigation."

I collected the forms, logged off then turned back to the ladies to hand them out. "I take it none of you have been to the police about your own situations?"

There were a few uncomfortable and indignant looks. How much of their reluctance was Brian Senior's gag order? How much because they had some reason not to trust the police? And how much because they had something to hide?

I could see this wouldn't be easily resolved, even if the perpetrator was the same in all their crimes. Getting at the information and evidence to bring him – or her – to justice was going to be an uphill struggle, especially if they kept hiding things from me along the way.

"Look, I can't promise we won't have to turn over some of what you tell us to the authorities at some point, not if it will help them catch Lisa's killer."

"What about client confidentiality?"

I was tempted to tell Joy she'd been reading too much detective fiction, but I bit my tongue and explained patiently, "That doesn't always work. If the police think we're impeding the progress of their enquiry they can imprison us or subpoena our records. Like confiscating hardcore porn from a sex shop. If we keep everything above board, pass on what they need to know, look helpful, they leave us alone. For the most part your private business stays private. I'm not saying everything you tell me will be pertinent, but on the off chance that it might be, you have to be aware we can't conceal it. That would make us guilty of a crime too. Anybody who doesn't want to do this should leave now. It's all in the contract. Read it before you sign."

"Why are you making this so difficult? We came to you

for help!" This from another one of the unnamed girls.

"I'm not trying to make it any harder than it is. I know it's difficult for you to talk about things like burglaries, assaults, vandalism of your homes, or rape. You feel violated and rightly so! Tori will tell you that I haven't forced her to talk about what happened, I've let her deal with it in her own way. She's only said what she felt comfortable saying."

Tori nodded.

"But it wouldn't be legal or ethical if I let you sign under false pretences. Kindness doesn't come into it. After what you've been through I don't want you to feel trapped because I didn't explain something to you. If you say something in confidence that isn't pertinent it will stay between us. Nothing gets committed to paper that doesn't have to be."

Sammi looked at me. "Randall's right. She's just telling it how it is. Quit bitching and read the small print, Stace. Randall's telling you your rights, unlike the pigs."

I wasn't surprised to hear how negative Sammi was about the local constabulary.

"Why does it ask whether I have a criminal record?" Liu wondered.

What to say? I finally settled on, "So we can exclude your personal details from anything we pass on to the police if that will present a problem at a later stage."

It was also for our own records. If we didn't check our clients out, we could end up being used as the weapon to harass a completely innocent party. Knowing whether the person paying your bills was a victim or an abuser was a good place to start the investigation. Quite often the first place. Investigate the client before you investigate their story. Always.

I couldn't tell them that. The brighter ones among them had surely already come to that conclusion. It's what the police do. We operate the same way, albeit on a smaller scale. We can't afford to be any less impartial if we want to get at the truth, even though we are taking our clients' money.

Sammi wrote down a long string of convictions. I was happy to see her openness. Why lie? We'd find out. The internet means there's no such thing as secrets.

Most of them didn't feel they had anything to hide. They each read the terms and conditions, filled out the appropriate sections, together with a brief description of the complaint they wanted us to investigate, and signed the page. I signed below, dated it, then separated the duplicate and handed it back. Seeing their comrades so easily satisfied shamed the others into completing their own contracts. Once everyone had handed over the papers, I locked them in a drawer until I could get them to the office. Then I counted the money and wrote out a receipt. The money went into the drawer too. I'd take it to the bank the moment they were gone.

"What happens next?" Tori asked for all of them.

"We arrange appropriate times for interviews with each of you so you can tell us in detail what happened. It might help you to spend some time thinking about this, and putting some notes down to remind you of the salient points. Just as if you were going for a job interview. If you feel more comfortable, you can write the whole incident down, make a statement."

Some of them looked relieved.

"After we've read it, we'll discuss any points we're not clear on with you, and ask you questions to further open up the problem. This will give us a place to start. Once we have preliminary information and evidence, we'll begin the investigation. We may need to get back to you, so we'll use your mobile numbers to clarify any points. There may be times when we need you to come into the office. We'll arrange something that works for all of us."

"I don't know about the rest of you, but I don't feel comfortable talking to a man about what happened to me," Liu admitted. The others mumbled their agreement.

"OK, I'll see to it that I conduct the interviews, but I'll have to tape them. Dean is the real detective in this outfit, I'm still learning the job."

They seemed content. Having unburdened themselves of both problems and money they were reluctant to stay. Making polite farewells, they beat a retreat. I was left in a quiet apartment with only the smell of perfume and the dent in my floor to show for their presence.

Tori's arms slid around me from behind. She laid her head on my shoulder. "You OK? You seem shell-shocked."

"It's the suddenness of it all. Last night you told me they hadn't made a decision. Now I find we've got two more clients than I'd originally bargained for."

"Stace and Terri. They heard us talking and spilled the beans – told us they'd had stuff happen to them too. Watching you last night decided them. It's OK, isn't it?"

"Of course. Dean will be thrilled to see that much work and that much money drop into his lap." I thought about it. "You're sure it's the same kind of thing?"

"From what little they told me."

"It's not going to be difficult for you, is it? Having to talk about what happened? Once we've eliminated the obvious suspects we're going to have to go into things in more depth."

"It won't be easy, but if it stops this, it'll have been worth it.

Until I mentioned it to Sammi, I never knew it had happened to other people. Everyone at the club seems to confide in her. I wanted to keep it to myself, forget about it, get on with my life. You know."

I clasped her hands and squeezed them, saddened that she hadn't felt able to discuss this with me before the other girls got involved.

"Sammi made me realise it was important. What I'd seen and heard could be used to stop it from happening to anyone else. Staying quiet could allow it to happen to someone else! That would make me as responsible as the person who did it. I couldn't live with that."

"If it's any consolation, you've done the right thing."

"Thanks."

We stood like that a few moments longer then Tori disentangled herself and made noises about having a shower and getting ready to leave. I'd promised to take her back to her flat today. My time was going to be limited. I had to go into the office, rearrange the work schedule with Dean and bank the money before meeting my client at two.

An hour and a half later, after dropping off the contracts with Dean, giving him a sketchy explanation of the morning's events and leaving him to bank the money, I picked Tori up and drove her home.

She was happy with what I'd done at her flat. She tried to press money on me for it, and when I wouldn't let her she insisted she'd make it up in kind! I took her through the security arrangements, then she dragged me out shopping for new curtains and bedding to replace those ruined during the break-in. When we got back she insisted on christening the new bedding as part of making it up to me: an offer I couldn't refuse! Finally she cooked me an early lunch.

While this was all very sweet and domestic, it firmed my resolve never to live with anyone. Not even someone I cared about as much as Tori. I was looking forward to having my home to myself again. I'd relished the hour I spent on my own while Tori got ready to leave, setting my apartment to rights, eradicating sights and scents of another person's habitation and our impromptu visitors. I'm fond of my own company. Doing what I want when I want and how.

Tori had been sensible enough to say nothing. She didn't press me about living together. I liked to think her thoughts on the subject were the same as mine. Maybe she hoped she'd persuade me differently if she didn't nag?

I left Tori happily cleaning and restoring her home with the prospect of visits from her parents and friends and the promise that I would return for dinner if my client didn't keep me too late. Failing that, I told her she should eat without me and I'd pick her up to take her to the Paradise. Knowing she was as safe as I could make her, I forced myself to concentrate on my new client and the money that would keep the business afloat.

8

"You want to go round the council estates on Grange Park?"

The man was deranged.

"I'm told many people are at home during the day. A large proportion of the unemployed in this town live there," he said, plummy tones dripping feigned concern.

Dean looked pained. "Which is precisely why you shouldn't go there."

"I must go where the voting public is."

"Only if you want to get lynched," I muttered.

"Which is what you're supposed to be there to prevent."

Bugger! He had good hearing.

Dean glared at me. It was all right for him; he didn't have to risk life and limb going round Rider Haggard Court escorting a public school twit.

Things went downhill from there. The only reason I'd given the suggestion house room was the money he was offering. It was good. Very good.

The following afternoon I left Dean figuring out the schedules for our new clients, changed my clothes and joined my Principal, the Liberal Democrat MP, on a walk around one of the most dangerous parts of town with his entourage of flunkeys and hangers-on.

I wondered what the adventure writer would have made of his namesake as I shepherded my charges around young can-kicking children playing truant from school and steered them clear of proto-gang adolescents, to the centre of a grass verge strewn with dog shit.

This is the sort of place where if you're fortunate

enough to find the chassis when you get back. The car will be on blocks and someone will have nicked the wheels, battery, stereo and anything else not bolted down.

We'd left his campaign bus four streets away. Which made me popular with his flunkeys who had to lug the PA system. I offered to help until we got to a workable spot, but as his lordship pointed out, I couldn't do much protecting with my hands full.

Setting up beside an empty Glasdon bin, he checked the sound level and started his pitch. He sounded convincing. Pity he didn't believe a word of it.

Then he held babies, posed for pictures, fielded heckling and answered questions from the people he drew from the flats.

They were as fascinated by the bulge of Kevlar under my jacket as they were with anything he said. Body armour was unusual, even around here. I stood more or less in front of him, (possible, as I'm not tall and he was) while he orated. His wage slaves with the sound system protected his back.

Time to leave. We started for the car.

A guy in a filthy barbour staggered out of an alley in front of us talking to himself. His smell preceded him. The MP's flunkeys, products of a lifetime ignoring oddballs on the London Underground, pretended the apparition wasn't there and hurried on. My Principal was not so well prepared. Either never having seen the like in his privileged life, or so high on his success that he saw another opportunity to proselytise, he hailed the fragrant vagrant.

"Excuse me. Yes, you, sir! Might I ask what brought you to this pass? Could it be…"

I didn't listen to any more. I was already moving. When

Stinky (not very PC, but this was hardly the time) turned around, shaken out of his own little world, I saw how wide the pupils of his eyes were dilated. This hopped-up hobo wasn't going to take any bullshit from a politico. Not even one as slick as my Principal.

I got in front of him and threw an arm across his face just as the crackhead lunged forward. From beneath his coat he pulled a knife as long as my forearm. It skidded along one of the leather protectors that fit from my wrist to elbow adapted from archers' bracers.

It cut a slice through the fleshy part of my arm over the triceps, scoring across the muscle. "Go!" I roared, pushing the stammering MP towards the car.

You shouldn't yell at your clients, but my purpose was twofold: galvanise the Principal into action and scare the druggie. Blood spattered the pavement. Mine. The MP fled, cronies in hot pursuit.

I had no one to protect but myself. I concentrated on disarming the headcase. My yell had given him pause. He staggered back, blinking. I didn't wait to find out if another attack was forthcoming. I kicked the knife out of his hand. He nursed his wrist, swearing.

The blade clattered into someone's front garden. Net curtains twitched, but self-preservation kept the house-holder inside.

Stinky turned tail and lurched back down the alleyway. I toyed with pursuit but let it go. I had a job to do. Following a nutter wasn't it.

I started to reach over the gate to secure the knife when a mutt the size of a pony raced into the garden. I decided if the hell-hound wanted the knife that badly he could keep it. I backed off before it hurdled the gate and added to my bleeding.

Back at the car, I jammed an oversized handkerchief on to the wound, exerting firm pressure the way you're supposed to, until I could get it looked at. I wasn't looking forward to what came next. The knife had been as filthy as its wielder. That meant a trip to A and E, stitches and a tetanus jab. The perfect end to a perfect day! And I still had to babysit the MP back to his hotel and do my stint at the Paradise.

Sometimes I wonder why I do this job. Am I as mad as the junkie? I don't have the excuse of being on something. It can only be the money. And it was a lot of money. The politico's white face when I got back the car made me swallow a satisfied grin; it might be a great deal more now that he knew how I earned it.

"…and bloody hell did I earn it!" I muttered around a mouthful of fusilli pomodoro.

Dean tried to pretend I wasn't talking with my mouth full. He refilled my glass with red grape juice, his own and Craig's with ruby Cabernet. Tori took a sip of her own grape juice. No vino for her because she was working. None for me because I have a problem with the sauce.

"It was a good job you were wearing the bracers," Dean mused.

It certainly was. Even so, I had another ruined suit and a three-inch gash on the underside of my left arm. Without friends like Craig I would still be sitting in A and E now.

"Do you think you should work tonight?" Tori worried.

"Not wishing to come over all macho, but I've had worse. I'll be fine as long as no one hits the stitches."

Craig chuckled evilly. "They'll wish they hadn't if they do."

"Damn right!" I have been known to get very angry with people who hit my stitches.

Tori collected up our plates and whisked them into the kitchen. I wasn't sure, but I thought she might have been crying. I made to go after her, but Dean grabbed my unsewn arm and Craig shook his head. "The last thing she needs is the Lesbian Avenger. Trust me, she just has to come round to these things. Like I did."

I sat down. I wasn't aware that Craig had 'come around', but let that pass.

I took the opportunity to ask about our investigations while Tori was absent.

"All of the ex-girlfriends have alibis. I'm sorry, Randall, you're going to have to look elsewhere for your culprit."

I swore softly and rolled the empty long-stemmed glass between my hands. It's at this point in television crime that the beautiful cop goes undercover and acts as bait. But I was neither beautiful nor a cop, and nobody was going to take me seriously getting my kit off. I haven't got the body for it and nothing on the planet will persuade me to have my legs waxed.

"So where does that leave us?" I asked.

"If you could get me the membership register of the club, I could check into the men's backgrounds. We might find somebody with a criminal record, or at least a medical record for impotence," Dean pondered.

It was a long shot, but I didn't know what else to do. Knowing a few of the clientele's secrets might give us some links to the attackers after we'd heard the girls' stories. It wasn't going to be easy. I couldn't think of a way to persuade Brian Senior to give me the list. This was going to require subterfuge, or something outright criminal. Breaking and entering and violation of the Data Protection Act for starters.

"I can get you that," Tori said softly from the door. I

stood.

"Not if it gets you fired," I told her.

"Randall, I've been working there two years, I could probably tell you the names from memory! Most clients aren't secretive about who they are and where they live and work. They tell you all sorts of things to try and impress you. Most of them either need to talk, are drunk, or want you to do more than dance for them in the club. They don't usually lie to you. They have to be quite well off to afford a full membership fee. That attracts a certain type of man. They all want to brag about the size of their equipment and their bank balance."

"Then how do you account for Randall? That is where you met, isn't it?"

Dean didn't like stereotyping, even though she wasn't alluding to men in general.

"The women are different. There are only four of them that come on a regular basis - aside from Randall – and all but one of them are very sweet and reserved. They don't talk much, they just watch you with round eyes and sweating palms."

"Do Randall's palms sweat?" Craig asked mischievously.

"Fuck off, Craig," I said, blushing.

"I've never private danced for Randall," Tori admitted.

Craig got out his wallet. "How much would that cost?"

Dean swatted him, and I swore at him again. But Tori considered me very carefully. A good deal more than my palms were sweating under the stress of her regard.

"Oh, I think I'd do her for free," Tori said, swaying her hips in a slow bump and grind as she oozed across the floor towards the table. Dean went very quiet and Craig watched in fascination, but I took her by the arm, spun her round and escorted her out of the room.

"We have to get ready," I said, firmly, keeping my back to D & C.

"Spoilsport," Craig called.

I didn't care. There was no way I was sitting through one of Tori's performances in front of my friends, no matter how much in jest it was meant to be.

Tori waited until I got her into her bedroom before wrenching her arm free. "Are you ashamed of me, Randall?

"No!"

"Ashamed of what I do, then?"

"Of course not."

She put her hands on her hips and glared at me. "Then what was that all about?"

"Sex is very private to me. I don't want my friends to know what turns me on, or gets me off. Or more to the point, I don't mind them knowing, as long as they're not getting a ringside seat. Watching you at the club is different, anonymous. Watching you in front of my friends… I couldn't do it. I won't. It's not about being ashamed of you or what you do."

"You're ashamed of yourself," she decided.

"Tori!"

"You're ashamed of being a lesbian. I see the way you squirm when we have to go somewhere together publicly. It's no touching, holding hands, kissing, or affection. You're not with me until we're behind closed doors, unless I force the issue. Or you think you're losing me. Or someone makes a play for me."

"I'm just not very demonstrative in public."

"You have an answer for everything, don't you?"

"It's the truth!"

"Prove it."

"How?"

She looked at me hard. "I'll think of something."

9

I got another unpleasant surprise in the car on the way to the Paradise.

"What?!"

"It happens one night in every three months. It's members only."

"That's not the point!"

"You told me you weren't ashamed of what I do."

"I'm not! But you didn't tell me once every three months you take everything off!"

"That's because I guessed you'd react precisely like this. It's only the difference of a g-string, Randall. They hardly cover anything to begin with!"

That was true. I was hard pressed to explain the difference myself, but somehow there was one. I wondered how she felt able to do this after what had happened to her. I didn't say any more though. Her life, her choice.

"Customers still can't touch us. I'm still going home with you at the end of the night."

I concentrated on driving. I couldn't stop this. I was committed to working in the club. There was no point arguing about something I couldn't change. But I didn't have to like it.

The Bird of Paradise was full when we arrived. Every chair was taken. Part of me wanted to rage and hit out at them all for being so prurient, knowing that they'd be seeing that much of my girl. Another part, the voyeuristic part that had brought me here to watch Tori originally, understood them completely, sympathised with them and felt the same electric buzz of excitement and expectation.

The thought of all those eyes getting off on what was mine when only I could have it at the end of the night. The thought of a girl that close, totally nude. Even though you couldn't touch her, she could touch you. And you could smell her... If I wasn't ashamed of myself, as Tori suggested, maybe I ought to be.

I got myself under control and saw Tori to the dressing room. This was going to be one hell of a difficult night and not just for me.

Brian Junior confirmed as much when I reached the balcony. "I hate these nights," he moaned. "The customers are always more aggressive, and most of the bouncers walk around with permanent hard-ons. It's bloody difficult to concentrate when you've got a boner. And the last thing you want to do is get into a fight."

I could well imagine.

"Because it doesn't happen all the time, you can't get used to it," he went on, eyes helplessly tracking a girl as she went by. "After you've been working here a few months you're just about over the fact that topless women are walking all over the place but..."

"I suppose the private dance booths get a lot of use?"

He nodded. "And the number of men thrown out of them defies belief."

We talked as we walked, quelling some ticklish situations just by our proximity.

"How's the training going?" I asked to get his mind off things.

"Fine. They had us doing something they call Formation Walking today."

I remembered. Working in a team of protection agents is a bit different from what I do. It's like a perfectly choreographed ballet. Moving around the client in fixed patterns. Keeping fans and fanatics at arm's length. Deciding who's a threat and who's just enthusiastic.

"I'm having a hard time seeing how it can help me in what I do here..."

"Depends on whether you're content to be a bouncer for the rest of your life."

"You mean they're teaching me to do what you do?"

"That's what you asked for, isn't it? It's one of the ways you learned to overcome your fear so you can defend yourself or somebody else. And tackle a head case wielding a knife." The hole in my arm from the tetanus shot itched and my stitches twinged, reminding me I could use some practice at that area myself.

"It's good money?"

"Yes. You're risking your life. I can't think of any other reason to do it."

It hadn't been that way for me to begin with. The sad, chauvinistic part of me enjoyed playing the hero, even if it was dangerous. The feminist in me got a kick out of doing what was traditionally a man's job, as well as or better than they did. This business with Tori was bringing out the worst in me. I was revisiting all my bad habits. It isn't wise to encourage these attitudes in trainees. It tends to get them killed. So I didn't 'fess up.

"They've arranged an Aggressive And Evasive Driving Techniques Course tomorrow."

"If you can afford it you should go. Even if you never use it, it's a great excuse to do handbrake turns and drive like a Formula One racer without getting arrested."

They'd also cover Ramming. Nothing can prepare you for that if you've never been in a car crash. They give you head gear and padding to practice in; he'd probably have a lot of fun. If he wasn't the nervous type. And if he didn't get whiplash.

"Do we get to go on a skid pan?"

I nodded. He grinned his enthusiasm.

"Cool! Thanks, Randall, I really appreciate this! This could be the start of a whole new career for me. It's not that I don't like working here, I do! But I'd like to prove I can do something for myself, not in dad's shadow, if you know what I mean?"

"I understand. Just don't quit this place until you're sure. See whether you're cut out for the life. Once you've got your first stab wound or the first bullet hole, then you can make some hard decisions. It's not a glamorous job. They're a good bunch of blokes to work with, though. Get them to show you their scars. Once you get them talking, they'll tell you how they came by them, how many times they nearly died, and how many of their friends actually have. I'm not trying to dissuade the competition – I wouldn't have given you the address otherwise – but to be truthful, there's not a lot of call for what I do round here. You have to be flexible, willing to move around the country. Sometimes even abroad. A lot of call for bodyguards in the Middle East at the moment, as I'm sure you can imagine."

Brian looked thoughtful.

Then somebody yelled for assistance…

The night was every bit the bitch Brian had implied.

A drunk got creative and decided to take a walk on the balcony railing. Before anyone could fetch him down, he fell off – on top of one of the bouncers. We had to call an ambulance to come and take both of them away. The drunk had nothing but bruises. The bouncer had a broken collarbone.

I broke up three fights, two on the mezzanine, one on the balcony – and this on a night when the Chief

Superintendent of Police was sitting in the front row. He didn't lift a finger to help. Everyone, both staff and rabble-rousers, pretended he wasn't there.

During the second fight my stitches tore. That guy definitely got more than he bargained for. Even Craig's best work has its limits. I had to borrow some tweezers to tighten things up and swathe my arm in crepe bandage.

We had to evict one guy for spiking a girl's drink with the date rape drug. The girl became inclined to do much more than just take her clothes off, and so friendly that she had to be sent home with an escort.

One of the dancers broke her ankle when she slipped on a wet patch on the floor. She had to be taken to the hospital too. The remaining dancers had to do double shifts on stage to cover for her, just as we had to scramble to cover for the absent bouncer.

When I thought things couldn't get any worse I was called into a Star room to supervise a private dance with Liu and one of the only female members of the club's clientele: the one who was not the 'sweet and silent' type Tori had described. She and her husband, both swingers, both bisexual, had been laughing loudly, getting very drunk, at a table near the front of the mezzanine, not far from the stage.

The dance itself went well – until the woman tried to stick her fingers in Liu near the end. Of course I acted to stop her. That was when the trouble began.

I grabbed her wrist and yanked her fingers back just short of actual penetration. "I'm sorry, ma'am, there's no touching," I told her politely.

"Fuck you!" she snarled.

Then she realised that I was a woman too. All her attention fixed on me. She pushed Liu off her lap, grabbed

126

my other arm and pulled me forward in Liu's place.

The music stopped. Liu hurried to rearrange her hair and turn off the CD, leaving me to take care of the problem. And it might have become a problem too. The woman was much stronger than she looked and very determined to have somebody if she couldn't have Liu.

"Dance for me."

"Ma'am, I don't dance. I'm a bouncer."

"I'll pay you."

"Ma'am, I'm already being paid, to do my job." I let go of her wrist and shifted my balance so that she wouldn't pull me over.

"I'll pay you more."

"Ma'am, I don't dance."

The hand I'd loosed stroked up the inside of my leg towards my crotch. I stepped back. The weight of her clinging on my arm wouldn't allow me to go far enough to escape her.

"Shall I get some help?" Liu asked.

Shit! How would that look?

"I'll manage," I told her with confidence I wasn't sure I felt. The woman chuckled throatily and reached for me again.

I decided I had to treat this like any other defence problem. Instead of pulling away, I moved into her space and reached down towards her. She was surprised I'd taken the initiative, and slackened her grip on my arm, not sure if she wanted to continue the game when she'd ceased to be the predator and become the prey. While she was emotionally off balance, I plucked her up, put her over my shoulder and started for the door. Liu applauded, then hurried to open it for me. The woman cursed me all the way back to her table.

The paying customers thought it was all part of the show. Her husband gave me a huge tip, much to his wife's chagrin.

If that wasn't bad enough I was told to sit in while the Chief Superintendent of Police sampled a private dance with my totally nude girlfriend.

He'd been staring daggers at me all night. I know I'm not exactly popular with the boys in blue, but prior to last summer I'd never had any dealings with him at all. I couldn't believe a couple of glasses of his favourite malt and the frenzy which seemed to be overtaking everyone had made me public enemy number one.

I was on the point of calling Dean, asking him if he knew of any reason why I was getting the evils, when of the girls let it slip that the first of them had been interviewed by the Murder Squad in connection with Lisa Moran's death earlier that day. Somebody had dropped the dime on our involvement. I was once again the spawn of Beelzebub in the Lancashire Constabulary's eyes.

Needless to say I was more than a little wary when I approached the door to Star 1. More so when I discovered he'd asked especially for me as well as Tori. Why? It was unheard of for a punter to request a specific minder; only the girls did that.

I started running through ways this scene could play out. Maybe I could short circuit whatever he had planned? I didn't get the chance. He had an unusual punishment for whatever my perceived misdemeanour was in mind.

He chose the music she would dance to. And just like the last time I had sat in on a dance with Tori, her client was almost completely sober.

The difference was, Tori knew about our problems with the authorities. She was also trying to show me that it was only me she was interested in, to lull my fears about this night of complete nudity.

Every time she turned her back on him, grinding her beautiful behind into his crotch, or sliding up and down his body, lying back on him and rotating her hips in a slow swivel, or arched her back as she sat in his lap and blew in his ear, her hot eyes were upon me. I was ready to rip her off him when he suggested I take his place.

"I c'n see she has the hots for you. I want to see what she does with you in this chair."

His voice was warm and friendly but there was ice in his eyes. Fuck! What was this all about?

"I don't…" I began. He cut me off.

"It isn't against any rules that I c'n remember."

He was facing me, not Tori. His voice was all Mr Congeniality, while his look said something else entirely. Shit. I tried again to persuade him not to do this. Whatever it was.

"I can't d…"

"If you don't, I'll fuck yer girl in front of you."

And there is it was. Either he watched two women perform for his pleasure or he hurt the woman I loved. He'd just moved from irritating bastard to suspect.

I didn't want to do this but he gave me no choice. I stood up to confront him.

"D'you ken who I am?" That was clearly for Tori's benefit.

"Of course I know who you are."

"And who d'you think they'll believe when I tell them you attacked me unprovoked? After you shot those men not long since? After yer girlie didn't tell the polis about her rape? Mebbe she liked it better than what you give her, eh?"

I have never felt such incoherent incandescent fury.

Nobody calls me a crap shag and gets away with it.

Tori started towards me, but he caught her wrist. He reeled her in with ease. Her whimper of fear was a bucket of ice-water thrown over me.

"It isn't much I'm askin', hardly an onerous task, letting yer own girlfriend do you."

Two women together. Voyeurism. A straight guy's dream. A lesbian's nightmare.

He swept an inviting hand at the spotlit chair.

"What's it to be?"

I started for the door to call his bluff, but a sound of pain from Tori told me that the bastard meant every word. He would hurt her. I couldn't let her be hurt again. Not if it was only stupid pride standing in the way. Not if I could prevent it. Especially if he had something to do with hurting other women.

I turned back. I would have hit him, but Tori's pleading eyes caught mine. That was what stopped me: that and the thought of the charges he could fabricate against me if he really put his mind to it. He was hell bent upon this humiliation: a taste of what would happen if the dyke detective and her pansy partner didn't keep their noses out of the big boys' business. I walked stiff-legged to the chair and sat down.

My eyes were on the carpet. I never saw him reset the CD, but the next thing I knew the music was back at the beginning and Tori was crouching over my lap. I looked up, tried to see around her. She caught my jaw and made me face her.

"No," she whispered. "Look at me, Randall, keep looking at me. He isn't here, he doesn't exist, we are the only two people in the room, you and I."

She started to move. I made a wordless noise of protest.

She put a finger to my lips, then leaned forward and kissed the tip of my nose, just as if we were at home, in bed.

"We'll give him a show he'll never forget." She pressed against me in a way I could not ignore. She made it easy to concentrate on her. She undulated her pelvis over mine. Licked the outer shell of my left ear. I closed my eyes.

"If I so much as smell you near my murder enquiry, I'll toss you and yer faggot friend in prison," he growled in my ear. "Judging from what I'm seein' that'd make yer girlie sad, though I'm no so sure about you. Prisons bein' full of yer sort."

My eyes snapped open and I twisted about trying to see him, trying to stand, only to find my jaw gripped again. Tori moved on to my right ear.

"Down, boy!" she ordered for our audience, then she whispered softly in my ear, "I won't let you go to prison for me."

Her hands started doing things to me she'd never do with a client. I gasped.

"You have to trust me, Randall."

She slowly began unfastening my tie. My jacket. My shirt. I could feel his breath on my neck and his eyes on the two of us.

Shit! How far did she mean to go?

She pressed her breasts against me and pumped herself against my right pant leg. A streak of gooey wetness appeared on the cotton/wool mix. Then her hand went down between us. The sound of my fly unzipping coincided with a lull in the music. I made a noise of denial and at the same time need. One of her hands cupped my skull. Pulled my mouth to her. Her other found its way through my underwear. I pulled away from her, cried out, closed my eyes, my fingernails carving crescent moons in the leather of the chair. She ground herself into my lap, squeezing her hand between us. Then the room was gone. I was in that other place as I came.

The extreme arch of my body must have bucked her off. I came to myself to find her drying her fingers, sitting on the floor, the music gone, our audience too.

I tried to get to my feet, determined to go after him and do... I don't know, something! As so often happens my legs would not support me. I collapsed back into the chair helplessly with a curse of frustration. She climbed into my lap, zipping up my fly, running her no longer sticky fingers through my hair.

"Let him go," she urged me.

"That bastard..."

"I know, I was there, remember?"

"Tori..."

"No, Randall. It's just what he wants. He's just like Anderton two decades ago – God's Cop, clearing the streets of the undesirables. You'll be playing right into his hands. I meant what I said. I won't see you go to prison for me. Not finding the sicko that raped me and not in revenge for this. If he's as corrupt as he seems, fate will find a way of tripping him."

"Tori, what he did was blackmail! And with what's going on here..."

"I know! I'm asking you to drop it. Please? For me?"

She tilted my face up, stroked her fingers up and down my throat. Tori is a whole lot of woman. I challenge anyone to deny someone when she asks you like that.

"I mean, what did he get really? A few moments of humiliation from you. Seeing the woman he paid for masturbating someone else to climax. He got to see two women fucking! One of his grubby little fantasies fulfilled!

He got to vent his anger about your involvement in his precious murder enquiry on both of us! He got to misuse his power and position! Neither of us are hurt. Far from it! It could have been worse."

"I wanted… I just wanted to…"

"I know."

She kissed me again.

"If it helps at all, he looked jealous to death when you came."

"He did? You're not just saying that?"

She shook her head. It did help. A bit. I still wanted to kill him, though.

I ran a finger over the shiny patch on my pants. Tori had the grace to blush.

"Looks like I got the full service."

"I don't do that for the clients!" I looked at her questioningly.

"I don't!"

"OK."

"OK! Just OK?"

I smiled and she swatted me. "I wasn't going to let you have all the fun."

"Sounds fair. That was what I was thinking, actually. I was wondering whether you'd like to finish what you started."

She blushed again, her coffee complexion pinking all the way down to her breasts.

"Randall, we're working."

"I have a reputation to restore."

"You don't. Really. You know why I didn't go to the police. It was nothing to do with how good or not you are in bed."

"Why don't I prove that? Doesn't seem like anybody's in

a rush to use the room."

I could see her resistance was weakening. I ran my hand slowly down her spine and stroked her coccyx in a slow circular motion. Blew gently across her suddenly erect nipples.

"I'll ruin your pants."

"Shit happens." I kissed the pulse in her throat.

"With you around it certainly d…" Breath went out of her in a rush at what my fingers were doing to her. She found something better for her mouth to do than talk.

I had just come out of the Ladies, got myself together (it isn't often I get to combine work and play), when Sammi cornered me.

She pinned me easily between the wall and the phallic-shaped bar on the mezzanine. One of her blunt-fingered, taloned hands pressed my right shoulder into the glittery plaster work with deceptive strength. One long leg forced its way between mine before I could move to stop her, her knee caressing my very damp crotch. She smiled a predator's smile.

"Mmm… What a nice boi. Ready for me I see."

I couldn't help it. I flinched with instinctive physical revulsion at her touch.

She must have felt my tension, or seen something in my expression, because she let up and traced her other hand gently down the side of my face.

"What's the matter, baby? I'm only playing, I know you belong to Tori. Aren't I attractive enough for you?"

"It isn't that." I shuddered.

"It's because I'm a trans, isn't it?"

There was no point in denying it. "Yes."

She stepped back, game over, obviously hurt.

"I never pegged you for a bigot." She started to turn

away. I needed to explain.

"Wait. Please. I don't mean to be insulting. I'm not! It's just…" How to describe it?

She gave me a look that said I had about one minute to say my piece before she either wiped the floor with me or walked away.

"I find it hard to get my head round the idea of someone who already has everything to satisfy a woman, has it all taken away and still wants to have sex with them."

"Don't tell me you don't understand how it feels to be trapped in the wrong body, boi. I've seen how hard you try to be a 'man'."

I couldn't disagree. "Yes, I know how that feels."

"Then aren't you just jealous, because I've done something you're too afraid to?"

"No. I looked into it. F to M gender reassignment isn't too successful. I'm not prepared to lose feeling in lovemaking to look the part. It's a poor exchange."

"If you're not a bigot and you find me attractive, what's the problem?"

"You won't believe it."

"Try me."

"They can do a lot of things with the knife and you can do more with clothes, make-up and hormones, but you can't change body chemistry. You look like a million dollars! But you don't smell, taste and feel like a woman. It's as simple as that."

She didn't try to stop me when I walked away.

Negotiating that minefield was never going to win me friends. But it did make me think about another uncomfortable possibility. I'd cavalierly tossed off 'isn't anybody straight anymore?' while contemplating my own lot. What if all of the women attacked here were lesbians?

Tori was. Liu certainly was. To an outsider, Sammi was a woman. Even though *she* had once been a *he*, not everyone was as quick to pick up on the tell tale signs. With her sexual preferences, that would make Sammi a lesbian in a stranger's eyes. I wasn't sure about Joy, Terri and Stace. And a bouncer's throwaway gossip had already furnished me with the information about Lisa Moran. (In light of this, it would be in my interests to check his alibi for Lisa's death.)

Was this whole business a hate crime? I'd have to run this by Dean. Perhaps it was somebody associated with the club after all. He was going to be unbearable if he was right.

It didn't seem right to march up to Joy, Terri and Stace to check my theory, and it was some time before I could catch up with Tori again. Meanwhile I had other things to worry about. Something strange was going on. Every time I walked past the girls they stopped talking. At first I thought it was my admission to Sammi: that they had all decided to ostracise me because I'd hurt their Agony Aunt's feelings.

That didn't pan out. Whenever they got me on their own, they either flirted with me, or were warmly polite, according to their gender preferences. What was going on?

It wasn't until the evening was nearly done that I overheard a snippet of conversation which made everything fall into place.

"Who'd turn down Stringfellow's? Pete might be a bit of a poseur, but think of the money you'd earn and the celebs you'd meet! You'd really be on your way then."

"I'd never have guessed there'd be talent scouts in this audience. Just goes to show. You never know who these clowns will bring as guests."

I know that old saw about eavesdroppers. I edged closer. I couldn't help myself.

"After what happened to her, it would be the best way to get a fresh start. It's a pity about her affair. But looking the way she does, she won't have a problem finding someone to warm her bed and take her mind off the break-up…"

Then they saw me, blushed red as beetroot and scuttled away.

You know the feeling. As if someone has pulled the rug out from beneath you and substituted the banana skin.

I had to get outside. I pushed through girls, customers, bouncers, with the same disregard, and fled up the steps to the outer doors. I couldn't breathe until I was outside in the cold night air.

It was pissing down.

I staggered down the steps into the car park and managed to make it to a pile of dustbins on the edge before I threw up everything she had cooked me that night, into the black, plastic lined interior.

"Randall?"

Don't ask me how she knew. Somehow she'd found out I'd heard, guessed where I'd be. I couldn't face her. Wasn't I supposed to be the strong one? And here I was puking up.

She'd followed me out of the club with no regard for herself.

She'd put on one of those tiny little hostess dresses that leave nothing to the imagination. She stood shivering in the falling rain, white marabou and high heels making her look like a bedraggled Page Three angel.

I wiped my mouth, stripped off my jacket without thinking and put it round her shoulders. Then she saw the stain.

"You're bleeding!"

"My stitches tore while I was breaking up a fight."

"And you didn't say anything?"

"I bandaged it up. I didn't want you to worry."

Her hands caught mine before I could move away. "Randall…"

"When were you going to tell me?"

"I was only approached last night. I haven't decided what I'm going to do."

"Stringfellow's want you and you haven't decided?"

She looked away.

"It would be a clean break, a way of escaping what happened to you. This place can't offer you a chance like that, money like that. And I can't complete with the lure of the city."

I was parroting the words I'd overheard. It didn't make them less true.

"Randall…"

"I've always known it couldn't last. Someone who looks the way you do could have anyone she wanted. What can I offer that would keep you?"

"More than you know. You're always running yourself down." She brushed rain out of my hair and off my shoulders. "Can we go back inside and talk about this? I don't know about you, but I'll catch cold if I stand here much longer."

I was about to reply when a long shadow fell over us. I turned to see the bouncer I'd insulted on the first night, Villiers, the one I thought was responsible for the knife-throwing incident. He was standing expectantly with two 'friends'. Shit. Just what I needed.

He pulled out a blackjack, tapped it thoughtfully on one hand. From the sound of it, the home-made cosh was filled with loose change. The others were similarly outfitted. Without the Kevlar this was going to hurt.

"This is to teach you to stay out of things that don't concern you."

I pushed Tori behind me. "Go inside."

I admit it was chauvinist. But this wasn't her fight. If she stayed out of it they would leave her alone. They wouldn't let me walk away. I either did this now or they'd get me later on ground that favoured me less. From what he'd said this wasn't just about macho pride and the bouncers 'union' staking their territory. They might have something to do with what had been happening to the girls. No time to worry about that now. I rotated my shoulders to shift the stiffness put there by my emotional state and the rain and walked forward to meet them.

Footing was uncertain. That could work both for me and against me.

The bouncer's friends ran towards me. The left one slipped on the slicked tarmac and went down. I kicked him in the head. He stayed there.

The first to reach me met my fist in his balls. He gave a high-pitched scream and folded over the injury. I almost joined him as my stitches took another wrench.

My crouched position helped me avoid the bouncer's cosh, as I twisted, lower than he'd aimed. The coins crashed into the fleshy place below my left shoulder blade and the top of my ribs. Using the momentum of my punch and twist, I drove my right shoulder into the bouncer and propelled him back, jabbing two rigid fingers into his extended arm. He lost his grip on the cosh. Coins spilled out across the parking lot, making footing more treacherous.

The first man got up wearing an ugly expression. I couldn't blame him. That didn't mean I was going to stand around and let him take his revenge.

I cut off his roar with a kick to his throat that sent him gasping down next to his friend.

A noise behind me spun me round. Tori. Why do women never do as they're told? She stood over the fallen men with a dustbin lid, the promise of a swift strike in her eyes if either of them showed any sign of getting up. (OK, I can't say I was sorry to get some back-up.) I turned to tackle the last man standing.

He hadn't been twiddling his thumbs. A handful of the loose change in my face was followed by brass knuckles to my ribs. Pain drove the breath out of my lungs as effectively as the thought of Tori leaving me. He blocked the jab I made at his groin. His fist caught me alongside of my head. My already blurred vision swam further out of true. I dropped to my knees in the wet.

As he locked his hands to bring them down on the back of my neck, I grabbed his ankles and yanked. He went down with a satisfying crash, hitting his head on Brian Senior's BMW and setting off the alarm. I used the side of the Porsche to pull myself to my feet, then dropped on to his ribcage with both knees. The sickening crack more than made up for the pain in my arm, head and ribs.

Tori dropped the dustbin lid and raced to support me as I staggered away.

"What's going on?" Brian Senior roared over his car alarm from the top of the steps.

Quick as a flash, Tori shot, "Randall stopped these pricks stealing your Beemer."

I blinked blood and rain from my eyes and stared. I couldn't find anything to say. Which was as well. I'm crap at lying. Which makes me a good bet as a girlfriend but a liability when it comes to PI work. Or so Dean tells me.

Members of the crowd pushed their way outside. This

whole scene – from overhearing Tori had been headhunted by Stringfellow's, to the end of the fight – had taken us past closing time. Brian Senior swore, got everyone back inside with the promise of free drinks, then hurried down to turn off his alarm before it attracted unwelcome attention.

Tori rummaged in the pocket of my jacket for my car keys, got the door open and sat me on the seat. She sorted through the jumble of clothes in the boot and climbed into the baggy, newly washed sweatshirt she'd worn before, and a pair of my sweat pants, the only thing that would go over the strappy shoes without her having to take them off.

Squatting beside me, she explored my head and ribs through the bar door and didn't like what she found. She settled my jacket around my shoulders and swung my feet inside, turning on the heater.

"Randall, promise me you'll stay there. I'll only be a minute. I have to go in and collect my stuff. Don't fall asleep, OK? It's dangerous with a head wound. I can't drive. I need you to stay with it long enough to get us home."

Sensible girl.

Appearing in A and E when the other three had been taken there would generate questions neither the club nor I would want to answer. Her boss had already removed the wounded, with the help of a few other bouncers, to another forecourt. An amusement arcade. Only then did he phone an ambulance for them and allow the customers to leave. Tori secured my promise and pushed her way back inside.

Brian Senior sensibly did not question Tori's take on events. We escaped after minutes, though it felt like hours. I sat nursing screaming ribs and watching my face swell in the mirror.

When we arrived home Craig and Dean were waiting. Tori had called them from the club, when she'd gone inside to fetch her things. While Dean saw to the car, Craig helped Tori hustle me in to deal with the medical side.

He was able to allay her fears about my sleeping. I did not have a concussion. The fist had only laid open the top of my cheek and temple. My resident nurse washed and closed both cuts, strapped up the one broken and one cracked rib even though it's an unfashionable practice these days, re-sewed my arm then gave me something to make me sleep to allow everything time to start knitting together.

She shooed them out as fast as politeness would allow when Dean showed signs of wanting to interrogate me about what had happened. I assured him I'd fill him in tomorrow. He wasn't happy, but grudgingly accepted now was not the time to press the issue, and left with as good grace as can be expected of a nosy queen thwarted in his desire to get the goss.

Finally alone, Tori stripped me of my remaining clothes and pressed me into bed.

She treated me to the second free strip of the evening, which I was in no fit state to appreciate, considering she was probably going to leave me. Pain does funny things to a girl.

"If you wanted me to stay so badly, you could have found a less dramatic way of persuading me," she mused, crawling into bed beside me.

The drugs kicked in. I was too groggy to argue. I put an arm around her, let her cuddle up to my uninjured side and fell into a deep and dreamless sleep.

10

"Where do you think you're going?"

"Work," I mumbled, muzzy from whatever Craig had dosed me with.

"Back to bed, soldier, you've been relieved of duty."

"I have?"

"Brian Senior came round this afternoon. They've found a replacement for Spink. They tried to phone, but I'd turned the ringer off. You needed to rest."

I sat heavily on the swivel chair. The bedroom seemed too far just now.

Tori indicated a neat stack of twenty pound notes on the desk. "He left last night's pay, severance and a bonus for saving his car." She chuckled. "I hadn't the heart to tell him the truth. He's so tight, getting anything out of him is blood out of a stone." She flourished a membership card with my name. "He also left this. Unlimited Membership, no expiry date. I'm impressed. The only other person who has one of these in the Chief Superintendent."

"Not sure I'm going to need it if my reason for going there is gone," I told her honestly.

She set down the membership card, knelt on the floor and began fussing with the buttons on the shirt I'd been trying to get into, unable to meet my eyes. I caught her hands.

"You really should go back to bed," she mumbled.

"So you can kick me when I'm down?"

Her eyes snapped up, annoyed. "No!"

I dropped her hands and caught her face instead. My knuckles were split.

"Talk to me. Are you leaving me?"

"It doesn't seem right discussing this with you when you're…"

"Bad news doesn't get better for putting it off. When do you go?"

Her eyes were on my lips, her hands making impotent fists on my knees. "They want me to come down and try out on Saturday."

Five days. I let go of her face. My hands had started to shake. I didn't want her to see.

Now I was unable to meet her eyes. I didn't seem to be able to draw breath. She sensed my distress, caught my hands in hers and stroked the backs, avoiding the split knuckles.

"Randall, I may not make the grade! I might not like the place, or the way they want me to do the job. It's very different…"

She was trying to convince herself. I knew what was coming next.

"If it pans out, you could come down, too. I'm sure there'd be someone more than happy to employ you, with your reputation. Maybe you could even persuade Dean to relocate! Or if that doesn't work, we could always meet up at weekends…"

What made it worse was she believed it.

"Tori, I can't. My life is here. Not because I want it to be here, because I can't afford to go anywhere else. The only things mine to sell are the Porsche – which isn't the genuine article – and the furniture in this apartment. I don't own the place. I'm a tenant. I have no savings. All the money I have is tied up in the business. I had to get a loan to buy into that when I became a partner. I owe the credit card company a mint from the bender I was on when you met me. I'm still trying to settle with them. Doing high risk jobs is what keeps the business and my head above water. I'm sorry. If you go, you go alone."

"God, Randall, I didn't know!"

"It's not something I advertise."

Tears leaked out from beneath her mascaraed lashes.

"This is one hell of a chance. It will never come again."

"What about you?"

"I'll stand by whatever it is you want to do. You know that. I love you, Tori, but you can't let that stop you, or hold you back. This is your time."

She climbed into my arms, on to my lap and wept.

Eventually she dabbed her eyes, bathed them in icy water to take down the swelling, reapplied her make-up, changed, got into a taxi and left. She refused to let me drive her.

Now I was up I couldn't countenance the thought of retreat to the doubtful security of sleep. I took more painkillers, peeled out of my eclectic mixture of sleep- and street-wear, took off the bandages and stood under a scalding shower. By the time I stepped on to the duck-board the medication had kicked in. I was able to apply new dressings without turning the air more than indigo. Food and clothes made me feel better still. Fortified, I called on the only person I could count on never to let me down.

Even during our falling out, Dean hadn't completely refused to speak to me; he'd just made sure I knew I would pay and pay until he was satisfied. I was glad that was behind us. I had a feeling I was going to need his help soon. If Tori left for good, I couldn't afford to crawl back into the bottle. Neither the business nor I could afford it.

D & C's place is out in the swank area of Blackpool real

estate near Stanley Park, not far from De Vere's health club, of which they are both members. As I said before, it's a very nice place, tastefully furnished and maintained. An early frost had made the garden look like Santa's grotto. Only thing missing were gnomes.

I paid the taxi and crunched up the driveway. Dean answered the door after two rings. He didn't look surprised to see me. Gay men don't do surprised, only jaded.

"Not at work?"

"They found someone to replace Spink."

"Pity they didn't tell that to your fan club last night. How are you feeling?"

"In pain, but I'll live. Look, can I come in? I've learned a few things, possibly about Tori's attacker, maybe about what's been happening to the other girls. I'd like to run it all by you, since you're the brains of this outfit."

"Nice of you to notice!"

"Are you telling me you've got some real work to do, or are you busy socialising?"

"No, I was about to settle down to a quiet night in front of the TV with Craig. Some of us only work from nine to five."

Shit.

"Never mind. It'll keep." I turned to go.

"Wait. You look like hell. Heaven knows what the neighbours will think if I let you walk away in that state. You didn't drive here, did you?"

He scanned the road nearsightedly for the Porsche – not wearing his contacts – alarmed at the thought. What do you know? He does care!

"I'm not that stupid."

"Sometimes I wonder." He held the door open.

"You really know how to endear yourself to a girl."

I raked my Rockports over a boot scraper, stamped my feet on the step, then stepped inside on to his real sea grass Welcome mat. If I was going to ruin his evening the least I could do was not mess up his house.

"Who is it?" Craig's voice drifted from somewhere in the warm interior.

"It's only me," I returned.

"Bang goes my night!" He stuck his head round the doorway and winced at the sight of me. "You look worse! Should you even be up?"

"You tell me, you're the nurse. Whatever you doctored me with knocked me out for what was left of the night and most of today. I only got up a couple of hours ago. I still ache, but do I feel better, even if I don't look it."

"Bloody lesbians! Your macho crap gives us pretty boys a bad name. Why can't you wallow in the attention and let Tori nurse you, like a real patient?"

"Jealous?"

"Fuck no! You're putting me out of a job as well as buggering up my evening!"

"You'd only whine that I was behaving like those straight bitches you work with." I put on his affected moaning voice: "They're always away looking after their kids and having days off for their gynae problems."

He glared at me.

"I suppose this means we can forget the Shiraz and *Titanic*?" This aimed at Dean.

"Sorry," Dean said, managing to sound contrite. Craig gave one of his overblown Gloria Swanson 'I'm so put upon' looks, sniffed and flounced back wherever he'd come from.

"*Titanic*? Again?"

"Just because you can't stand it…"

"Let's not get into a fight over a film. I haven't got the energy. Besides, I know you only watch it to drool over Leo."

"I do not! Well, not entirely."

I grinned, then wished I hadn't. God, my face hurt!

"Tell Craig I'll buy him another bottle of vino to make it up to him."

"Don't worry about it. He'll drink this lot by himself. He won't remember you were here by the end of the night."

Convenient. I tried drinking to forget, and just my luck, it didn't work. The memory was there sharp as ever in the morning, with a hangover to accompany it. That, my health and the money are why I stopped. Now I don't drink. Ever.

Dean let us into the kitchen/breakfast room and poured us both something non-alcoholic, while I peeled off my coat and settled into a chair.

"Before you start in on what brought you here, perhaps you'd care to explain how you ended up in this state. Tori told me one of your attackers was a bouncer at the Paradise. I thought you were trying to be one of the boys?"

"It might all be connected." I told him about the first night, the altercation I'd broken up on the balcony, the arrival - too late - of the cavalry, Villiers and Grey. I omitted the knife-throwing incident but followed up with what the bouncers had said last night before the fight.

"That's what you get for showing up the inadequacies of the help and being bloody smug about it," he summed up.

"Yeah."

"You're your own worst enemy."

"Don't bang on. My ribs and head are reminder enough."

He winced, eyes flickering uncomfortably over my face. He decided I was suffering enough without making me sit through one of his lectures.

He took a pull at his coffee. "It could just be a pissing contest. But it seems like too much of a coincidence. I take it they knew the other reason you were working at the Paradise?"

"Not at first. After Brian Senior spoke to me about it I don't think my looking into the attacks on the girls was much of a secret."

He tipped his chair back to retrieve a stub of pencil from a drawer and a legal pad which had clearly been doing duty as a recipe book.

"Where are these pricks now?" He found a fresh page.

"The hospital, I presume; they came off worse than I did."

"I'll get Craig to look into it. Do you have their names?"

"Only the bouncer, I don't know his friends, they didn't work at the club." I spelled it out for him. He pencilled it in his usual careful hand, ripped out the page and pocketed it.

"I'll pay our friend a visit. Even if he isn't responsible he might know who is. Nothing like the threat of a little pain to sharpen the memory. Want to play bad cop to my good cop?"

"You certainly know how to show a girl a good time."

"Just keep it to yourself. I don't want to spoil my reputation as a nice boy."

"Whatever you say."

"I'll find out which ward he's in and we'll arrange a visit. You looking the way you do might actually be an advantage. Tomorrow afternoon?"

"Can't be too soon for me."

"Just don't get carried away."

"Moi?"

He rolled his eyes, freshened his coffee and took another

sip. "All right, let's hear the rest."

I shared my thoughts about the possibility of it being a hate crime. He listened carefully without interrupting, then paused before he replied. Never a good sign.

"I'm not saying it isn't possible, but..."

I started to protest but he forestalled me. "It's true that the victims appear to be lesbians, though until we conduct the interviews we won't be sure. And as yet we don't know enough about Lisa Moran to know where her sexual preferences lie. The bouncer mouthing off probably had no more involvement in Lisa's death than us. But in light of your latest revelations... Go carefully. Don't accuse him of anything! It'll probably come out that he chatted her up and she rebuffed him. You know how straight men are: 'If a woman doesn't fancy me she *must* be a dyke!' Vic is probably just a hettie prick pissed off because he didn't get a shag."

"I know it's pat. It would just be nice to wrap up a case simply."

"I'm not discounting it. You may be right. All I'm saying is investigate. Don't judge."

"Whether it's true or not, all it does is add to the number of possible suspects."

"Don't get despondent, Randall. You're new at this game. Sure it's easier when there are fewer suspects. A case of proving whodunit, how, where and when. Means, motive and opportunity. But it gets dangerous when they know you're closing in. They start thinking of desperate solutions to get out of the hole they've dug. We become collateral damage."

"OK, I get that. But don't we have too many suspects in this case? And not just for the murder? And perhaps more than one perpetrator?"

"Perhaps. But believe me, it's better when it's like this. Lots of possibilities to look into. I know you don't want to hear this, especially since you have a personal stake in things, but the longer we can legitimately work the case the more money it brings in."

"That sucks, Dean. These women are afraid! They need a quick answer to their problem. They don't have much spare cash. They want to know that the person who did this can't do it any more. Whatever it takes to stop it."

"If you're thinking of doing something rash, I'm having nothing to do with it."

"What happened to letting me kick skittles of shit out of the culprit and providing me with an alibi?" I challenged.

"Now there's murder involved. I won't let it become two and see my best friend go to prison into the bargain."

We glared at one another over the table.

"Should I referee?" Craig wondered, draped round the doorpost.

"No," we both said.

"Good, then keep it down. You're interrupting my viewing pleasure."

He wandered back to the lounge.

"Sorry. I was overreacting. Drugs."

"Me too. Though I can only blame the coffee. Damn."

We grinned ruefully at one another.

"I promise not to be a shit about this if you promise not to milk the girls."

"In so much as it's possible. It will take as long as it takes, Randall. You know that."

Sadly, I did.

"The first of the interviews is tomorrow at ten. Will you be in a fit state?"

After what I'd just said about the money, I'd have to be.

"I'll be there."

"I have an appointment. You'll have the place to your-selves. I'll be back at two."

I was about to ask him what I should do until then when he revealed, "You have a second interview at 12.30. With any luck you'll be in a position to fill me in on whatever you learn over a late lunch. Then we'll visit our friend in the hospital. If everyone keeps their appointments, we should have a preliminary picture of what went on in two days' time."

I'll give him one thing: jobs move quickly once he's committed.

"My contacts in the media will have come through with the rest of the goods on Lisa Moran by then. You arrange to speak to that bouncer and get the skinny on the club members, then we'll have everything we need."

"There's more." I filled him in on the memorial service. I'd been so pushed for time the other day it had completely slipped my mind. "We're invited. Tori thought we could watch who turns up in case the killer came to gloat."

"Along with half the police force, I'm sure," he sighed. "Oh well, there's no getting around it."

Shit, I hadn't told him about my run-in with the Chief Super either. As well as everything else I now had to wonder whether a corrupt cop had anything to do with this mess! I absolutely was not mentioning that possibility to him until I had evidence! He'd think I was being paranoid. There's no love lost between my partner and the constabulary, but Dean likes to believe the good guys really are good. It takes proof to shatter his illusions.

"That Scottish twat will have us in for obstructing justice before they've finished the requiem mass. You did know she was a Catholic?"

"No, I didn't. Does that make a difference?"

"Heathen! It will if you're going to sit in that church."

He explained.

"There is no way! No hats. No kneeling. No praying. I'll wait outside."

"I never know when I'm going to run into one of your sacred cows. All right. I suppose it's either that or try passing as a bloke. In any other company you'd fake it easy, but with those apes all six foot wide and six foot tall you'd stick out like a sore thumb. I'll do the good deed and watch the grieving mourners. After all, you're doing the interviews. Your nearest and dearest probably has a point." Then, seeing my look, "What? What have I said now?"

"She may not be my nearest and dearest for much longer." I told him about her audition.

"Oh, Randall, I'm sorry."

"It isn't a done deal, yet. Still..."

He looked on in sympathy. There wasn't much to say. We've all been there. He knew my financial straits well enough to know I couldn't up sticks and follow her, no matter how I felt. He set aside his mug to grip my hand across the table.

"I know I'm not her, but if you need me, you know where to find me."

"Thanks. I won't crawl back into the bottle."

"I never thought you would," he lied.

Comforting fiction. Nice to hear anyway.

"Hi, you've reached Randall McGonnigal. I'm not here right now. If you don't object talking to machines, leave a message after the tone. I'll get back to you ASAP."

Beep.

"Hello, Randall, it's Tori. I hope you can hear me!

153

I thought I'd call and check on you. You either took my advice and went back to bed or you're with Dean. Either way, I hope you're feeling better. The club has an extension till four. I'd forgotten about it till I arrived. As you're hardly your usual self, I'm going to sleep at my place, rather than chance waking you whenever I finally crawl home. I've arranged for a White Knight to take me home, so don't worry, I'm safe! I know you have an early start, conducting interviews, so I'll see you tomorrow night. For dinner, if that's OK with you? Eight o'clock, my place. Call me if you can't make it. Gotta go! It's my set. Love you."

Beep.

Shit. Alone! We only had four nights before she left. I played the message a second time, just to hear her voice, then wondered if I'd be doing that when she was gone. I made myself erase the tape; I wasn't going down that road again.

It was five to midnight. I felt wrung out from pummelling my brain with the intricacies of the case, thinking like a detective instead of a bodyguard whose girlfriend has been raped. The painkillers had worn off. I ached all over. I stripped, took a couple more and got back into the shower. I stayed under the water till it cooled and the hurts had died to a dull ache.

"You don't look as bad I thought you might."

"Thanks, I think."

Liu smiled and cocked her head on one side. "Give it another day and no one will notice it at all unless they're right next to you."

To my surprise I'd fallen asleep the moment my head had hit the pillow. The only visible signs of the fight I'd had on waking were multihued ribs and swelling at my temple.

"We should get on."

"Of course. You have Sammi at lunchtime, don't you?"

She made it sound like we'd be doing more than just talking. That was deliberate. I saw I would have to take a firm stance if I was to prevent this getting out of hand.

"Liu, we have very little time."

She pouted.

"Considering the unpleasant nature of the subject I thought the least we could do was have a little fun."

"Liu, I have a job to do. It hardly makes me sound professional! Have a heart, my partner has to listen to these tapes!"

"I'll behave."

Verbally, she did. Visually it was a completely different matter.

"What do you want to know?"

She leaned back. Her already short skirt rode up. I forced my eyes back to her face. She smiled.

"I need you to tell me exactly what happened. Start with the day, date and time, then everything you can remember."

"It was a Saturday, in August, the very end. I'm sorry, I don't remember the date."

Glad of the chance to look away, I flipped through the calendar and noted the date of the last Saturday in August. Liu continued,

"I was on my way home from the club. It was three, maybe three-thirty in the morning. I was wrecked. One of the girls was ill. We'd had to cover more routines on stage."

I nodded in sympathetically.

"The cab dropped me at the end of the street where I live. There were roadworks blocking the way further up. It was raining. I paid, then ran up the street to the house so

I wouldn't get too wet. While I was standing in the porch, fumbling my keys out of my bag, I heard footsteps. High heels. I clutched my bag and spun round, so I didn't get hit from behind. I thought it was a mugger!"

"You did the right thing."

"From you, that means a lot."

She did that Sharon Stone crossing and uncrossing her legs thing. I definitely wasn't going there! Tori hadn't even left yet. I kept my eyes firmly on her face.

"I didn't get a good look at her. She was wearing a coat with the hood pulled low over her face. She was taller than me and white. Definitely a woman. She hissed, "Bitch!" and threw something. I flung my arm in front of my eyes. I heard her running away and felt something dripping down my hair. Eggs! I counted myself lucky it wasn't worse. I found my keys, fled inside, got my coat off, emptied the pockets and dumped it in the washer. Then I rinsed my head under the tap to get the eggshell out of my hair. I made sure I'd put the dead bolt on the door and went upstairs. I lit candles and had a bath and a stiff drink."

"Has anything like this happened to you before?"

"No."

"OK, let's go back over the events in a little more detail. You didn't hear footsteps until you were at your door?"

"Well…"

"I know you were running. That tends to block out other sounds, and the rain wouldn't have helped, but try to remember exactly what you heard when you got out of the taxi."

She thought about it, eyes closed, conjuring the moment.

"I don't remember hearing any feet but mine while I ran, but now you come to mention it, I do remember hearing a car engine as I turned up my road. Do you suppose she was following me? Following my cab?"

"It's possible. You say she was taller than you?"

"Yes. Five seven, five nine. I know she was white because she wasn't wearing gloves. I saw her hand go back to throw the egg in the streetlight. There's one outside my house."

She shivered and hugged herself.

"I'm sorry, I know it isn't easy for you to revisit this."

"I thought I was over it. Then Tori came in last week and told Sammi what had happened to her. Suddenly everyone had stories! It was horrible! We'd all had things happen to us that we just swept under the carpet hoping they would go away. That it was a one-off. That it must have been something we'd done. That we were to blame for what had happened. How fucked is that? Why do we blame ourselves?"

"I don't know, Liu. You're not to blame. I do know that."

"I am. If I'd mentioned it earlier, maybe Tori wouldn't have been…"

"You mustn't think like that."

She began to cry. I pulled open a drawer and grabbed a handful of tissues Dean keeps for female clients who come to report on their philandering husbands. I turned off the tape and came around the desk to kneel before her, take one of her hands, press the tissues into the other. She sniffled into them with mumbled thanks. I sat back on my heels and waited it out. I didn't dare get any closer, even though she needed comfort. She clutched my hand until she felt able to talk.

"You don't blame me?"

"No more than Tori does."

She tried out a smile. I returned it.

Why do women think themselves to blame when something like this happens? I'm sure psychologists have a name for it. All I know is how angry it made me to keep hearing it when someone else was to blame. Angrier still to know that at least one stalker was another woman.

Sammi had been in her flat when the doorbell rang. Foolishly she hadn't checked the intercom, just buzzed her visitor up. Glad of the company? In a mood to take risks? When she opened the door, her ski-masked attacker forced his way in, bounced her head off the wall a few times, and while she was too stunned to fight back, bent her over the armchair back and raped her. When he was finished, he'd smacked her head one more time for good measure on the wooden frame of the chair and fled.

Sammi's attacker was a man. She was sure. He hadn't used protection and she'd caught the clap. She was also the only one to report her attack.

"And a fat lot of good that did," she complained. "All it got me was an unsympathetic WPC, who they changed for a bloke as soon as they found out I'd originally been a man – and he was even more obnoxious than she was." She made a face at the memory.

"They left me in one of those surgical gowns. It felt like hours. Sitting around, cold and aching, first in A and E with a police registered surgeon. Then an intrusive examination that hurt almost as much as the rape. Then in a police station. And all they had to say was I brought it on myself. Bastards!"

The first thing that hits you is disinfectant. It almost but not quite covers the smell of sick people. I hate hospitals. In my job I see the inside of the places more than most.

Our quarry was located in a bed near the doors on a

ward near the psychiatric wing and the children's ward. Thanks to Craig's insider knowledge we made our way straight there from the outside, using a shortcut that avoided going through reception and advertising our presence.

Of the three men I'd fought, only the bouncer, Villiers, had been kept in for observation. According to Craig my dropping on his ribs had sent a broken bone back to puncture a lung. They'd had to drain it and re-inflate it. I tried to feel sorry for him. He could have died! But I looked worse than he did and what they'd intended for me would have been far worse. That made my part in this affair much easier.

Dean walked over in his smart suit, clutching his clipboard as if he belonged there. Nobody questioned him. He looked like a consultant. Anyway, it was visiting hours. I waited until he'd drawn the curtains round the bed to ensure privacy then slipped through the door into the shrouded enclosure with a suitably malevolent expression. It strained my acting abilities when I saw the bouncer's face go from polite inquiry to pale as his sheets when I followed Dean in.

Before he could buzz for assistance, Dean slid the pager away and grabbed one wrist. I grabbed the other and clamped a gloved hand over his mouth to stop him yelling. His body bucked against the bed.

"We can do this the easy way or the hard way, Mr Villiers. Which is it going to be?"

He took a long look at me and subsided.

"Sensible choice. All we need are some straight answers then we'll leave you to recuperate in peace. But if I think you're lying to me you'll be doing something else in peace. Do we understand each other?"

I put pressure on his wrist until I could feel the bones grind together and watched his face pale further. After that he nodded vigorously. Dean let go of the man's wrist and straightened his suit fastidiously.

"My business partner will let you go now. Bearing in mind what you and your friends did, I'd advise you don't scream for help. She's understandably a little over-enthusiastic in the physical persuasion department just now."

"What do you want?" Villiers muttered.

For once I didn't have to work at looming menacingly. When the person you're intimidating is lying down it's easy to be impressive at just over five feet tall.

"Before you and your goons laid into me, you said, 'This is to teach you to stay out of things that don't concern you.' What did you mean?"

"I don't know what you..."

Dean looked away as I slapped my hand back over his mouth and began to squeeze a nerve cluster near his throat: what Trekkers think of a Vulcan nerve pinch. "I may not have a dick, but I do have total recall. What did you mean? Or do I have to get really nasty?"

"Fuck," he gasped as I freed up his mouth. "What do you think I meant? You made me look like a right pillock in front of people I'd worked with for years! I couldn't just let the insult go by without doing something."

"Knife throwing wasn't enough?"

Dean looked at me sharply. Thankfully he didn't blow things by picking me up on it. But this guy wasn't the only one who'd be having a difficult conversation today.

"That wasn't me!"

"Who was it then?"

"Grey. He thought you needed to be taken down a peg

or two."

I'd caught Grey looking at one or two people in an ugly way, Sammi and myself included. It wasn't too hard to believe. I stepped away from the bed.

"If I find out you've lied to me I'll be back. And you'll wish you hadn't."

I did the dramatic exit through the curtain and set off down the stairs at the hurry up. I'd wait for Dean outside. This was one scene I didn't want to have anywhere we could be overheard.

He exploded as he burst out of the doors, clearly having built up a head of steam on the way down. "Someone threw a knife at you and you didn't tell me?"

"Because I knew you'd react like this."

"You could have been killed!"

"No I couldn't. I caught it. I can do shit like that."

He started to make a snappy comeback, then thought better of it. He knew it wasn't a boast. When he stops to think about it he knows what I'm capable of. And hadn't he just watched me torture information out of someone? (Not something I was proud of, but a salutary lesson all the same.)

He exhaled noisily. "All right. I overreacted. I'm sorry. Are you going to be OK? With what you just did? I mean… It goes against everything you've been taught. Martial arts codes and what have you."

"It was necessary. I'm not about to make a habit of it."

"That's good to know."

Dean fell in beside me as I started back to the car. There was more. I waited in silence. He'd work himself round to it. And he did.

"Look, Randall, I'm not going to go on about this, but you need to tell me everything. It might seem personal to

161

you but it might just be significant to the case. You haven't been doing this long enough to make the judgement call. You're too close to see the big picture clearly."

I thought again about my run-in with the Chief Superintendent. I would tell him. Just not yet. "There are just some things I need to get straight in my head first, OK?"

He sighed. "Just don't leave it too long." Realising he wasn't going to get any more out of me now he asked. "Why are we leaving? What convinced you the man upstairs was telling you the truth?"

"I was right in his face, Dean. I know how much I was hurting him. It was the truth. Villiers –" I stabbed a finger in the general direction of the ward "– is just a prick full of his own machismo."

Grey was another matter. I told him so. "He feels like a prospect. He's weird. Not that that's a reason! Half the people in this town are weird, but they're not guilty of anything more criminal than non-payment of a parking ticket. I'm used to folks looking at me a bit off, so I didn't think anything of it. But if he's capable of throwing knives, what else is he capable of?"

"Maybe he isn't the only one. I think we need to widen the scope of our investigation. I want the names of all the bouncers, Randall. Maybe your Mr Grey, Lisa Moran's detractor and our friend upstairs aren't the only ones who are weird."

Hearing Tori speak of her incident – coherently – was almost more than I could bear. I'd wanted to do it at home, but that evening Tori came to the office just like everyone else.

"Why should I have special treatment? Isn't what

happened to everyone else just as horrible? I don't want to taint either your place or mine with such a vile memory. Besides, I want to see where you work."

I don't know what she thought of the place. She eyed the strip lights on the stairs with a smile and ran her hands along the furniture, which – thanks to Dean's family money, which also put him through law school and helped to buy his house - is leather instead of cheap stacker chairs. She refused my offer of a drink and stood looking out of the window in the main office for some time before allowing herself to be persuaded to a seat to begin. I can't say I blamed her for her reluctance.

We made one concession. I sat beside her instead of across a desk.

She started out by handing me a typed list. "The names and as much of the addresses of the club members as I could find out. I hope you don't mind. I used your PC. I didn't think you'd be able to read my scrawl."

"This is great, thank you. You're sure you won't get into trouble about this?" She gave a shrug that said 'What if I do?' I suppose since she was probably leaving she had a point. She took a moment to order her thoughts then began.

"I was walking from the bus stop to my parents' house. I had my hands full with the flowers I'd bought Mum and some real ale chutney I'd picked up for Dad. For a wonder the sun was out. I remember it glittering off everything reflective. Funny how stupid things stick in your mind, isn't it?"

"Something like this imprints everything indelibly."

"You think I should see someone professional to talk about this with, don't you?"

"I'm not convinced talking to a counsellor will help. It

163

can't make it never have happened. You've always been level-headed and practical. If you think you've found a way to deal with it, go for it. But if things start to feel as if they're coming unravelled, do something about it. If that means getting professional help, so be it. I told you I wouldn't force you to do anything. I meant it. I'll stand by you, whatever you choose."

She hugged me. "Thank you, Randall. I don't know why I didn't just speak to you in the first place. You always make me feel so grounded."

I held her until she felt able to go on.

"As I walked, I ran into all these people I used to know. Neighbours, postmen, old Mr Clement from three doors away who used to be kind of the local handyman. It's a very close community in Cleveleys. Mostly OAPs. I was just turning into their street when I saw a car I thought I recognised. It looked like Lucinda's. My ex, two before you. A blue Vauxhall. Same rainbow sticker on the bumper and the rainbow flag we brought back from Amsterdam in the back window. Well, I wondered what she was doing parked there. She doesn't live anywhere remotely nearby – last I knew she had a rented cottage out in Presall – so I went over to have a nosy. It was at the edge of an alleyway. As I peered through the window to see if I recognised anything, someone came up behind me. I thought it was her. There was a blast of perfume. Lou Lou. I started to turn around and something hit my head. I saw stars, then everything got sucked down a tunnel." She shuddered. "You know the rest."

"I'm sorry, babe, I need more detail than that."

She flinched. I took her hands.

"You're very good at this. Did all the girls get the same treatment?"

I winced. Dean had asked exactly the same thing after hearing the first two tapes. "No. You're a special case. Aside from Sammi, you're the only one who suffered sexual assault. That needs more delicate handling. And I'm not in love with them."

I turned off the tape and took a few moments to show her how much of a special case she was. Before things could get out of control she pushed me away.

"All right. You've convinced me," she growled. But I could tell she was pleased.

I started the tape again. Tori frowned, trying to recall details that would help us. "I woke in a wrecked garage. The corrugated iron sheets of the roof didn't meet. Neither did the doors. But the sun was too bright to see anything through the gap. The concrete floor was cracked. Petrol stained. There was nothing in there except the sawhorse I was taped to. I was fastened up with duct tape so tight my hands turned white. There was tape round my head, over my mouth. It tore hanks of hair out to remove it. I was on my knees. My panties were shredded on the floor in front of me. My clothes were ripped, but whoever had taken me didn't remove anything else." She shivered.

"They only spoke once. I suppose they were making an effort to disguise their voice. It was a rasp. I'll never forget it. If someone speaks to me that way again, I'll recognise them. But who it was? I don't know, Randall. I really don't."

"It's OK. I'll find them, I promise you."

She looked at me sadly.

"I will!"

She swivelled out of my arms and turned away. She began picking at a loose thread on stitching of the chair. I hadn't the heart to stop her.

"After they'd spoken to me, they just started fucking me."

"Tori, that wasn't fucking. It was rape. It was assault. Never think what happened to you was sex. It wasn't."

She swallowed hard.

"I don't know how long it went on. First they used something metallic. That cut me. I tried to scream but my mouth was taped too tightly. Then a splintery piece of wood. Then something plastic. Rotting fruit. Rubber. Something icy cold that felt like Pyrex."

She shuddered again.

"Honestly, Randall, if it hadn't been for you and that bath, I'm sure I'd have all kinds of infections now. They didn't use any lube. And they only put things where they should go. Never anally. It was scary how practised they were. As if they'd done it before. They wore latex gloves. I felt them when they opened me. Whoever they were they came prepared."

I'd balled up my fists as she spoke and realised I was snarling. I tried to smooth out my features and give her a sympathetic face. It was hard. I wanted to smash something. She knew I wasn't angry with her. There wasn't much more to tell.

"When they'd used everything they'd brought they hit me again. The next thing I knew I was in a sack on my parents' doorstep. The bell rang. Then my parents pulled me out. They'd cut all the tape off except over my mouth. I don't know how I got there. I don't know how I got to the garage, or where the garage was. I know it isn't much help. I'm sorry."

"It's more help than you know. It was the middle of the day. There were people about. Somebody must have seen something! Whoever it was couldn't just wander around with a body-shaped sack over their shoulder, without someone seeing and questioning them!"

Dean spent a day ringing doorbells in Tori's parents' street. He spoke to all the people she'd mentioned. Nobody remembered anything unusual.

There were no derelict garages nearby. The blue Vauxhall was nowhere to be seen.

Even though I knew more than I ever wanted to know about what had happened to the woman I loved I was just as powerless to bring her abuser to justice and give her peace than I'd been at the beginning.

Over the next two days between other tasks Dean and I started looking into the client list. Interesting. A magistrate. A head teacher who wouldn't have been any more, if his school governors found out where he spent his evenings. More police than just our Chief Super. A few prominent clergymen. And a high court judge! But even Dean had to agree that they were unlikely to be who we were looking for. We also went over the private lives of the bouncers: disturbing, but most of them equally unlikely as perpetrators, though we weren't discounting Grey, yet. And of course we went through all the women's stories.

Two attacks had taken place outside. One on the street – the girl walking home after being dropped off. (Joy.) One in the doorway of her home. (Liu.) One woman had had dog excrement posted through the letterbox. (Terri.) Two women had vandalised flats. (Tori and Stace.) Sammi and Tori had suffered sexual assault, both attacks very different.

Even without the testimony of Lisa Moran we reluctantly had to conclude that we had at least two perpetrators.

11

I stood in the pouring rain outside the church of Our Lady Of The Assumption at Lisa Moran's memorial service, wondering just how many of the colleagues of the innocent-looking girl in the newspaper photograph had known about the sex-games she regularly indulged in.

Dean's media buddies had come back with the rest of the goods on Lisa. What they'd found – if it was true – was the stuff of sensationalist tabloid wet dreams.

The scene the landlady had walked in on was exactly that. A Scene gone wrong. Bondage. S & M. Call it what you will. Lisa Moran had been spread-eagled on the grubby carpet of her flat, fastened by wrists and ankles to the legs of her bed and the butane gas powered stove, with two pairs of fishnet tights. She had recently been flogged and was wearing the shredded remains of a latex slave playsuit. She had sex toys stuck in every orifice. In fact it was one of the huge silicone dongs which had suffocated her. The official cause of death was Erotic Asphyxiation! According to the coroner's report (you can get your hands on anything if you grease the right palms) she was no novice with any of these, except the whipping. Which hardly surprised me. She couldn't dance at the Paradise with her back laid open. The remaining injuries – she'd been badly beaten with fists – had been afflicted post-mortem. Possibly by her lover, angry that she died before she could finish their little game. There were neither fingerprints nor bodily fluids at the scene. Whoever her playmate had been, whoever the murderer was, whether or not they were the same person, they'd been meticulous in their clean-up.

I don't know much about BDSM. I'm not a player. Which is why when Cecily's love play had become violent I'd called the whole thing off. If I wanted inside information, I'd probably have to talk to her, since players were reluctant to talk to outsiders. Not a conversation to look forward to. Cess being Cess, she'd probably insist that the only way she could properly explain was with a practical demonstration.

So who was the abuser? According to the other tenants, the only people she ever had up to the flat were women. An endless parade of them.

"I even found her with her tongue down somebody's throat on the landing!" one outraged former lodger was quoted as saying.

No prizes for guessing what theory my money was on. Every victim was a lesbian.

As soon as this memorial was over I was going to have words with Vic, the bouncer I'd heard bad-mouthing Lisa. He might not have done the deed, but he might know who had. If nothing else, he might know who Lisa had been seeing in the last days of her life. In spite of the plethora of information we'd gathered we still had no idea where to go next. Frustration was eating me alive.

I was thinking very hard about ignoring Dean's warning and bulling straight in, shaking the tree to see what fell out. Only two more days before Tori left for London. I badly wanted to bag her attacker. What else could I offer that might make her come back to me?

Before I had the chance to storm inside and do something that would cause Dean to reconsider our partnership or get me landed in the local lock-up, the church doors opened. The service was concluded; I scanned the mourners on their way to cars waiting to take them to the reception. I didn't see anyone looking anything but miserable about Lisa Moran's death.

I didn't recognise everyone. Hardly surprising. Even if I had known all the participants there are always ambulance chasers at funerals. What did shock me was the appearance of someone so recently in my thoughts. Under a dark umbrella and keeping subtly to the back, Cecily stepped lightly down the church steps into the rain. Pushing as politely as I could though the mourners, I made my way to where she was standing. Gripping her elbow, I steered her, unresisting, away from the crowd.

"What are you doing here?" I hissed when I judged we were far enough away not to be overheard.

Carefully disentangling herself, she countered my question with another. "I might ask you the same."

"I'm here with Tori. What's your excuse?"

"Here I was thinking you were a bodyguard. Are you qualified as a PI now?"

"Just answer the question."

"I knew the deceased."

"In the biblical sense?"

She slapped me. The sound rang out like a pistol shot in the wet churchyard. Mourners turned to us with frowns. Face burning, I ignored them until I was sure their attention was on their own concerns and schooled my temper.

"I probably deserved that. This is a memorial. Tell me I'm wrong and I'll apologise."

I watched her switch hands with the umbrella then smooth the free one down the front of the raincoat. Her silence confirmed my suspicions. She'd slapped me because she could and because she enjoyed hitting me.

"We played once or twice. She wasn't really my type." She looked straight into my eyes daring me to ask what her type was. "I still miss you, Randall. You're so strong. You can take so much punishment."

I took a step back in spite of myself. Slowly she unfastened her coat. Stroked bare flesh. Shit! She wasn't wearing anything underneath! I took another step away. This wasn't going at all the way I'd planned.

"Tell me you don't miss the excitement of our trysts. If you were still with me we could escape this sad little charade and do something more exciting. Over there, in that crypt. I'm sure your imagination can supply details."

Another step away put my back to the church wall. She smiled and closed in.

"Randall? Are you coming? I thought you were driving us to the reception?"

Tori.

Cecily's smile became a grimace. She reordered her raincoat and her expression to something appropriate for the occasion before she faced off with my lover.

"Victoria, always a pleasure."

"Afraid I can't say the same."

Cecily started to make some caustic remark then Dean loomed up out of the rain and her mouth shut with an audible snap. You don't get into a bitching contest with a gay man if you know what's good for you. She knew when she was outclassed and withdrew with what grace she could muster.

"Must be going, no time for chit-chat."

"You aren't going to the reception?" Tori enquired sweetly, cutting wide of her to take my arm. It wasn't quite possessive but it came close.

"I just came to pay my respects. Some of us have real work to do."

"What a pity. I was so looking forward to continuing

our conversation."

"Another time."

"Count on it."

Cecily walked away, swinging her hips. I masked a shudder.

"What was the bitch up to?" Tori asked as we started for the car.

I wasn't going to tell her Cecily had propositioned me. "That's just what I was trying to find out. She says she's slept with Lisa a few times. I don't know how much is true and how much was to get a rise out of me."

"Ignore her," Dean advised wisely. "Let's get out of here. We have a reception to go to. And I'd like to arrive before my clothes are completely wrecked."

Interrogating bouncers was becoming a nasty habit. I wasn't sure I liked the person this case was turning me into.

Frustration that Tori was leaving me, that the case was going nowhere, that Cecily seemed to be stalking me, came to a head just after we arrived. Vic was standing in a corner cracking inappropriate jokes with his friends.

I hung around with Tori and Dean, listening to their small talk with half an ear until I saw the guy leave for the toilets, then made my excuses and followed. I gave him just long enough to do what he came there for, and incidentally to let another guy leave, before I pushed in through the door.

Either he'd had a conversation first or he pissed like a horse; he was only just putting it away when I arrived. Another man in a similar position looked up at my entrance and did a double take in the mirror. He opened his mouth to protest, saw the masculine cut of my suit, the determined expression on my face and the purpling bruise from the fight, thought better of it and fled, almost catching himself in his zip in his earnest desire to be anywhere but here.

"What the..?"

"Lisa Moran."

"What about her?" Said with enough bravado to make himself feel better, but enough respect to show he'd heard about the fight even though he hadn't seen the results until today. So far so good. I stepped closer, invading his body space threateningly.

"Cast your mind back. First night I worked the Paradise. We were queuing to get paid. Lisa hadn't been into work for the third night running. 'That dyke bitch is going to get her ass fired,' were your exact words. Didn't sound as if you liked her very much. Now she's dead. See where I'm going with this line of thought?"

"I didn't! I'd never! You think that I..?"

He crossed himself and pulled out a rosary, then fell to his knees and started praying. Right there on the bathroom floor!

"Holy Mary, mother of God..."

Tears spilled down his face. The door opened. Two slightly tipsy men sobered abruptly on seeing our tableau and backed out. Shit! I had to get control of this situation.

"Get up! I'm not your priest. If you need absolution you're not getting it from me." I hauled him to his feet. He was weaving. He must have got tanked before he went to the memorial; no wonder I was on the receiving end of his emotional outburst. Oh well, *in vino veritas*, perhaps?

"I didn't hurt her. I swear! I asked her out. She was really vicious. Told me I didn't have the right plumbing. I didn't know she was a d..." He looked at me. "A lesbian. She made me look stupid in front of my mates."

How many more times was I going to hear this adolescent excuse to do or say something cruel? I wondered if this was what Lisa's murderer had thought. Or Tori's or Sammi's rapist. Disgusted, I left him sobbing and praying to his unforgiving reflection and went back to report my findings to Dean and get something to eat. At least this reception could be good for something.

"Well, that was a turn up! The Bitch-Queen of St Annes at the funeral. What did she really want? Aside from butch-baiting, that is?"

I should have known Dean wouldn't let Cecily's appearance go. I told him.

"So she was just here to annoy you."

I didn't tell him how close to my own thoughts that came. "Then how did she find out about it?"

"Obits column like everyone else. Really, Randall, don't buy her 'I'm here to pay my respects because I once slept with the deceased' excuse. Cecily wouldn't piss on someone she thought was a crap shag if they were on fire." He bit into a carrot stick viciously.

Where was this animosity coming from?

"Look, I know you hate her from when she and I were going out. But this sounds personal."

He considered his immaculate manicure as if considering whether he should divulge some great truth, then said quietly, "Did I tell you I went to law school with Cecily?"

"You never mentioned it."

I was getting shades of *Basic Instinct* about this conversation and told him so.

"You and your trashy movies," was his rejoinder.

I grinned. "Unlike you and Craig with *Titanic*?"

He made a face. "As I was saying before I was so rudely

interrupted! I went to law school with Cecily. She was a brilliant student, but she had a bad rep. She wasn't into anything violent then. Just swung both ways and had a lot of lovers. She wasn't backward at coming forward with the details of her affairs. I thought when she got the CPS job I'd seen the last of her. Then she turned up on the scene with you. I couldn't say anything. I knew you'd get over her once you discovered what she was like. And you did. I wish you'd come to your senses earlier. Still… I have to tell you I questioned your taste for a while. Gina, Cecily, that string of women…"

"Dean!"

"All right! As you say, I'm not your mother. Sometimes I worry about you."

I wisely let that lie. Though I appreciated the sentiment.

Dean nibbled on a triangular sandwich.

I sneezed. I hoped I wasn't getting a cold after standing around in the rain. I glanced over at Tori, standing with the girls from the Paradise, coolly elegant in her little black dress. She'd keep me at arms length so she wouldn't get infected. At T minus two and counting I didn't think I could bear that.

"You were right about the bouncer," I said around a mouthful of sausage roll. I filled him in on my conversation in the washroom. He raised his eyebrows but didn't comment. "Pissed off because he didn't get a shag."

Dean sipped his brandy and looked pointedly at my piled plate.

"What?"

"Randall, it's a funeral reception, not all you can eat for a fiver."

"The food's got to be eaten, the caterers will throw it away if we don't. I'm cold, wet and hungry. Where's the harm?"

"Ever heard of respect for the dead?"

"And people think it shows more respect if you don't eat the buffet?"

"Irish," he muttered.

Yes, I've Irish blood. What did you expect, with a name like McGonnigal? My family would be having a wake with much carousing and feasting at the deceased's expense at this point. It's traditional to try and outdo the lavishness of the last send-off. Better than sitting around soggy in a sad little two-star hotel, talking in whispers as if we're in a library or moping.

"We're being more disrespectful talking business than eating the food," I said by way of defence, starting on a chicken leg.

"You'll get salmonella."

"I'll risk it."

He made one final attempt. "We could circulate, ask a few questions." Anything else he might have added was drowned out by a commotion at the bar.

Remember what I said about ambulance chasers?

"All we're asking for is a comment!" a trench-coated reporter pleaded, thrusting a micro-cassette recorder in Lisa Moran's father's face.

His colleague was on the floor clutching a bloody nose with one hand while he scrabbled to salvage his own machine. One of the bouncers was stomping on it with an ugly look on his face and no regard for the guy's fingers.

"Bloody vultures! Let my daughter rest in peace!"

Lisa's mother tried in vain to grab her husband's swinging fist as he let fly at the second man. Unlike his partner, this reporter was quicker on the uptake. He dodged the punch, only to back into two plain clothes police officers. They strong-armed the troublemaker out, closely followed by the man on the floor. Seemed there was a point to police at funerals after all. Speaking of which…

"I thought I told yous to keep out of my investigation?"

Shit. Shit. Shit.

Even though he was sitting down, Dean somehow managed to look down his nose at the man. Completely unfazed. Wish I could have said the same.

"Do you investigate funerals now, Chief Superintendent? Who are the suspects and what might they be accused of? Poisoning the guests? Bad taste in paper napkins? I fail to see how attending a memorial service and reception qualifies as interfering in a murder investigation. We are here as moral support for someone acquainted with the deceased."

"Amazing how they always start with the legalese when they're rumbled, don't you think, sergeant?" my nemesis mused to the lackey at his elbow.

"That might be because I am a qualified solicitor. Now, if you'll excuse us, my colleague and I were discussing our business before you interrupted us."

Even seated, the weight of Dean's stare was formidable. It always is when he's in the right. I was so not looking forward to the conversation we'd have when they were gone.

The Chief Super knew when continuing would just make him look like a point-scorer. He turned and stalked away. His oppo couldn't resist trying for the last word though. "Just watch it, you."

"One more word and I'll be filing a harassment suit, officer… Just what is your monkey's name, Chief Superintendent?"

The man grabbed his blustering subordinate's arm and pulled him away with a stare that could have melted steel.

I noticed Grey drifting over to join them as soon as they were clear.

The look Dean turned on me after they'd gone was no less blistering. My appetite was completely ruined. I set down the paper plate.

"Warned us to stay out of his investigation, did he? When were you going to tell me?"

I told him now. He looked shocked.

"I knew you'd want evidence. I couldn't begin to imagine how to go about it."

"I take it this was the thing you had to get straight in your head?"

I'm not the only one with near perfect recall.

"Yes."

"If Tori didn't seem convinced her attacker was a woman, after what you've just told me, he'd be top of my suspect list," he began, tucking his notebook away.

I was surprised to hear him agree with my thoughts. And after the way he'd threatened Tori at the club... Who would know better than a police officer about not leaving traces forensic could pick up?

A caterer was circulating with a bag and I emptied our table of rubbish. "Even if she wasn't, I am. The other women who saw their assailant have confirmed they were female. Tori's attacker wore Lou Lou! There is no male equivalent of that."

"I hate to disabuse you, but I know a man who wears it."

"You're shitting me!"

"Cross my heart. But he's gay, so I think we can rule him out."

"Tasteless bastard."

"I won't tell him you said that."

"Like I'd care if you did."

For a time we sat there gloomily. Then Dean mused, "I don't suppose any of the dancers at the club wear that perfume?"

"No, they don't. I've been close enough to know. And neither do any of the women clients. All except one tend towards unisex perfumes that smell similar to aftershave, like me. The odd woman out wears scent so expensive that Lou Lou would be slumming. Even if she was trying to make a point, she'd do it extravagantly; she's that kind of woman." I thought of how I'd embarrassed that particular woman, carrying her back to her husband after she propositioned me. She was drenched in something worth about £1000 an ounce.

"Could be a red herring. Maybe a man who got the scent on his clothes from his wife!"

"At this rate we may as well start accusing ourselves and our friends, since nothing is narrowing down the suspects!"

He went quiet for so long that I thought I'd hit another nerve.

"I think you're right."

"Excuse me?"

"I said, I think you're right."

While I was trying to digest this he continued. "I wasn't going to mention it. I just wanted to forget the dinner party fiasco. You know Greg's wife, Sharon? Well, she's become the Scorned Woman from Hell. She's done all the text book stuff - shredding his clothes, dropping his car keys down the drain, destroying his CD collection... This may be the first case I've heard of where the guy gets the house after a break up! The police have had to be called in several times."

"Get to the point, Dean."

"She's started following him around. Greg filed for a restraining order. Said she was making him paranoid."

"Tori said he's been at the Paradise more than usual since they broke up."

Dean winced. "I know. And two nights ago she assaulted him with his cricket bat. Craig saw him in A and E. He needed five stitches! The most disturbing part is, the same night Greg says she was screaming about his infidelity with 'those dancing sluts.' And I don't have to tell you what perfume she was wearing at the dinner party, do I?"

I couldn't believe we'd overlooked such an obvious candidate. Who had a better excuse for power-motivated revenge? Tori's attack had not taken place until after the dinner party revelations. And most rapists are familiar with their victims. Who had more reason to attack the other girls than a scorned wife?

Had Sharon known her husband was visiting the Paradise all along? Had she been attacking whoever she could before her husband had been outed?

Perhaps she'd had no one specific to blame before the dinner party. But her husband's reaction to Tori – and Tori's stories of how he behaved, in lascivious jest – had pushed her over the edge. Perhaps then she felt compelled to take the final steps?

Energised by the thought that the mystery might be solved, I collected Tori and drove her and Dean home. Despite the memorial, the show had to go on; it was business as usual at the Paradise.

I didn't tell Tori or the other girls our thoughts. They were just possibilities, nothing more. Once I had evidence to support the theory it would be different. But getting it…

Back in my flat, I caught sight of the membership pass

Tori had given me. It sat where she'd left it, on the desk beside my pay.

Maybe I could confront this woman? She might be out there waiting to strike again! Could I afford to stay away? And after my run-in with the bouncers, it could get back to the wrong ears, suggest that I might be a coward, easily scared off. Never mind that I had been legitimately replaced; I knew how it would look. And no matter what happened between myself and Tori, I wasn't about to let her down. I cared too much to let that happen, and I'd made a promise to her father. I knew how it would look if I reneged on that, too.

I rummaged through my wardrobe. A silk shirt and an Armani suit. Evening gloves to hide the split knuckles. The bum ribs wouldn't show. I might be battered but I was not cowed. Collecting money, pass and keys to the house and car, I set out to prove myself one more time.

12

I parked the Porsche in the usual spot, set the alarm, and sloshed my way across the sodden parking lot and up the stairs. At least it had stopped raining.

I didn't recognise either of the apes on the doors, and decided they must be Spink's replacement and whoever they'd drafted in to cover for the bouncer I'd hospitalised. They looked as if they were about to give me a hard time, so I flashed the Unlimited Membership pass under their incredulous noses and sauntered by.

Inside was different. My reception was guarded but cordial. Nobody wanted to be unfriendly, knowing what I was capable of. Similarly, nobody wanted to get on the wrong side of the bouncers' union. I didn't blame them. The cashier swiped my card and waved me through.

I walked around the balcony, looking for Brian Junior to pay my respects.

"Sharp suit," he said, by way of greeting.

"Thanks."

We walked companionably for a while.

"I didn't expect to see you back so soon."

"Can't keep a good woman down. You've had no trouble since my run-in?"

He shook his head. "Thanks to dad's quick thinking and Villiers keeping his mouth shut. I don't suppose he liked to admit a woman cleaned his clock. What he did wasn't officially sanctioned, if you know what I mean".

"Yeah."

"I'm sure you're glad to be back to working regular hours. Back to bodyguarding?"

Not that I'd ever really stopped, but he didn't need to know that.

"It pays better. How's it going at the gym?"

He winced. "Hard, but I'll live."

We stood watching a situation that might have turned nasty, each with the same balls-of-the-feet readiness, until it blew over, then continued where we'd left off.

"Thank your dad for the pass. He isn't in, or I'd have told him myself."

Brian squinted at the locked door and darkened glass a little way along the balcony. "We've been having a bit of bother with the brewery. He was hoping to be back before we opened, what with the memorial and everything, but looks like he's still negotiating."

"So you did the honours? Opening up, I mean."

He nodded. "Dirty job, but somebody's got to do it." Looking around him he added, "Since you're here as a guest, we should get you a decent table. The Chief Super isn't here yet. You've got a Platinum Card. You get first dibs on the best seats."

"I sense a wind-up going on. I take it you're not a fan of the Scottish git?"

"Let's just say he's given me a few uncomfortable moments."

"OK. I've already been beaten up. What's a little police brutality among friends?"

"Ah, that's the beauty of it. He can't touch you in a public place. I saw the grief he gave you at the reception. I thought you'd appreciate getting back at him, in a small way."

"Especially since you can't?"

He just looked at me. I think we understood one another.

"Lead on."

I know it was childish, and would probably mean our

problems with the local law enforcement would escalate, but this was one of those offers you can't refuse. Besides, if Tori and I were breaking up, how could I resist the opportunity to watch her set the stage alight a final time from the best seat in the house?

I followed the boss's son down to the mezzanine and let him install me at the centre table, exchanging the Reserved sign for one that said Private Party. He left me with a scantily-clad waitress to take my drinks order. Knowing prices were high, I presumed upon my association with the ladies and asked her to get me a bottle of mineral water hidden in an ice bucket. Coupled with a tinted glass, no one would know what I was drinking.

The girls trickled by to visit me. Some chatted, others flirted. I handed out as much money as I could afford and as they would accept, before I caught sight of Sammi.

She didn't seem to be having much luck tonight. She noticed me as the rush cleared and stared to see me sitting at the reserved table. I beckoned her over.

"We have come up in the world!"

"Payment for services rendered." I showed her the pass. "Would you join me?"

"Don't do me any favours!"

"You'd be doing me one. Tori won't think I'm trying to sleep with you."

One of the girls began a number on stage and a few of the audience sitting behind us began heckling, because Sammi was in their way. I stood up and drew a chair from the table for her, giving the shouters the finger. Smiling, Sammi allowed me seat her before I returned to my own chair. We sat in silence, watching the slow bump and grind to its conclusion, before I snagged a passing waitress and asked for a fresh glass.

"Last of the big spenders."

I blushed. "I thought since you were working…"

"What's your excuse?"

"I don't drink."

"Ever?" The spin she put on it let me know she'd guessed the truth. I inclined my head.

"Even big bad bodyguards have deep dark secrets!"

My flaw pleased her. She sipped, drawing rings in the condensation on the table top with a long nail. "I wasn't sure I'd be welcome."

"Why? What you are doesn't mean I can't be sociable."

"You know, if you closed your eyes and breathed shallowly, you'd never know the difference…" She slid her hand up my thigh beneath the table.

She did it just right, but… Nothing fired in my brain. I clamped a hand about her wrist, probably with more force than was really necessary, and removed her exploratory fingers. "Believe me, I'd know."

"Spoil sport." She pouted, rubbing the mark on her wrist where I'd grabbed her, and retreated behind her drink. No doubt thinking up a new gambit.

After a while she started stroking the curve of her ample breast through the thin strip of material that almost covered it. I couldn't take my eyes off her hand. I couldn't pretend I didn't wonder. She smiled, catching my embarrassed eyes.

"You can look but you can't touch?"

"Something like that."

"I'll just have to be content imagining how it would feel to have your fingers inside me. I'm very tight…"

"Please!"

She chuckled.

"I couldn't resist. If you could only see your face!" One of her large hands covered mine, and the look she slanted at me was all devilment. "You do use your hands, don't you?"

I snatched my hand away feeling the blush creep up my collar. A familiar figure in regulation tux sauntered past, giving me the excuse I needed to change the subject.

"Do you have any problems with him?"

"Grey? He's an odd bird. Asked me out when I was transitioning, before I started at the Paradise. I turned him down. I don't date men. I can't say he was happy about it. When I came to work here he raised the subject again, but he stopped after he caught me with my tongue down Liu's throat. I suppose he finally got the picture."

"Was that before or after your rape?"

Sammi blinked then her face paled. "My God. You think..?"

"He was the knife thrower. It occurred to me that I might not have been his intended target. I don't have any evidence – yet – but I thought you should know."

"Fuck! You won't find evidence. He's tight with the Chief Superintendent."

My response was drowned out by the music as another act came on.

It was Tori. She caught sight of me at once. She likes to pick out one of the audience, to direct her routine at them. I've noticed some dancers stare into the middle distance when they're on stage, but Tori is very present. When she looks at you, you know it's you she's seeing, not some fantasy partner. That's reflected in her takings. As thirty per cent goes back to the club, the Bird of Paradise was going to be worse off for her going as well as me.

A truly blistering routine that had me dripping with anticipation was the result. It wasn't until the music faded, the applause shuddering the floor, that I came to myself and remembered we weren't alone. A lump in my throat prevented me from speaking when Sammi enviously asked me if Tori was that good in bed. All I could do was nod helplessly.

"No wonder you never have eyes for anyone else. Do you really think she'll go?"

I found my voice. "Yes."

"I'm sorry."

I focused properly upon her. She looked sincere. "Thanks."

"Will you still come here? Afterwards."

"I don't know. Listen, about Grey, I…"

"No, I need to think about this. Thank you for finding out. For telling me. You're the only one who's ever bothered to try. I promise I won't go off and do anything daft. If I can think of a way to get him, would you be up for helping me?"

I nodded.

"Thanks."

Tori, clothed in the minimal fashion usual here, flushed with the success of her dance and maybe even lust, was making her way across the floor towards me. I stood as she approached. It seemed like the right thing to do. Sammi rose as well.

"I'll leave you lovebirds to it. Thanks for the drink."

"Any time."

She gave Tori's arm a sisterly squeeze. My lover spared a moment to smile at her before she was in my arms and wrapping herself around me. Wolf-whistles and complaints rang in my ears when we finally broke from the passionate clinch and she allowed me to seat her at the table. Just in time to piss off the newly arrived Chief Super. I paused to look at him long enough to drive home my point, before ignoring him completely, focusing all my attention on Tori. I was peripherally aware of him having a brief altercation with a member of staff about the seating arrangements, before he retreated sulkily to a less well appointed table to glower at my back. The flames of revenge warmed me. Sad, but true.

"Thank you for coming, Randall. Are you sure you should be doing this?"

"How could I not?"

She looked pointedly at the ice bucket and its hidden contents. I handed her my glass. She accepted it, sniffed, then sipped.

"Perrier?"

"Highland Spring. It seemed appropriate." I indicated the disgruntled Chief Super.

"Is this wise?"

"Probably not. I've learned you have to take risks in life to get what you want."

"And what is it that you want?"

She leaned across the table, her hands doing just what Sammi had done earlier. Funny the difference pheromones make. I was still trying to think of an excuse to haul her off to the bathroom and show her exactly what I wanted, when she stopped.

"Later," she promised. I tried to get my brain back in gear.

"I came to watch you because I may not get another chance. To drive you home so you'll be safe, tell Sammi I think we know who her rapist is and to show those who need to know that I've not been beaten by my beating."

"Four birds with one stone?"

"Yes. Do you mind?"

"Of course not. I like having you here. I know how you

feel about your reputation, and being driven home means no worries about being followed by a psycho with a grudge." She paused. "Wait a minute – you figured out who..?"

She grabbed my hand and dragged me to one of the Star rooms. Someone was just coming out as we arrived. She pushed me inside and locked the door.

"Tell me!"

I explained what we had learned.

"Dear God, all this time. You really think it's him?"

"Sammi does. That's more important. That isn't all. You remember the dinner party?"

"How could I forget? But what does that have to do with..?" It dawned, exactly as it must have on Dean. "Lou Lou."

I caught her before her legs gave out and sat her in the chair usually reserved for the clients. When I tried to let her go she clung to me.

"Stay with me," she insisted. I had to hoist her again and sit in the chair myself with her on my lap before she was satisfied.

"How..?" She interrupted herself with a shiver. "Never mind. At least I can see why. Are you sure?"

"We're looking into it. We need evidence before we go to the police. Assuming that's what you want?"

"I'm not sure, Randall. What are the chances we'd get a conviction?"

"Slim," I said, honestly. There would be juries who'd consider what goes on here provocation and wouldn't consider what she did rape. Even with the 1992 changes to the law to recognise spousal rape, the definition of rape hasn't changed much since 1956. According to that you have to be a man to rape someone. "You could bring an assault charge. She abducted and attacked you, whatever provocation she thinks she had."

"And proving it?"

"Will be next to impossible. You didn't report it and neither the police nor a qualified medical practitioner examined you."

"So whether she did it or not, she's still going to get away with it?"

"I didn't say that."

She looked at me long and hard.

"You can't be contemplating an eye for an eye. I know you, Randall McGonnigal. You could no more rape that woman than I could."

Then she had another thought. "You're not carrying your gun?"

"We've been through that."

She looked relieved.

"Then what?"

"First we make sure we've got the right woman. Confront her with what we know! She was Dean's friend. Maybe he has some idea about hitting her where it hurts? I don't know. Yet. But I promise that I won't shoot her. Even if I did know, I'm not sure I should talk about it."

She stared.

"You can't just tell me who did it then leave me in suspense!"

"Tori, it's not your problem any more. You're leaving the day after tomorrow. You'll be out of it. It'll be better that way. If the legality of what I do becomes questionable, you can't be blamed. You won't know anything."

She sprang off my lap, bristling.

"How dare you take that highhanded attitude with me! Who was it that got raped? Don't I deserve some say in what happens to the person that attacked me?"

"You're not objective enough."

"Damn straight I'm not! Are you?"

"More than you are. I've had time to think about this. To find some distance. And as you quite rightly point out, it didn't happen to me."

"It's just another job to you!"

"It will never be that. But it is what I do. And if we don't try and stay within the law we become no better than vigilantes."

She looked at me. Somebody hammered on the door. I stood. "She will pay, I'll see to that."

Tori turned her back on me. I tried to hold her, but she walked stiff legged with anger around me to the door. I followed her, put a hand on her arm. "Tori?"

She ignored me and unlocked the door. Brian Junior stood impatiently on the threshold with one of the girls and a client. Tori pushed past them.

"I thought you said customers couldn't touch?" the client muttered. I didn't quite catch Brian's explanation as I followed her out, but I knew it would be something pithy.

"Tori!" I had to shout to make myself heard over the volume of the music.

"Go home, Randall. I need to think about this. I'll take a cab, a White Knight, or something. I want to be alone." Then she was gone.

Shit! Sometimes nothing goes right. She left in two days. I'd blown one of our last nights together by doing nothing more than telling her the truth. To top it all, the Scottish git was sitting at my table when I got back. I knew when to quit. I left.

I wasn't fit to drive. A walk to clear my head? I hung a

left and started for the sea.

Dean swears by the sea as the cure to all his problems. If pressed, he'd say, as a water sign, he's being true to his nature. I don't believe in astrology, but there's something soothing about watching the repetitive motion of the tide and the shushing of surf.

Five minutes and three main roads later I was on the promenade. It was quiet and dark at this time of the morning. I strolled until I found a spot I liked, then let the North Sea work its magic. It was icily perfect beneath the moon and the streetlights. The Illuminations had been turned off. Tourists gone to their beds. I stood near the bandstand – filled with skateboarders by day – and breathed deeply, letting the tension flow out of me along the path of moonlight.

Someone, gender not immediately apparent, shuffled up beside me and tried to bum a cigarette. When I admitted I didn't smoke, they asked for the money for a cup of tea. From the smell that was a euphemism for a cheap bottle of booze. I refused. They swore loudly as they shuffled away.

The moment was broken. I started back, not having resolved anything, except that the world had more losers in it than me.

The rain started again. I flipped up the collar of my jacket against the icy drops trying to slither down my neck and trudged to the parking lot.

We like to think we're in control of events; the reverse is true. Look at tonight. I'd thought Tori would be happy to see an end in sight, let me handle her problem, achieve closure and move on. It didn't look as if that was going to happen. Dean and I thought we had the situation under control; we'd get the evidence we needed, tidy up the situation to everyone's satisfaction and get on with our lives. We were probably wrong about that too.

I'd been staring at the moon-drenched water longer than I'd thought. The cleaners were leaving the club when I drew opposite. A couple of the girls were standing in the lot, sheltering under a golf umbrella waiting for their rides home, Tori among them. Brian Senior was locking the doors.

While I was vacillating about going over, two taxis arrived from the top of the road. A waste disposal truck clanked from the bottom road between us. By the time the traffic had cleared, Brian and his car were gone. So were the girls. Almost. A leg kicked out of the alleyway alongside the club, then disappeared as if dragged.

I know what you're thinking. I wasn't in one piece, and it wasn't my problem. You should know me better. I was born to play good Samaritan.

I darted across the road. The rain made me skid the remaining distance into the alleyway. Luckily I kept my feet.

The single street lamp, coupled with the rain, illuminated the struggling women. I hardly had time to take in more than a glimpse of auburn hair and the flash of a knife, before I piled into the fight. Instinct made me protect the woman I loved. Training made me seek to disarm the knife wielder. It wasn't until the blade slashed my hand I realised they were one and the same.

Tori gasped, dropped the knife and took my bloody hand between both of hers.

"God, Randall, I'm sorry!"

"What were you doing?"

"I've been carrying the knife with me since the rape. Whenever you weren't there. In case she... I never meant..."

She looked down at my bloody hand, then let go, turned aside and threw up. I wanted to go to her, but there was her attacker to deal with.

I turned to the other woman.

Sharon had a cricket bat in her hands. (The one she'd attacked her husband with?) She must have left it nearby to drag Tori into the alley, not realising things wouldn't be so easy this time, not knowing Tori had a knife. My distraction had allowed her to arm herself again. She raised it. She looked more scared than angry.

"Go ahead, hit me," I told her. "If it makes you feel better."

Tori made a strangled noise then lunged. With my uninjured hand I held her back.

"Go ahead," I said again, making a sweeping gesture with my slashed hand. Blood splattered on to the tarmac. Sharon couldn't take her eyes off it. "Violence won't bring your husband back. It won't make him be what he's not."

She choked back a sob. Tori stopped fighting to get past me, seeing her pain as clearly as I did. She dropped the cricket bat and fell to her knees, crying, in a puddle.

I handed Tori the car keys.

"Go and get the Porsche unlocked and the heater on."

I gave her the knife, too. It was a kitchen knife, one of a set. She looked at the thing in my hand as if it might bite her.

"Take it. If you dump it with my blood and your finger-prints all over it, the police will be knocking on your door tomorrow asking you who you killed."

She shuddered, accepted it, took a look over her shoulder at the weeping woman, then back at my hand. I fished out a handkerchief and bound it while she watched.

"I'll live."

She didn't seem convinced but she went. The cut didn't

feel deep. I hadn't time to find out. I slopped over to the sobbing would-be-attacker and squatted beside her. "I'd loan you a handkerchief, but I'm afraid mine's otherwise engaged."

Sniffling, she looked up.

"Could we discuss this in my car? Catching pneumonia would be letting him win, don't you think?"

I stood and offered her my good hand. She looked at it, swallowed hard, accepted it and allowed me to pull her to her feet. She wasn't dressed for the cold. The thin coat was wet through, her skirt plastered to the back of her soaked stockings. She shivered as a gust of wind threw rain into our faces with a vengeance.

She took one look at the cricket bat and left it, allowing me to lead her out of the alleyway towards the parking lot.

She seemed dazed, as if just waking from a bad dream. What she didn't look like was a woman who had raped another woman. I felt sorry for her. She was as much a victim as Tori. I didn't believe she was responsible, for either the rape or her actions.

When we reached the car Tori was sitting in the passenger seat, legs curled under her. Her eyes bore dark circles that might have been mascara. She'd been crying. The knife was on the dashboard. Cleaned. The evidence was sticking out of my ashtray.

I took back the keys and popped the boot. Sharon stood passively while I stripped her out of her skirt, stockings and wet coat and wrapped her in the duvet that, along with the clothes, formed part of my surveillance gear. Then I installed her in the back of the car, took off the sodden suit jacket and climbed in the driver's side.

With the doors closed, the heater on full, the windows steamed and covered in rain, the three of us were isolated, in our own world. Not an ideal place to have this conversation, but I couldn't think of anywhere that would be. Tori and the woman were looking warily at one another, neither willing to start. It was up to me to get the ball rolling.

"I'm going to rehash some history, then we'll all know where we stand. Not long ago my business partner and friend, Dean, invited me and my girlfriend, Tori – " I nodded at her but my eyes stayed on Sharon "– to a dinner party with his friend, Greg, and his wife. You, Sharon. Dean didn't know Tori was an exotic dancer. None of us were aware your husband had been slipping off to the Bird of Paradise, where she worked, without your knowledge. That he was one of her most frequent customers in the private dance booths."

The way I'd presented the facts was making an impression.

"When Tori ribbed him about it, Dean was shocked to discover what my girlfriend did for a living. You were shocked to find out where your husband had been going those nights when he said he was working late. Tori was shocked to find out that you didn't know what he'd been doing."

I paused to let that sink in. Now for a little subterfuge. "She thought you knew. Plenty of wives do. She wasn't trying to show you up in company, Sharon. She doesn't do dishonesty. Or cruelty. To Tori, what she does fills a niche, helps marriages, doesn't destroy them."

I sighed.

"We were saddened to hear that you hadn't been able to reconcile your differences and divorce proceedings had started, but we understood. He couldn't be trusted. He'd lied to you. We didn't hear about this until later. Dean blamed me for not telling him about Tori's job. Which caused a rift between us. In the meantime Tori was raped."

Tori shivered and looked at her hands. The woman gasped. Started to reach towards her. Not the reaction of a rapist. Tori looked into her eyes and saw that too. She turned to me in confusion. I hurried on. "We think her rapist was another woman. A woman who used foreign objects to violate her. A woman who wore Lou Lou perfume. The perfume you wore to the dinner party."

"No!"

It was the first thing she'd said. The word, like her expression, proclaimed her innocence. In the light of what I'd witnessed, she would have to do better than that. Clearly she thought so too.

"I can see why you thought it was me. After what I've done. But it wasn't! I am guilty of attacking your girlfriend tonight. Stalking other girls from the club. Posting dog mess through one's door. Following another home. Vandalising their places when I could get in. It wasn't fair – they used their beauty to snare men and lure them away from their wives. I'm not pretty, I never will be. I thought if I took away their security, made them suffer like other women, it would stop. They'd leave. Get other jobs. Our men would stop coming and see we're all the same. A bit of love and affection would make their wives blossom. I haven't…" She swallowed and rubbed her eyes. "I haven't been thinking too clearly lately."

"Attacking temptation isn't enough," Tori said, softly. "You have to make yourself over in the likeness of the temptation. If that doesn't work you have to move on."

The two women looked at one another. I wondered whether I should get out and let them thrash out their differences or cement an alliance. Tori broke eye contact and turned to me.

"You should get your hand seen to. Why don't we go to my place?"

Then she turned to the woman again. You've been forced to leave your home since you attacked your husband and he took out the restraining order. I've a comfortable sofa, if you'd like a place to stay the night?"

Tori wound the crepe bandage round my hand and tied it off. "How's that?"

I flexed my fingers. "Good."

"I'm really sorry."

"So am I. I thought I'd wrapped the whole thing up."

She took my face in her hands. "You've found Sammi's rapist. Discovered who's been harassing the other girls. And got cut up. Again. Isn't that enough for one night?"

"I wanted to deliver your attacker before you left. I wanted you to know whatever happens next I will always think about you, worry about you, love y…"

She clamped her mouth over mine.

"I know," she told me when we came up for air.

"Are you sure about her sleeping in there? I mean we don't know for certain that she…"

"I do. It wasn't her, Randall. She was wearing it again tonight, the perfume. It's not the same. Whoever it was, their body chemistry made it smell sweet. Lou Lou doesn't smell like that on Sharon. Besides, Sharon's straight. She wouldn't have the first clue about what to do with a dildo. Whoever raped me knew exactly what they were doing, and came prepared. Trust me, we're perfectly safe. You won't need to spend the night on a kitchen chair. Not that I'd let you."

She slid her hand inside my open shirt and down.

I glanced at the locked door and our impromptu guest. She gripped my chin and twisted it back to face her.

"Forget about her. Your only thoughts should be giving me something to remember you by, as quietly as possible."

"You're the one who makes all the noise!"

"We'll see about that…"

13

"...It was the strangest thing. The following night, Tori took her in, introduced her to the other women, let her tell her story and apologise. And they forgave her! They were crying over her! I got pushed out of the dressing room."

"Honorary man?"

"Yeah. She stayed the rest of the night, watched what went on at the club. Then went home with Sammi!"

"Well," Dean mused, "I suppose if anyone knows what a straight woman wants it would be someone who'd been a man. Though I use the word 'straight' very liberally in this case. Is she still at home with Sammi?"

"Far as I know."

"Another convert."

"Looks that way."

I dug in my pocket and handed over a pile of cash with a receipt.

"What's this? Not that I'm not happy you're giving me money, Randall!"

"Severance payment from satisfied customers for services rendered."

He began separating bills like with like, and flipped open the drawer that contained his favourite toy: an electric banknote counter, the sort you see drug lords and money launderers using in hip crime movies. He set it on the desk and powered it up.

"Is there enough, do you think?"

"Since we're doing the ladies a discount, there will probably be some change."

I flexed my hand.

"You should let Craig look at that. You should have come round."

"It's OK. I didn't want to wear out my welcome. It was very late."

Dean looked at me. I turned away.

"She's gone, hasn't she?"

"This morning."

"I'm sorry, Randall."

"Thanks." I swallowed past the lump in my throat and forced back tears. "I keep wondering if Craig was right. If we'd been living together, would she have considered Stringfellow's offer? Would she have gone?"

"You'd both have been unhappy and broken up not long after in angry recriminations. It would have been 'you only stayed with me out of pity' versus 'you held me back when I could have been somebody.' You wouldn't have been comfortable with the compromise. You're not cut out to live with someone, even if you're sharing your life with them. No matter what Craig says! I saw how antsy you were during the days she was staying with you, while she was recovering and we were fixing up her place. And I know you. You did the right thing."

"If you love somebody set them free?"

"Yes."

"Then why does it hurt so much?"

I threw myself into work. By night I spelled Dean on a surveillance he was running at a big computer place on an industrial estate. It had been burgled three times in the last month.

Surveillance is one of the most boring, uncomfortable jobs on the planet. This one was at the South Shore end of Blackpool, near the airport. Aside from hangars, the terminal and warehouses that make up the estate, there are were no other buildings. Dean and I were forced to camp out in parked maintenance trucks or squat behind the dark corners of the warehouses.

Weren't the buildings covered by CCTV? Yes, they were. The thieves had found a way to avoid the cameras, or hack into them and persuade them they hadn't seen anything. We had to wait around turning into ice cubes for the villains to arrive. Catch them in the act.

It was autumn. October. Cold or wet by turns. At the end of the first hour I was aching and miserable. More stretched ahead to contemplate all the things wrong with my life.

We were no closer to finding out who raped Tori. At least one woman was capable of raping and maybe killing, if Lisa's murderer and Tori's attacker were the same person. That and Sammi's rape were the most important unresolved things in my life. Even with Tori gone I couldn't let it go. I'd made promises. I always keep my promises.

Time to look at the suspects.

Tori's certainty aside, Sharon stayed on the list. The perfume was right, she had means, motive and opportunity. And she had no alibi for the time of Tori's rape.

Then there was Grey. If he was capable of one rape, might he not be capable of another? And since Grey was in with the Chief Super, who better to know how to throw investigators off the scent (literally!) or create a false trail altogether?

Which brought me to another point. In spite of the news report trumpeting Lisa's murder, there had been a distinct lack of action in investigating the crime. No suspect in custody, no arrests pending. Couldn't this, too, point at police involvement? A cover-up. Or an attempt to sweep an unfortunate mess under the carpet for someone well connected?

If Grey wasn't responsible for either the murder or Tori's rape, shouldn't I be looking elsewhere? At someone who was a constant visitor to the Bird of Paradise? Someone whose private dance with my girlfriend had had decidedly sinister connotations?

The coroner's time of death was too vague to pin anyone down for Lisa's murder. I had no way of knowing where he been at the time of Tori's rape, and it certainly looked as if he was guilty of covering up Sammi's rape. What more was the Scottish git responsible for?

Our investigations into the girls and the bouncers had been fruitless. None of the girls had motive or opportunity. Villiers was the only man with a criminal record, and he had an alibi for the time of Tori's rape. He'd also had no motive for revenge until I came along.

Likewise the patrons, both male and female. Greg and Sharon had their own agenda, and all the recent disturbances we knew of had been handled on the premises. There were visitors to the club and tourist members, but we had no hope of tracing them and they were a long shot anyway.

We had only three real suspects and no proof. Try as I might, I couldn't gather enough evidence to put all the pieces together and make a whole – though I couldn't escape the feeling I was overlooking something. Pondering on the problem took my mind off the cold and the boredom of the surveillance. Two hours and incipient frostbite later, I still hadn't a candidate.

I left without spotting any burglars, but with numb toes and a sense of frustration.

I came home in the morning to find my building up for sale.

This was the first I'd heard! Hammering on the owner's door produced no response.

"He isn't home. He moved while decorators overhaul it. He's hoping for a quick sale."

I looked up to find my other neighbour, Ashley Hayes, sitting on the stairs.

"When did this happen?"

"Couple of days ago. I left a message on your machine."

"I've been keeping pretty irregular hours, I haven't had time to pick everything up."

I'd been working so hard, out so much, that when I got home all I could do was fall into bed. I had text, ansaphone messages and e-mails from Tori in the first few days. Which made it feel like she was still down the road. Since then, just as it had been when she was here, we were working such contradictory hours we couldn't hook up. Now I tended to skim through the other stuff to find hers.

"What brought this on?"

"Property market boom. He thinks he can sell the building with tenants. I don't know if the new owner will let us stay when our contract expires. Mine's the end of next month."

Mine was the month after next.

What was I going to do? The rent was high, but a good deal compared to other places.

"I've been looking at my finances to see if I could afford to buy him out. These days I'm just a student. I couldn't do it alone. I have savings. With a partner or as a co-op I could."

He gazed at me with puppy-dog hopefulness. I was sure he'd melted plenty of ladies' hearts with that trick.

He didn't have the right plumbing to interest me so it didn't work.

"I have some pretty heavy financial commitments, Ash."

"Don't we all? But if we can generate the capital, the mortgage can't come to more than we're already paying in rent. We'd own the place then. It wouldn't be dead money."

It was tempting. But I couldn't think where I was going to find the money for a down payment - nor anyone who'd offer me a mortgage considering what I did. It was bad enough getting the loan to buy into the business with Dean. And life insurance? Forget it!

I accepted his offer of a non-alcoholic drink. (Does everybody know I'm on the wagon?) And since Cecily was out, I went up to his flat to talk some more, in spite of my misgivings. Mainly because I couldn't see any alternative. Partly because he was so enthusiastic and hopeful, I didn't immediately want to dash his hopes. Also I admit because I was curious.

As we talked I began to see why Cecily liked him. He was warm, friendly, easy to chat with and though he was six feet tall and bodybuilder broad, he didn't crowd you with his physical bigness. He was so pretty that if I hadn't known better, I'd have said he was gay. The guy could charm birds out of trees. He'd make a great brief.

"If you don't mind my asking, how the hell did you end up with Cecily?" (OK, it was rude, but I had to satisfy my curiosity.)

He laughed. "I don't mind. I always hoped we'd get around to talking about this one day. I know you were together. She still misses you. Some days you're all she talks about."

My skin crawled. Ever wish you hadn't asked something?

"You were the main reason I moved here. I wanted to

take a look at the competition!"

Fuck! More shades of *Basic Instinct*. "And now you have?"

"I like you. I don't feel threatened. What you had with Cecily is different from what she has with me. I think you did the right thing, breaking it off. Cess can be obsessive. You and Tori look good together. I think Cess has a healthier sex life with me, no offence intended."

"None taken." Though now of course I wondered what Ash considered a healthy sex life. Ruthlessly I thrust those thoughts out of my head. I wasn't going to ask! He'd get the wrong idea. He was already flirting with me – perhaps unconsciously, perhaps by design. Maybe he thought my sexuality was as fluid as hers? I'd have to nip that in the bud.

"But you asked me how I ended up with her. It's pretty cliché, I suppose. Eager student; sexy, successful tutor. We were both adults. So…"

If things between him and Cecily were as rosy as she painted it, why wasn't he living with her? I didn't have to ask.

"We both like our own space. She has her place and I have mine. I was a dot com millionaire. I got out just as the market crashed. Lost some, so I'm not rolling in it. I decided to use the money to retrain. That's how I have some readies to think about buying out the old moaner downstairs."

I've been working with a detective too long. I see conspiracies everywhere.

We batted the idea around. Made some calls.

We were still talking, he reluctant to return to studies that were boring him, me disinclined to return to a flat that seemed too empty, when sadistic Cecily of the flexible sexuality walked in. I made my farewells and fled.

I had one of those uncomfortable meetings with Cecily on the stairs a day later. She blocked the top of the stairs from side to side. In order to get past I either had to talk to her or physically remove her. Which was, of course, her intention. We'd hardly spoken since our run-in at the memorial.

"I hear Tori left you."

"She didn't leave. She's in London. Trying out for Stringfellow's."

"If you say so, Randall. We both know she isn't coming back. Her flat's been on the market for a week."

That was news to me.

She reached out. I shot backwards so quickly to avoid her touch I almost fell down the stairs. She smiled indulgently.

"Like a skittish thoroughbred race horse."

I hated that she was getting off on my revulsion.

"You will come back to me, Randall, we were made for each other."

"Never!"

"Never say never, Randall. Did I tell you I've put in a bid for this place? I'll let you stay for a price. I've been thinking of some interestingly painful things to do to you. If you co-operate, I won't raise your rent..." She leaned close "...much."

"I'd rather live on the street."

She laughed cruelly. "Be careful what you wish for, Randall."

When he heard about the latest earthquake to shock my life, Dean watched me like a hawk to see if I'd crawled back into the bottle. It was tempting. But it wouldn't solve anything. I had no money for booze. If the worst happened and Cecily or another unsympathetic landlord bought the apartments, I'd be out, without time to prepare. I needed money for the bond on a new place. The amount I'd need to drink myself into oblivion was on the way to half a week of my current rent; I couldn't afford to drown my sorrows in a bottle.

Cecily was right. A For Sale sign was up on the flat Tori owned. I called her to try and talk to her about it, without success.

The next night on surveillance was colder still. I stamped around as quietly as I could. A bottle skittered along the tarmac. Our computer thieves putting in an appearance? Despite the disturbing turn my thoughts had taken I set them aside to deal with business.

Dean extrapolated a pattern from their earlier hits which suggested they'd be here one night out of these three. He's good. The noise was him, arriving with a thermos of something to stop me becoming a popsicle, but we had to abandon our drinks. Our likely lads had arrived. Once the culprits were inside we padlocked the doors and called the cops. Dean's thermos disappeared during the ensuing scuffle. Guess there were more tea-leafs around than just the computer boosters.

I missed Tori. I missed being able to pick up the phone and hear her voice. Dropping round, with flowers, just to be with her. I left messages in cyberspace for her to collect at an internet cafe whenever she had time, tried to call her mobile, but she'd either turned it off or was out of range. I could feel her slipping away from me.

It was political conference season, and I had more work

than I could handle, thanks to the Liberal Democrat MP I'd saved from being knifed.

By day I accompanied them to and from their accommodations: the Cliffs, the Imperial, the Hilton. To working lunches in a number of swish restaurants where all I got to do was smell the food. I either stood behind their chairs, or sat at a small side table with nothing more exciting than a glass of fizzy water, alert to the nuts and celebrity stalkers politicians attract. I also drove them to and from the conference hall at the Winter Gardens.

By night it was a different story. I was inconspicuous while one MP lost his shirt at roulette in the Norbreck Castle Casino. Sat through an appalling production of *Turandot* at The Grand. Refused to procure prostitutes on several occasions. And twice I had to go to the Paradise in my capacity as Personal Protection to two ministers, which was hard, but not as hard as I'd expected.

The town was only just our own again when all the work Dean had been 'awaiting developments' on came to fruition. I'm ashamed to admit I was short-tempered with Dean, when he was trying to ease me through what was rapidly looking like a break-up. We stayed late much of the next two weeks writing reports and closing cases with our clients.

Then, less than a month after she'd gone, the For Sale sign turned to Sold on Tori's flat. The final nail in the coffin. She wasn't coming back.

Dean was unfailingly kind. He invited me to dinner every night when I wasn't on a job.

I finally put my foot down. "Enough! I have to deal with this on my own."

"I'm trying to help."

"I know. You have. Don't think I don't appreciate it. But

I won't be responsible for ruining your relationship with Craig. We both know that if we carry on like this, I will."

He looked at me sadly.

"You know I'm right."

"Promise me you won't lose it if I'm not there to hold your hand."

"I promise."

I tried going out on the scene. With Craig and Dean. Alone. I revisited my old haunts. The Flamingo, the Mardi Gras, Bar B's. I even hung out on Canal Street, Cruz 101 and Vanilla in Manchester.

I couldn't get Tori out of my head.

December arrived. Two months post Tori, I arrived home, aching from a beating I'd received, protecting an abortion doctor from a 'peaceful' protest to find For Sale had turned to Under Offer on my own building. The axe had fallen.

I'd checked out the estate agents. I didn't have nearly enough for the bond on a new apartment. Dean wasn't in a position to give me a loan. And the bank? Forget it.

Cecily, in a negligée, smiling in Ashley's doorway made my stomach somersault. She must have seen the desperation on my face as I climbed the stairs. Known I didn't have anywhere else to go. She glided towards me and pinned me against my door.

"Ready to come and see me, Randall? I'll forgive your insults if you beg. I have a real dungeon. Completely soundproof. I look forward to hearing your screams. Then again, you always were the strong silent type. I wonder how long you can last against my new toys?"

"And Ashley?"

"Can watch. Did you know he finds you attractive? Maybe afterwards I'll watch while he does you."

I shuddered.

"Still a virgin, Randall? Not for very much longer. I'll enjoy breaking you in myself." Her hand caressed my crotch, and I flinched. She chuckled and stepped away. "Must go, I'm busy. I'll leave you contemplating how best to please me."

At the last minute she turned back. "Randall? Get a hair-cut. I like you better with short hair and you really can't afford to disappoint me now, can you? I'll be seeing you. Soon."

I unlocked my door. A simple note typed and unsigned, requesting an interview at seven the following evening, to discuss my continued occupancy, lay on the floor. Cecily was right. She would be seeing me soon.

"Hair's a bit severe, Ran."

"Barbers! All think they're Sweeney Todd."

"You OK?"

"Yeah. Look, I might not be in tomorrow."

"Are you moonlighting on me?"

"No! I'll be back as soon as I can."

"Please tell me you're not going on a bender."

"I give you my word. No booze."

"Then what..?"

"Somebody's bought the house. They want to see me to 'discuss my continued occupancy.' I think it's Cecily."

"Psycho bitch? I'll come with you."

"No."

"Randall! Be serious! Ever since you finished with her all she's wanted was to get you back in handcuffs, and after what I've been finding out… Bloody hell! That's it isn't it? The hair… Randall, you can't do this!"

"I don't have any choice. I can't afford to move out. The

bank won't advance on my loan. She's got me over a barrel."

"She'll have you over a lot more than that. Her house has a fully equipped dungeon!"

"I know. She took great pleasure in telling me about it last night."

"Randall, pack your bags. You can stay with us."

"You haven't got the space."

"We'll make the space!"

I shook my head.

"Damn it! I won't see you go through that again. And I won't stand by and watch you get yourself maimed. You're my friend."

He grabbed me and pulled me into a fierce embrace. I disentangled myself.

"You'll let me come with you?"

"No. This is something I have to do alone or she'll smell a rat."

He glared at me. I jumped in before he could start again. "I'm going prepared. Letting her think she has it her way. Then springing it on her and telling her to go fuck herself."

She was waiting for me in the hallway when I got in at six. Her business suit skirt was so short it could have been reclassified as a belt.

I'm not much of an actor, but my illusory fear must have been convincing. I watched her predator smile rack up a notch, while I pretended to fumble for my keys.

"Love the hair. I'm glad you took my advice. I think perhaps the Boss suit would be best. With one of your silk shirts, white, and a silk tie. Do you still have the one I bought you?"

My hand went instinctively to my throat.

"No."

She smiled. "Never mind. I'm sure you'll find something suitable. I'm looking forward to it." She ran her hands over her ample curves and licked her lips. She opened the door. Sultry jazz was playing.

"Later, Randall."

With a smile she was gone.

I took my time getting ready. I showered and dressed just as she'd ordered, and applied a cologne she and Tori had both, ironically, loved on me.

When I let myself out, there was no reply to my knock on Ashley's door. I presumed she'd decided to play this whole landlord thing to the hilt and was waiting downstairs. I arrived with a minute to spare before the deadline. I knew what a stickler for punctuality she was.

I could hear music inside, so I knocked then tried the handle, in case she couldn't hear me over the love songs. Love? The woman doesn't know the meaning of the word. I guessed she'd chosen those deliberately to hurt me too.

The apartment was big and dark. I'd never been inside before, but I knew it took up the whole bottom floor. I closed the door behind me and walked through the rooms.

The redecoration had turned out nicely. The smell of ancient cigarette smoke from its former owner was gone, along with the cheesy 1970s decor I used to see through the uncurtained front windows. It was remarkably pleasant. I was surprised that she'd left it as it was. Her tastes ran to something distinctly darker. Perhaps this was a façade. Was there a dungeon in the back room?

I hadn't seen any sex toys or torture implements by the time I reached the bedroom. The place smelled of perfume and was lit with candles. I was confused. Was she playing with me? Trying to convince me she'd changed? When the door closed behind me and hands fastened over my eyes, I felt on steadier ground.

None too gently, I flipped her over my head on to the bed. She landed with a whoosh of expelled air, in *deshabille* that, if it had been anyone else, might have excited me.

I turned away, about to deliver the beginning of the scenario I'd planned, when the voice behind me froze me in my tracks. "Is that any way to welcome me home?"

"TORI?!"

I spun round to find her lying on her stomach, ankles crossed in the air behind her, chin propped on her laced fingers, watching me.

"I sincerely hope you weren't expecting anybody else!"

I didn't know what to say, what to think. My head reeled. I had to hold on to the door for support as everything came unravelled.

She leapt up and grabbed me and sat me down where she'd just been. Her hands were soft on my face, the way I remembered, her hair a curtain around us as she fussed over me.

It was really her! This wasn't a dream!

She left me long enough to fetch a glass of water which she forced me to drink. The cold reality in my mouth and throat brought back a measure of stability to my knocked-sideways world. She stayed close and watched me recover, her face all concern. When she thought I was as close to normal as I was ever going to get, she took the glass from me, setting it aside as if I was a child, or a mental patient, who'd harm herself if she was left with such a dangerous object. Then she sat back and looked at me.

"You really were expecting somebody else." She took in the suit, my hair. "At a guess I'd say Cecily has been playing her games. Did she tell you she'd bought the place? Tell you that unless you met her you were out?"

"Something like that."

"And you were coming here to tell her where to shove her offer."

"You should be the one in the private detective business."

"That's Dean's affair. I just put two and two together. Dean offered to put you up?"

"Yes."

"He's a good man. A good friend."

I just nodded. I couldn't get enough of looking at her. She was so beautiful. She lit all those fires in me I thought had died. Reminded me of all the times we'd… She said she was home! What did that really mean?

"Tori, I…"

"I should explain."

"You're really back?"

Now it was her turn to nod. "I've come home, Randall. The last two months taught me where my priorities lay. What I really wanted. Who I wanted. You. If you can still feel the same way about me?"

"You have to ask?"

"I know what I see and what I feel. I didn't know if you would want to trust me again with your heart. I'd understand if you couldn't."

She choked up. This wasn't a ploy to get me back. I kissed away her tears. My lips found hers. She opened her mouth, devouring me with such need that I knew my nightmares of her finding someone else had been just that. Nightmares.

"I missed you so much," she breathed, between kisses, between touches. "I couldn't countenance the thought of being with someone else. I did try. Once. But they didn't kiss like you. Their touch didn't set me on fire. I couldn't go through with it. Being with you, here, now, I know that there's only you. Please, Randall, take me to bed."

I've never taken my clothes off so fast. Tori helped, but there was no finesse. I just wanted to feel her skin against mine. I'd have done anything to have it. I've never felt that way about anyone else. Then our hands and mouths were on each other. For the next hour, I was nothing but sensation.

I came back to myself when she caught my new crop of stitches. Pain was such a contrast from what had gone before that it woke me up. She kissed the place with her soft mouth when I flinched.

"I'm sorry. I wasn't expecting this. You haven't been letting them get you because you felt bad about yourself after I was gone?"

Had I? I didn't think so and said as much. She wasn't convinced.

"Tell me how you came by these."

"I was asked to stand Personal Protection for a doctor at an abortion clinic. I didn't take her talk of threats seriously enough. I thought, since they were mostly women I wouldn't have anything to worry about. I went without the Kevlar and the bracers. I was wrong. One of the protestors charged us with a broken bottle. I did what she was paying me for. I took the bottle."

"With no protection at all?" She was horrified.

"I didn't have a choice. It was her or me. She sewed me up afterwards."

"That isn't the point!"

"It is. It's what I do. I won't be so stupid next time."

She stroked the sewn flesh gently, then her fingers slipped lower...

I caught her hand. I wanted what she was doing. But I

needed to know I wasn't being offered a taste of heaven only to lose it again.

"Please. I need to know how you come to be here. How you afforded this."

"Money I made there. Here. Savings. The sale of my flat. Mum and dad. A mortgage. The usual suspects."

I wanted to ask whether she meant to stay, but found I couldn't voice that fear.

"I'm not going back, Randall. I hated it. They're big and prestigious and they pay well. But it was… What was that word you used? Tawdry!" She made a face. "Businessmen looking down on you, treating you like furniture. They hold business meetings there! We might as well have been wallpaper. There wasn't an ounce of honest lust or respect for what we were doing. It pervaded the atmosphere and dragged you down. There was no excitement. No electricity. No incentive to do your best, dazzle the clients. By the end of the first week I'd given up hope."

She shuddered. I stroked her shoulders, urging her to continue.

"By the end of the second week, I'd had so many financial propositions – and they couldn't believe it when I turned them down – that I could have papered all the walls in this apartment with money and still had some left over, if I'd accepted. I didn't! I wouldn't have let you put your tongue to such magnificent use if I had."

She kissed me, in spite of the uses I'd put my tongue to.

"Even if I had been able to stand the drudgery, the property prices would have been prohibitive. Every penny I earned would have been spent on rent or mortgage. The reason all the girls are so skinny in London isn't fashion; it's because they can't afford to eat!"

Now I was satisfied. "So you came back." I moved my

hand from her shoulder to more intimate places.

"Um…" She pressed herself against my stroking fingers. "Yessss… I came back. I'm taking a few days off, then I'm back at the Bird Of Paradise. 'Direct from Stringfellow's in London' makes good advertising. I suppose it helped that I didn't ask for a raise! I saw this place had gone up for sale when I was coming to visit you. But you weren't here – I assumed you must be working. I remembered what you'd told me about your financial situation. So I went to visit the man who owned it. I made him an offer he couldn't refuse. Now I'm a property-owning member of the bourgeoisie."

"What do I have to do to convince you I'm a tenant worth keeping on?"

"Just keep on doing what… aaah!… you're doing right now. If I could persuade you to put your tongue to creative use again, I might give you a rent rebate."

"For a rent rebate you can tie me to the headboard, cover me in maple syrup and lick the stuff off."

She laughed that wonderful laugh. "I don't think that will be necessary. Give me time. I'll come up with something."

14

I was grinning like an idiot when I got into the office the next morning. Even the camp strip lighting couldn't shake me out of my good mood.

Dean had obviously been pacing for some time. He grabbed my arm and dragged me to the inner sanctum. Then he started trying to peel me out of my clothes.

"Hey! Did you turn straight overnight?"

He glared at me. "You went to see the Wicked Witch of the North and didn't phone me to tell me how it went! Now you're smiling like a loon."

"Moi?"

"Stop taking the piss! This is serious! You can't just waltz in here looking like the bloody Cheshire cat! What am I supposed to think? Either you're high on something, or you've learned to love pain. Whichever it is, there is no place for you in my business. You're my friend, but I can't afford to give you the benefit of the doubt. You'll either get yourself killed, or you'll get our clients killed. I care about you too much to let you to do the first and the second wouldn't benefit the business."

He was serious! "Dean, I have never touched Class A drugs. I'm clean and I'm sober."

"Then show me the scars."

"I don't have any! At least, no more than I did when I left last night. You really think I'd learn to like pain?"

He started to run his hands through his immaculately coifed hair, then thought better of it and stuffed them in his designer trouser pockets instead. "I sincerely hope not. But you're a bodyguard. You risk your life for total strangers."

"For pay! For a great deal of pay!"

"That's the only reason? The money?"

"Yes!"

Shit, how to explain?

He wouldn't be happy unless I gave him justification he'd understand. Like the man said, it isn't logical to take a punch, or a knife, or a bullet for somebody you don't even know, or care about. No matter how much you're getting paid.

"I don't enjoy the pain. I accept that it goes with the job. I try to find as many ways to avoid getting hurt as I can. I live with it when it happens, as shit inevitably does. And I make sure I get paid well enough to make it worth it. That makes it much easier to bear. But I've never liked pain with sex."

I said the last with fingers crossed. I had cause lately to question the truth of that.

"You sound as if you're telling me the truth. I've seldom known you to lie to me. It's just that I know the lengths you'll go to to get what you want. I know how much that squatty little flat means to you."

Then he frowned and looked at me hard, striking the heel of his palm against his forehead. It was a melodramatic move. Pure Queen Dean. "That's it! How can I have been so blind! You've found somebody else, haven't you?"

"I didn't have to. And I didn't have to become Sadomasochist Cecily's sex-slave to keep my apartment either – squatty or not! She's come back, Dean. Tori's the one who bought my building. She's the one living downstairs."

Dean whooped. "The clever cow!"

"Hey, that's my significant other you're calling a cow!"

"I wasn't maligning her at all! She has my undying admiration! Tori has just done the only possible thing to allow you both a happy ever after. She's found a way to live with you without actually living with you. And given you security with no strings."

"I wouldn't exactly say that. I still have to pay rent."

He gave me a penetrating look.

"She has a mortgage! I'm no freeloader."

"I never implied you were! But don't tell me she hasn't reduced the rates for you."

"Well..." His smug 'I told you so' look reminded me why he is the brains of this outfit. Queen's intuition. I wonder what our clients would say if they knew?

Days went by without sight or sound of Cecily. She was either off up country representing somebody professionally, or lying low.

I was told she was mentoring law students at college. I found that hard to believe. Aside from teaching Ashley, who she was fucking, I didn't think she had the patience. But it would explain how she came to meet Lisa Moran, who to my knowledge had never been on the scene.

But whatever the reason for her absence, I didn't miss her.

Tori and I settled into a comfortable rhythm. Life and work went back to normal. With Tori home, all was right with my world.

Except for two things. I still couldn't prove who'd raped Sammi even though we were sure who it was; and Tori's attacker continued to elude us.

Tori seemed to have succeeded in putting the incident behind her. I couldn't have done it. The spate of violence at the club had ceased since we'd dealt with Sharon. But it rankled that I was working for a detective agency and couldn't solve crimes this close to home. Sammi's presence was an unintentional thorn in my side because I couldn't bring her the closure that she needed. Tori's mother had paged me every couple of days at first, then once a week, now only occasionally, making me feel more guilty as the time dragged on without resolution. I felt I'd let them down.

Dean's dinner party 'domestic' was resolving itself in amicable divorce. They divided their assets equally and put the house up for sale. Greg stayed in the place waiting for a buyer while Sharon moved in with Sammi permanently.

I was looking forward to spending the best Christmas of my life. Then, arriving home from the office one evening, I spied a familiar car in the parking lot. Cecily was back.

Tori snagged me from her apartment as I was about to head upstairs and confront the bitch. A good thing too; I was already pushing up my sleeves.

"Yes, she's back. No, you're not going up there to get into a fight. She's a barrister, Randall, she'll have you in court so fast your feet won't touch the ground. Whatever her other shortcomings, she is good at her job. Think with your brain, not your fists. Besides, she'd probably get off on being beaten up."

She pinned me against the open door, the soft pressure of those curves a more effective captivity than strength. Her fingers brushed though my hair, which was growing into something we were both more comfortable with. I closed my eyes, anger draining out of me to be replaced with desire. Tori leaned into me, catching my lower lip between her teeth playfully.

"Better," she growled, sure she'd got my attention.

Then in an abrupt change of pace: "Your rent's due."

"Shit! Our last client's cheque won't clear until tomorrow."

"That isn't good enough."

I blinked, desire gone. Money isn't a game to me. Sometimes I can be too literal. "I can give you half of what I owe…"

"It's all or nothing!"

"What can I do? I don't ha…"

Even pinned against a door, her breasts crushed up against mine, it took me a moment to shift gears and see what she'd been driving at all along.

"If we can close the door I'll do anything you want."

"Promises, promises!"

"Try me."

We ended up on the kitchen work top. Or rather I did. Pants round my ankles, shirt and jacket open all the way down, tie looped round a copper pan on the overhead rack, watch in the sink. Fuck it! The damn thing was supposed to be water resistant to a depth of fifty metres; I'd find out if they were lying now.

Tori straddled me wearing nothing but her long hair, an ankle chain and a satisfied expression. "Ummm… You really did mean anything I wanted."

She trailed chocolate sauce, the kind you get for ice-cream, around my left nipple then leaned forward to suck it off. I lay back and let her. Sex and chocolate: who can beat it?

"Promise me you won't do anything stupid about Cecily."

I didn't want to promise anything of the sort. But she just kept dribbling the stuff on. It was maddening without her mouth to follow. And it was sliding towards my expensive white shirt. It would be ruined if… "Yes! OK! I promise! Please! Just…"

She grinned and applied her mouth in the nick of time.

Later, after a shower, she sat in front of the mirror with damp hair in a glorious rippling cloud around her.

"Let me brush it."

"Randall, that is so cliché!"

"So?"

"We'll never have dinner at this rate."

"You're cooking me dinner? You didn't have to."

She blushed. "I wanted to make something for you."

Tori was a great cook. When she cooked for us I was properly appreciative. "Thank you." I kissed her. "What are we having?"

"It's a surprise."

"OK, I can wait. I still want to brush your hair."

"It never stops at that though, does it?"

That was true. The feel of the weight of her hair in my hands, the smell of it, the feel of it when it covered us both… "If that's all I'm allowed to do, that's all I'll do."

She gave me a look that said she didn't believe me, but she didn't say no. "Let me do what I need to in the kitchen. I'll join you when I'm finished."

Since I was being honoured with a Tori original I didn't argue. I busied myself arranging the stool from her dressing table so that I could sit on the bed while I worked and she could see what I was doing in the mirror. When she came back she'd towelled her tangled auburn locks and slipped on one of those transparent baby doll nighties that always made me want to ravish her. So much for just brushing her hair.

It did start that way: de-tangling, smoothing and arranging, using my hands as often as on the brush. But the revealing nightie had slipped by the time I was finished. Whether by accident or design, one café au lait nipple was begging to be noticed. When I grazed it with the bristles it rose to violent prominence. She moaned, snagging my hand and drawing it down the front of her body, watching us in the mirror, suggesting in a breathy whisper that there was other hair I should brush.

One thing led to another. We found our way to bed.

And a new use for the hair brush which I'm sure the manufacturers never intended.

"Ladies and gentlemen, live from Stringfellow's, London, the Bird of Paradise proudly presents, Miiiissss Tori!"

The whole place blacked out. A single spotlight hit the stage, illuminating Tori in a feast of skin-tight leather adorned with glittering silver chains. The opening guitar chord of Michael Brown's *Black Leather* slid down the scale. The audience roared their approval. Slowly she raised her head beneath the peaked cap and began to strut toward them. I wasn't the only one holding my breath.

"Breathe, Randall. It's nothing you haven't seen before," Sammi drawled, sliding into the seat across from me, a faux cocktail in her hand.

"It's something I'll never get tired of." Tori's welcome back performance. Could I be anywhere else? "Is there something I can do for you?"

"You don't know how long I've waited to hear you say that!"

Her words and her hand on my thigh snagged my attention as surely as a bucket of cold water dowsing me. I removed the hand.

"I want to talk to you."

Something in her voice made me give her my undivided. "All right, I'm listening. What?"

"You still looking into who raped Tori?"

"Every bit as much as I'm trying to find evidence to prosecute yours."

"Thanks, I'll hold you to that. But that's not…"

I wanted to watch Tori but something in her voice said *now*.

She smiled bitterly. "Now you're interested! Story of my life! OK. Don't know why I didn't think of this before. Remember that bitch at Lisa's memorial?"

"Cecily?"

"The very same. Well, about the time you and Tori got together she had an… encounter with her." She sat back and gave me a speculative look, to make sure I was really listening. I was.

"Myself and some of the girls at the club asked Tori to go out on the scene one weekend. You had to go up to, where was it? Glasgow? You had a client who thought he was going to get shot hiking or something."

It was the Cairngorms, but the rest was about right. The idiot had some *Thirty-Nine Steps* fantasy. Nothing came of it. As far as I know, he's still very much alive. But if somebody is willing to pay me the going rate for my services, why should I complain?

"We went to Funny Girls, then Bar B's. While we were taking in the show, Tori kept twisting round. She said she could feel somebody watching her. She couldn't pin down who, but after we'd paid in next door, they came up to her. It was your Cecily."

"She isn't my anything except ex."

"Glad to hear that." She twirled a paper umbrella from her drink.

"Sammi!"

"Your green eyes flash so beautifully when you're angry."

I growled. She wriggled like a happy puppy. "God, if

neither of us was taken you and I could have such fun!" I gave her The Look, and she tossed the parasol back into her drink with a sigh. "All right. She was charming and attractive and Tori was flattered. You hadn't made a commitment. You were getting over your last girlfriend. Tori wasn't sure how you felt about her or if anything was going to come of it. She let Cecily chat her up and flirted a bit."

I understood. "She was keeping her options open."

Sammi nodded. "But the more they talked, the more obvious it became that Cecily wasn't really interested in her. She kept asking whether she was with somebody. What were they like? Was she going to stay with them? What were they like in bed? I thought it was her hamfisted way of finding out if Tori was available. Then some woman in the loo told me she was your ex, and I twigged. It was you she wanted, not Tori. She must have seen the pair of you together. I reckon she wanted to know what her chances were of getting you back."

"Or decided to split us up."

"Whatever. Anyway, I told Tori and she blew her off."

"And you're telling me this now because?"

"I like you. Tori too. I wouldn't want it to happen again." She took a great interest in her long red fingernails. "And the bitch is sitting right over there."

Everything slid into slow motion as I lurched to my feet. Sammi's voice droned like a tape deck with exhausted batteries. The music groaned and faded out. Audience applause thundered against me, rocking me on my feet like a physical thing. And Cecily turned in her seat to look right at me, unleashing a slow smile with all the warmth of winter.

Why hadn't I seen it? All this time, all the stones we'd

looked under to find the villain in Tori's life, and the culprit had been right there in mine, laughing at me.

Time snapped back into its usual frame. Tori pushed through the tinsel curtain and disappeared backstage with her tips. I had missed her whole number. I turned back to Cecily's table and found it empty. Shit! Where had she gone?

"Randall? Are you OK?"

Sammi.

I needed to think about this before I did anything. What was it Tori had said to me only this morning? 'She's a barrister. She'll have you in court so fast your feet won't touch the ground. Think with your brain, not your fists.' And of course she was right. Especially as I didn't have a shred of proof.

"Sammi, I need you to do something for me. Find Tori. Stay close."

She frowned.

Please God, don't let her give me an argument. I could only work with what I had.

"OK. With a reception like she got any crumbs that fall from her table will be rich pickings tonight. You think Cecily..?'"

"I don't know. Don't say anything to Tori. I don't want her worried." Which was of course why I couldn't guard her myself; if I stood sentry she'd know something was wrong straight away.

"Mum's the word." Sammi smiled. "I'll keep an eye on her, I promise."

"Thank you." I lifted her too-big hand and gently kissed the fingers, then set her drink back into it, a large denomination bill wrapped around the stem of the glass.

She made a big production out of tucking the money in

a glittery garter, just as if I was a paying customer. Then she blew me a kiss and glided away after Tori.

I sank back into my seat and tried to scan the club nonchalantly for my nemesis. Just as over-protecting Tori would alert her to trouble, so would haring around after Cecily. I waved away a refill for my drink while I eyeballed the room and tried to come up with a strategy.

'Think with your brain not your fists'. Tori was right. Much as I wanted to beat Cecily to a pulp, I needed proof if I was to make assault charges stick and at the moment I had none. Tori's desire not to involve the police meant there weren't even any medical or photographic records of her injuries.

If I had spoken with Cecily about the sub/dom scene as I'd originally planned, would I have realised the truth sooner? My desire to avoid her at all costs had lost me a valuable means of collecting evidence. I was entirely to blame that we hadn't resolved this earlier.

That led to further grim thoughts. If Cecily was responsible for Tori's rape, might she not be responsible for the death of Lisa Moran, too? Sammi's attacker and the other girls' stalker had been identified; who else did it leave? She certainly had the means and the opportunity.

What about motive?

The attack had been frenzied and post mortem. The killer had been angry with Lisa. I cast my mind back over my own liaison with Cecily. Putting off speaking to her because she made my flesh crawl had got me into this mess in the first place. I couldn't scruple to examine my relationship with her now if it might yield clues to her behaviour. What had Cecily wanted from me? Initially she'd wanted me to hurt her, but when I refused she turned the tables. She craved blood and suffering with sex the way other women needed to be held and told you loved them when it was over. Yet it was my reaction to the pain that had pleased or irritated her the most. Had Lisa disappointed her in some way with her reaction to Cecily's games? Had Cecily's punishment for a perceived transgression gone too far? Might Lisa's death have been an accident?

I now felt certain Cecily was Lisa's killer, however it had come about. With Tori's safety at risk I could not afford to give her the benefit of the doubt. If she'd killed once she could kill again.

Which made the motive for Tori's rape – what? Because she was with me? To kill our relationship? To get back at me? Or was it vanity to assume it was about me? Didn't Tori and Cecily loathe one another?

Why she did it mattered less than whether it was over. I didn't know whether I should be fearful for Tori's safety now I knew her rapist might also be a murderer.

And I had no evidence to prove any of it.

I closed my eyes and pinched my nose against the onset of a headache. What was I going to tell Dean? More to the point, how was I going to tell Tori?

When I opened my eyes, the throb of pain counterpointing this new problem, I spied Cecily at the bar. She seemed to be with a group of women friends. I wondered if Ashley knew where she was. The anatomy of cheating has always escaped me. I watched her laughing and joking with her friends and wondered if she'd have the gall to come over and confront me. I doubted it. She'd always had one face in public and another in private. I suspected she'd save up some pithy comment for one of our uncomfortable encounters on the landing.

Perhaps that was how I could trap her? Could she be

cocky enough, confident enough to confess all, thinking herself safe and immune from prosecution? And could I manipulate her into telling the truth?

Which brought me back to motive. Shit. My head was really starting to pound now.

To further complicate matters, Christmas was only four days away. My lover and my business partner would kill me if I ruined the festivities for them. Both had plans I was to be a part of. Much as I loathed putting it off, I had to delay trying to resolve this. Maybe distancing myself would help me come up with a plan of action Dean would agree to? All I had to do was contrive a way to stick close to Tori over the next few days and she would be safe. I watched Cecily making her way to the doors, confident of having achieved tonight's objective: rattling me.

She'd achieved a lot more than that, and none of it to her advantage.

I set out to track down some painkillers.

I'd make it my New Year's resolution: bag Tori's rapist and Lisa Moran's killer. Find a way to get the goods on Grey and the Chief Super. Sounded good. Now all I needed was a plan.

15

"Tell me that you've cleared your calendar for Christmas."

"I promised I would and I have. I've a few things to finish on Christmas Eve morning, then I'm all yours till January second."

"You won't regret it."

My family estrangement meant I'd deliberately worked through past Christmases. Lack of a partner gave me nothing to stay home for. This year Dean was closing the office early to spend time with Craig, and for the first time I was spending Christmas with a lover and her family. My only reason for leaving my suspicions – no, certainty – till later was that Tori would kill me if I ruined things.

"I'll see you at eight for Dean's party?"

I woke from my distraction. "Hum? Yes, of course."

D & C were hosting their annual Christmas soirée. Now all was forgiven, we had been invited. I'd arranged to pick Tori up at eight.

My wool-gathering made me miss what she'd been saying. She repeated kindly, "You've met my parents, Randall, they don't bite."

Let her think it was nervousness. Better that than the truth. She changed the subject.

"What do you want for Christmas?"

"A new watch." The manufacturers had lied about it being water-resistant.

"I'm sorry about that."

"I'm not. That was the best sex I ever had! A buggered watch is a small price to pay."

She threaded her arms around my neck and wove her

fingers through my short hair, teasing out strands of it, wrapping it – and me – around her fingers. "Aren't you going to ask me what I want?"

"Nope. I already bought you something."

Her eyes lit.

"No. You'll have to wait till Christmas Day."

She pouted.

"What if I don't like it?"

"You will. Should I get something for your folks?"

"A bottle of wine to go with dinner would be fine."

"Red? White? Rosé? Sparkling? Still?"

"Buy whatever you like, it'll go with something. There isn't much they don't drink."

"If you're sure that will be enough. They are hosting and cooking for the whole day."

"What do you get for your parents?"

"My mother always wanted perfume or clothes, my father only wanted the money."

"You do still get them something?"

"A card."

"Randall!"

"Ask me if I've ever had one back!"

"Keep sending the cards, Randall. Some day we'll spend Christmas with them."

"I doubt it, but it makes a nice Christmas wish."

"Is a watch is all you want? How about some curtains to brighten the place up?"

I put my finger in my mouth and made gagging noises. It's a standing joke that my apartment is more masculine than D & C's house. Wood, marble and stainless steel make up the solid surfaces, leather and suede the soft furnishings. There are wood panels and emulsioned plaster walls – no wallpaper; no curtains – I have aluminium

Venetian blinds; and no carpet – it's cork floored through-out. I don't possess a vacuum cleaner. When it gets dirty, I take a mop to it. The only fabrics are the bedclothes, towels and my clothes. And the tailor's dummy the body armour lives on when I'm not in it.

It isn't a place I spend much time in. Tori was horrified at first, but she says it's grown on her. It doesn't distract her from the most important thing – me. (What a flatterer!) She still can't resist making jokes about the paucity of my possessions.

"I'll never persuade you to move in with me, will I?"

What had brought this on? "I like the arrangement we have."

"If you lived with me we could share a bed every night."

"We already do."

"Never the same bed two nights running!"

"I didn't know that bothered you. Does it matter so much where we sleep?"

"Think about it, Randall. Regular meals, cooked for you. Laundry done…"

"Tori, I don't expect you to stay at home and be the good little housewife while I'm the breadwinner. You'd hate it! I'm not saying I wouldn't mind somebody to do my chores. I'm just not prepared to make you my domestic slave to make that happen."

"Think of the financial aspect. We could rent your place out. Make heaps of cash."

"Is that what this is about? Money? Put my rent up. Don't stand on ceremony because we're a couple. I'm not going to demand a joint bank account. If you need it…"

"I don't. Much."

"Then what? Aren't you happy? Is it that you think I'm not committed?"

"I know you're committed. It's just…"

"Tori, I love you, you know that."

"Do you think I'll leave you again?"

"Yes… No! I don't know!" I threw my hands in the air. "I just can't live with anybody."

"Because of Gina?"

"No. Gina was just the proof."

"It always comes back to her, doesn't it?"

Shit! Shit! Shit! I really didn't want to be having this conversation.

"Tori, I'm over her."

"Really?"

"Really. I just need my own space. I don't want to resent you. I would if I felt I had no escape."

"So you need to escape me now?"

"Of course not!"

"Well, that's how it sounds."

I took a deep breath and silently counted to ten. "I meant a metaphorical escape."

The look of betrayal in her eyes told me anything else I said was going to be the wrong thing. I'd been so intent on handling her carefully, first because of the rape, then to ensure she was back for good, that she thought she'd tamed me. I was entirely to blame for the fix I suddenly found myself in, and I couldn't begin to think of a way out of it that wouldn't totally fuck up my life. So I did the only thing I could.

"I have to go to work."

I grabbed my jacket and left. I didn't dare look back.

I was distracted all day after my uncomfortable parting with Tori. I resolved to try and make it up to her at the party. It was something I would have to address, and sooner rather than later if what we had was to continue.

In my crap mood I must have swept the note aside when I opened the door. I was late. The only thing on my mind was a shower, before I threw on the Master Hand tux and collected Tori for Dean's party. If she'd forgiven me.

Towelling my hair and howling along to *Original Sin* by Pandora's Box, I came back into the living room, noticing the slash of white against the tan of the cork. I assumed that Tori had been up while I was in the shower and slipped a note under the door when she found the door locked.

Reading it disabused me. I sat down hard, missing the chair, ending on the floor. The message was simple but devastating.

"I don't think Tori likes my dungeon. Perhaps you'd like to trade places?"

It was typed and unsigned, but it didn't take a genius to guess who'd written it. I threw on the clothes I'd laid out, no time to find something more appropriate. What the hell would be appropriate anyway? I grabbed my car keys, turned everything off, locked up and raced out.

Cecily's new house wasn't far. I'd never been there, but I knew where it was. The place was in darkness, but I wasn't fooled. The door opened at a touch. It took me a while to find her dungeon. Like a fool I started at the top of the house; Cecily, traditionalist that she was, had converted the cellar. A door opened into it from the cupboard beneath the stairs. The only light in the house came from around the edge of the trapdoor.

I walked down steep, narrow, wooden stairs. The kind people end up with when they convert loft space. I was uncomfortably reminded of the Tori I'd found last time I used similar stairs. Was I more angry than afraid by the time I reached the bottom? I don't know. I do know I was wishing for Kevlar and my gun when I pushed open the faux gothic door and walked into her fetish room.

"Randall! Good of you to come. See, Victoria, I told you your beau would come riding to your rescue. Did you park your white charger outside?"

Tori, in the simple satin sheath dress she'd bought for the party, was fastened to the wall by twists of wire. Her spike-heeled shoes stood on a table top, spotlit like trophies. Her hair was dishevelled, but she seemed in one piece. She looked how I felt. Angry and afraid. Duct tape covering her mouth prevented her from saying anything.

"Let her go, Cecily. Stop this before you go too far."

"Ah, Randall, been there, done that."

"Tori's rape. Lisa Moran's murder."

Tori's eyes widened. She redoubled her struggling.

"Bravo! It took you a while to put two and two together. Was it the perfume that threw you? For shame. It was a ruse! Really, Dean needs another partner. All those lovely muscles have crowded out everything but average intelligence, I fear."

I started towards them. Cecily reached down and plucked up a mini blow torch, the kind cooks use to caramelise puddings. Lit. She held it dangerously close to Tori's hair. "You're mistaking who's in charge. Back, or Vicky finds out how Michael Jackson felt."

I backed up so fast I bumped into the door.

"I'm going to talk and you're going to listen. I don't really want to hurt Victoria again. She was always a means to an end. Do exactly as I tell you and I'll let her go."

"You expect me to believe you? After admitting to abduction, rape and murder?"

"Assault, not rape. And she didn't report it and is quite

over it, thanks to you. Abduction? Perhaps. Murder? Erotic asphyxiation was the coroner's official report, wasn't it? A regrettable accident."

"Semantics. I'm not convinced."

"Then you'll just have to trust me. I am, after all, the one with the blow torch."

"What do you want, Cecily?"

"What I've always wanted. You. Ever since we broke up, I've been searching for your replacement. Nobody came close. They either chickened out, went back to their safe boring little lives, or they enjoyed it. Where's the fun in that? In beating someone who wants to be beaten? Or cries like a baby when you flog them then thanks you for it! Only you would do. No one else has your tolerance for pain. No one else hated what I did to them but was still so in the moment that they fucked me masterfully while they bled."

Jesus! What must Tori think of me? I'd sanitised what had gone on between Cecily and myself when I told her about our relationship. While essentially Cecily was telling the truth, it hadn't happened the way she was spinning it. Not in my memories. Had I really fucked her while I bled? Tori would never trust me again!

"You should have seen her, Victoria. On the night I beat her black and blue with that paddle, she had the self-possession to get herself out of the cuffs. No begging or screaming. She swore a few times, that was all. She was magnificent! She's wasted on vanilla sex and airheads like you."

Tori snarled something through the duct tape. Cecily ignored her.

"You never did come after me, did you? That's how I knew you didn't hate me. You were just waiting for me to make the right move. Be clever enough to win you back. You even cut your hair for me. I appreciated that. I really did. Then she came back."

She glared at Tori, blow torch perilously close.

"Cecily…"

She wasn't listening.

"Set your car keys beside Vicky's shoes and go to that table over there." She indicated a long scrubbed oak trestle. "Put on the collar and wait for me. Since you care for her so much, I'll take her home. Then I'll come back and we can play. Together. The way we were meant to be. She doesn't know where this place is. A blindfold will ensure we remain undisturbed. She remains unhurt. We all get what we want."

"I don't want you."

"No? You'll change your mind. You want Tori safe, don't you? So you don't love me. I can live with that. Hate is as powerful. It will do just as well, and I can make do. It's either that, or Tori will have to learn to Moonwalk. I don't think they'd let her dance at the Paradise with third degree burns, do you?"

"You wouldn't!"

"Try me."

I couldn't let her do this. If she had both of us captive there was no chance. She'd completely lost it. Could I make it to Tori before..?

I didn't get the chance. When I didn't immediately comply, she turned the blow torch on Tori's bare shoulder. Tori jerked away, trying to scream through the tape. I did it for her.

"NO!!! Jesus! Stop!"

She turned her attention to me and moved the torch away. A patch of livid burnt skin, blackened in places, proved she wasn't willing to compromise.

"Keys, Randall. And if you aren't fast enough, it really will be her hair next time."

The smell of burned flesh convinced me of her sincerity. I threw my car keys at the shoes. One of them fell over but all three items stayed on the table. A post-modern still life.

"Very good, Randall; that wasn't hard, was it? Now the rest, please. I really will take her home. You have my word. Have I ever lied to you?"

I moved over to the table to show willing. The collar was like a dog's, leather, studded with metal. No way was I putting that thing on!

"Will you burn me too? When she's gone?" Keep her talking. Think. Buy yourself time.

"Perhaps." Shit! She really was considering it! "I have more interesting things I'd like to do to you. I've had a long time to think about it." She looked at me consideringly. "A mark of my good faith." She ripped the tape from Tori's mouth. An earsplitting shriek bowed my head in shame. I'd promised to protect her and I'd failed.

By the time I could bring myself to look at her, Tori was swearing. Cecily applied an ice pack to her shoulder.

"Do shut up, Victoria. You're trying my patience. I promised you'd be safe if Randall did as she was told. It's Randall's fault you were hurt, not mine."

"You were the one that burned me, bitch!"

I wasn't going to let her blame me for her sadism! Angrily I strode towards her again.

She went from solicitous to aggressive in the blink of an eye. I hadn't taken two steps before she turned the blow torch on Tori's injured shoulder. Tori's scream went through me like a blunt knife. My knees buckled.

"STOP! Please!"

Just like that, she was all sweetness and light and the ice pack was back on Tori's shoulder. Seeing me on my knees pleased her. Hearing me beg pleased her even more.

"The collar, Randall. Put it on." I looked at the ground. When I didn't move she tsk'd. "Maybe it's true what they say, you really can't teach an old dog new tricks."

Tori whimpered. The blow torch was perilously close to her burned shoulder.

"I grow tired of asking, so I'll just command. If you don't want Vicky to suffer put on the collar. Which means more to you? Pride, or the safety of the woman you profess to love?"

I brought it down. It would be a tight fit. I unfastened the bow tie and the top button of my shirt, then fastened the thing around my neck.

"Good dog! You can be reasonable! And to prove I mean what I say…" She unhooked Tori's wrists from where they were secured. She was still bound hand and foot, but it was one step closer to freedom. Cecily covered her with the blow torch, but tossed her the ice pack. With a fumble, Tori caught it, pressing it awkwardly to her shoulder.

"There now! Isn't it much better when we're civilised?" Cecily indicated a leash hanging over the table's edge. "I'm sure you know what to do next. I promise you I'll reciprocate."

She didn't give me time to think about it. When I didn't move immediately she sighed and swung the blow torch back towards Tori. Tori's gasp was enough.

"Don't! I'm doing what you asked! Look at me! Don't hurt her because I was slow."

"You see? Just right. Not a hint of fawning. Even with your health and safety at risk, on her knees, she's still fighting me. I like that."

I snarled and snapped the choke-chain leash on to the metal clip at the collar and held my hands away from my body. It wasn't surrender. I wouldn't give her that. It wasn't what she wanted.

Cecily smiled, as close to happy as I've seen her, then kicked a lever on the floor.

You've seen retractable vacuum cleaner cables. That's what happened to the chain leash attached to the collar around my neck. Whiplashed by the action, I was yanked back.

My head smacked against the table edge.

Fighting against blacking out, feeling blood from my opened scalp trickling through my hair, I was dragged up and back on to the surface of the table. To avoid being garrotted I went with it.

I clawed the collar, trying to slide my fingers between leather and skin. I gulped air into my labouring lungs. My neck made sickening popping sounds.

The speed and torque in the winch were too strong and fast for me to turn or get the collar off. I felt a wrench when I finally came to rest, sprawled across the table on my back. I wondered if I'd be going anywhere if I did get the collar off.

I was scrabbling at the leather, trying to remember how to breathe, when Cecily appeared above me. I felt a jab through the suit jacket and shirt into my arm. She smiled into my eyes with all the warmth of winter. Anoxia and whatever she'd stuck me with started to have an effect.

"I'm going to do it right this time," she assured me.

Then everything went black.

16

I opened my eyes to blood and handcuffs. I was spread-eagled over the scrubbed oak table, the way she'd once fastened me to my bed. Alone.

Low lighting and the drip of a leaky faucet somewhere added authenticity to the dungeon Cecily had created. I wondered how many people had sampled her hospitality while she formulated her plan to get me here for her pièce de resistance. I shuddered.

Shuddering hurt. Gingerly I began flexing muscles and joints to see whether I'd be able to escape if I got free of my bonds.

A mixture of drugs, suffocation and the crack on the head made my skull ring with jackhammers. Every time I moved it felt like my worst hangover. My stomach roiled with nausea. I'd have thrown up if there'd been anything in it. But none of it was fatal – nothing I hadn't had to deal with - and work through – in my worst moments of excess following the break-up with Gina. I probably had concussion, which was more serious, but again, nothing I hadn't had before. I'd just have to move slowly and carefully for a while.

Luckily, nothing seemed to be broken. Whatever had wrenched in my back as I'd been hauled up on to the table was quiescent for the moment. I'd cross that bridge when I came to it. It was important not to waste any more time. I didn't know how long I had before Cecily came back. I couldn't afford to be lying here helpless when she did.

I explored the handcuffs' mooring and wondered

whether she was keeping her promise to take Tori home. Another reason to get free. If she hadn't the sick bitch would get more than the taste of pain she craved. Thinking about the way she burned Tori made my blood run hot. Thinking about her raping Tori added fuel to the fire.

I had no picklocks. The chains were welded and bolted too firmly for me to pull loose, even with the fires of my anger warming me. I would have to try something else.

Acutely aware of time passing, I flexed my hands and shaped my fingers into points that would have been familiar to any practitioner of vaginal or anal fisting. I am blessed with double-jointed thumbs, and I can narrow the diameter across my knuckles to about the width of my wrist. Losing a couple of layers of skin was a small price to pay for freedom.

Next the collar.

The ankle cuffs weren't so easy. The chains weren't long enough to let me reach the floor. The best I could do was sit, legs dangling over the edge. Not enough. Unless…

This was going to hurt. I grabbed the edge of the table and rocked violently to one side. The bugger was well balanced. It took three tries to tip the thing over and spill myself on to the floor. As well as cutting into one ankle deeply enough to draw blood, bruising the hell out of the other and spraining the wrist I landed on, I hit some of her other equipment on the way down. I probably did more damage to myself than Cecily had. At least I could derive some pleasure from wrecking her fetish room while I cursed the pain and fought against passing out again.

When I recovered, I crawled to where I'd thrown my keys. I dragged the table behind me, and left a trail of blood from the cuffs cutting into my ankles. I got close enough to knock the keys off the plinth to the floor before the pain got too much.

I'm sure the Swiss Army suppliers who made the penknife on my key ring never intended it to be used to break out of handcuffs. But it worked. A mixture of the saw blades, knife, screwdriver, toothpick and corkscrew had me free of one binder and working on the other before I heard someone above.

I was still attached by one leg to the table. If Ashley was in on this I couldn't hope to fend them both off without freedom of movement.

There were footsteps on the stairs. I was out of time.

I switched the attachment to knife blade and dropped it – open – into my jacket pocket. Then I stood as best my hobbled state would allow and began kicking the table leg I was still attached to. It hurt. It hurt my tethered leg. It hurt my bleeding ankles. It hurt my aching head. It hurt my screaming back. But I couldn't stop. My only hope was to break the damn thing off. Dragging around a table leg gave me a fighting chance. Dragging around a table did not.

The sound of splintering wood covered the opening door. I stepped clear of the wrecked furniture, broken table leg dragging beside me, before I confronted my captor.

"You couldn't wait, could you?"

Mad as a stirred hornets' nest, Cecily coiled a length of bullwhip over one arm.

"I prefer to play games by my rules. Without a handicap."

She glanced at the length of wood dangling from the cuff around my ankle. Eloquent reminder that I hadn't completely succeeded. She looked at my skinned knuckles. The handcuffs still attached to the table. Back to the abraded flesh. Her expression was wistful. "You always were good with your hands."

Then she unreeled the bullwhip in a crack that laid open my right leg through the pants. I'm not proud. I howled.

"I don't suppose they teach you to defend yourself against something like this," she mused with cold academic curiosity, reeling the whip in, coiling the thing for another attack. I backed up, dragging the length of table leg.

Her second cut laid open my arm. She'd been aiming for my face. I'd moved just fast enough to cover it. Blood soaked through the slashed shirt, turning the white to crimson, making the wool mix of the jacket heavy. If I didn't do something quickly, I'd be in no shape to do anything at all.

How do you fight something as archaic as a bullwhip? My instincts screamed *Run!* But there was no where to run to. Cecily was between me and the door. A whip is a distance weapon. I should step into her space, so that she couldn't unleash it. Take it away from her. But the damage I'd sustain in trying…

She caught me a third time while I pondered. It sliced a fresh cut across my uninjured arm. I snarled with pain and snatched at the length coiled round me. By now both whip and hands were so coated with blood that it slipped through my fingers. She yanked it back for another strike.

Off balance, I lurched into something that chinked, dangling from the ceiling behind me. As she launched a fourth cut of the whip, instinct made me grab whatever it was and leap upward. Her weapon hissed by beneath me and clipped the swinging length of table leg. Cecily cursed and snatched the coils back.

My saviour had been a length of chain with manacles attached. The outfitters of Cecily's playroom built to last; it supported my weight without a creak.

That gave me an idea.

While she re-coiled her weapon and aimed higher, I flipped my legs back, hit the wall, pushed off and swung. I aimed right at her, feet out to kick.

I hadn't calculated for the table leg.

It swung out and caught her a blow that felled her like a slaughtered ox. I landed badly because of that same hunk of wood, but that hardly mattered. When I limped over to kneel beside her, Swiss Army knife in my hands, she was out for the count.

"I told you she wouldn't need saving twice."

Craig.

I looked up to find the three of them clustered at the bottom of the stairs. All were in their party clothes, Dean with a baseball bat, Craig with a candlestick, even Tori, shoulder swathed in a burn dressing, wielding a can of pepper spray. I've never been happier to see anyone.

Tori dropped the pepper spray and flew over. Covering my face with kisses.

"I've never seen anything braver. Taking my place. Letting her hurt you so I could be free. Wait till I get you home. I'll make love to you like you've never known."

"The only place Randall's going is A and E," Craig told her. After he'd finished skinning back Cecily's eyes and checking her pulse, he left Dean to cuff her with some of her own toys while he looked me over, what bits of me he could get to with Tori in the way.

"Those cuts need sewing, your wrist needs strapping, your ankles need bandaging and they may recommend traction for your back."

"Can't you..?" Tori began.

Craig shook his head. "Way beyond what I can do. And you should have that burn looked at properly. There may be something they can do to stop scarring. It's not really my field."

"What about her?"

"The hospital for her too," I said. "The psychiatric wing. This goes way beyond kinky sex. She needs professional help. Either she voluntarily sections herself for psychiatric evaluation, or the police arrest her for the murder of Lisa Moran. I'm telling them everything in the morning, no matter what she decides. It's either prison or an institution." God, I was tired. And aching. "Tell me you came in the Range Rover?"

"Of course!"

"Then bring her. When she comes to I'll explain her options. I'm fairly sure I know which one she'll choose."

I looked at Tori.

"I know this isn't the way you imagined this ending."

She looked at the unconscious Cecily.

"I can live with it. Knowing who did it so that I don't have to be afraid any more. Seeing you free under your own power, knocking the bitch out, was enough for me. I think it's laid a few of your demons, too."

I couldn't argue. Dean heaved the unconscious woman over his shoulder and started up the narrow stairs, Craig close on his heels. Tori and I followed more slowly.

"At least I'll have something positive to tell your parents," I mused as we trooped out of the house. Craig opened the car rear. Dean dumped Cecily none too gently into the back. Waiting on the road side for her door to be opened, Tori stood aghast, hands on her hips.

"Randall McGonnigal! Don't you dare ruin Christmas dinner with this horror story!"

"Joke, Tori. Even I wouldn't be that crass."

She broke into one of those smiles that lit up her whole

face. I'll always remember her like that. Then the drunk driver careered round the corner and wiped her away.

17

It was not the Christmas I'd planned.

I don't remember screaming as Tori went down. I recall my raw throat as I ebbed and flowed between consciousness and the quiet place the drugs had created where there was no pain.

I don't remember Dean's speed-limit-breaking drive to the hospital. I recall him and Craig singing Christmas carols at my bedside while I was in traction.

I don't remember being admitted to hospital. Yet I recall Tori's mother holding my hand, tears running down her face as she kept vigil at my bedside.

I missed Tori's funeral.

I missed New Year's Eve.

I hated myself for the former. I couldn't bring myself to care about the latter. All the joy had gone out of my world without Tori. I willed myself to die. Yet I didn't.

"It wasn't your fault. You did what you promised. You found the maniac who raped her. You protected Tori from her," Tori's mother said to me, in one of my moments of lucidity.

"Then why does it feel like I failed?"

"You can't fight fate, Randall," Craig said, fluffing pillows, straightening sheets on his rounds. "It was her time."

"Nothing personal, Craig, but fuck off, will you? It was not her time, it was not fate, it was a fucking drunk driver. Go and play nurse to someone who appreciates your platitudes."

Ashley came to visit.

"I know I'm probably the last person you wanted to

see."

"You've got that right."

"You have to understand I didn't know anything about what she was doing."

"And I'm supposed to believe that, am I?"

"I didn't think you would; that's why I'm leaving. I've submitted my intention to quit to the executors. I think it will be better for all of us if I move away."

An adult thing to do. I wasn't in the mood for adult. Still, I forced myself to be polite. "Where will you go?"

He looked sheepish. "Cecily's place. I'm looking after it for her until she gets out."

"You still think she can be cured?"

His eyes were shadowed. "Yes. I do. At least I hope so. I love her, you see, so I have to believe it. I'm going to work with her therapists, see if there's anything I can do..." Then, sensing this was not what I needed to hear, "I'm really sorry things worked out this way. I like you. I liked Tori. But I love Cecily, for all her faults. I have to try."

They tried to give me grief counselling. I told them to fuck off, too. It wasn't grief counselling I needed. It was anger management.

Drugs and pain had seen me through the grief, numbed the edge the way booze had with Gina. Now overpowering rage boiled in me: frustration at my helplessness, my inability to do anything about what had happened. There was only one thing that would ease that.

The gym. I had to be back on my feet to take advantage of it. Since death didn't seem interested in me, I decided to live.

Sammi and the girls came by, causing uproar. Dressed in skimpy Miss Santa suits they put on an impromptu show that stopped the ward. But their clowning was cover for something more serious. They all shed a few tears with me for Tori before they left.

"If you need us, you know where to find us," Joy told me hopefully.

Liu didn't say much, but she made it clear she would be happy to step into Tori's shoes. Flattering, but too soon. I couldn't consider that part of my life while the aching void of Tori's loss ate at me.

"Don't you think you've seen the last of us. You and I still have my little problem to sort out," Sammi reminded me.

"I hadn't forgotten. It's my new year's resolution."

"I'll hold you to that."

Their visit was the real start of my recovery.

They released me on January 3rd.

I got home, thinking I'd find an eviction notice. I found myself owner of the building.

Of course I called Tori's mum. It took me three tries. Her father wouldn't speak to me. Though the traffic accident wasn't my fault he held me responsible. After two hang-ups and an earful of abuse, I got through to the woman who'd sat by me as if I were her daughter. I hardly knew what to say. She made it easy for me.

"It's the house, isn't it? You got the deeds?"

"Yes."

"I came to deliver them myself. That nice young law student, Ashley? He let me go up and put them through your door. He was just going out as I arrived. He's moving, he tells me."

"Yes."

"Her insurance paid off the mortgage and paid us back.

She wanted you to have it. I'm sure she never imagined it would be this soon. She made a will when she bought it. We won't contest."

"You'd be well within your rights if you did."

"No. Victoria made it clear you were to be regarded as her next of kin if anything happened. She had documents drawn up in case she had an accident dancing or something."

I wondered if the 'or something' came about before or after her rape.

"It's going to take Rafe a while to deal with this. Me, too. Would you mind if..."

She was going to ask me not to call or write. The house was my pay-off. I interrupted her. She'd been kind to me. It was the least I could do.

"You have my number. If you need me. And the keys if you want any of Tori's things."

"Thank you, but no. I'll pop them through the letter box when next I'm passing. I know she'd want you to have everything. We have all we need to remind us of her here, in her old room." Where she belonged only to them, and was still an innocent child. A person who hadn't made a choice to have girlfriends instead of boyfriends, dance in what amounted to a strip club, get raped, or run over, in a world where they couldn't protect her. I understood.

After that neither of us could think of anything to say. Again she came to the rescue.

"I'm sure you have plenty of things to be doing. I really will phone, if you want me to."

"The ball's in your court. I meant what I said. If you need me, I'll be there."

"Thank you, love. You don't know what that means to me. You take care."

"I will."

I found myself listening to the dial tone. That summed up my life.

"McGonnigal, you're up."

I stepped on to the practice floor, bruised and sweating. None of the usual slurs followed me. Nobody lined up to take me down a peg or three and show me that a woman shouldn't be doing this job. For the first time their faces were sober and sympathetic.

Spink was back. It was the big black man who lumbered out to meet me.

"I'm not here to fight you," he said, before I could open my mouth. "You proved I can't well enough last time. Just came to say goodbye. I'm quit of the business. I've got a job minding my son-in-law's market stall on Abingdon Street. Made the wife happy to see me again."

Some of the men chuckled dryly.

"I just wanted to say sorry on behalf of us all. It doesn't matter what we think of you professionally or personally. It doesn't make it any better just to offer condolences. But we all know what it's like to lose someone. Most of us knew your girlfriend, because of her job. She was a nice lady. One of the best. Did they catch the bastard that knocked her down?"

"Yes."

"Good. Then it's time to get on with your life. You'll never forget her. It'll hurt for a long time. This won't help. Nobody is going to fight you. We can see the mood you're in. They don't want to die. There's a punch bag over in the corner. Or Eli will happily beat the stuffing out of you a bit longer. You want my advice? Walk away. Getting back on track doesn't start here."

"Spink…"

"We're rooting for you, Randall. You've got a good reputation. Don't blow it."

I looked round at them, my throat closing up.

"There'll be other days," one of them said.

"We'll be here," another agreed.

I did the only thing I could before the tears started. I nodded and walked away.

A lot more than soapy water went down the changing room drains. At least I didn't look like I'd been bawling my head off by the time I hit the street. Maybe I could go to the range? Shoot the shit out of some targets? Anything, rather than think. Or feel.

Dean was waiting. Leaning, grinning, against the side of his Range Rover. I don't know if Spink or one of the others had called him. I wasn't going to ask. I was just grateful.

"Going my way?"

"Depends on which way that is."

"The office, actually. I have a case I'd like to you look at."

"You know I'm not much of a detective."

"You're not so crap as you make out. But I'll be doing the detecting, if that's OK with you? It's unusual – for us, at least. Celebrity stalker. The police don't seem to have made any headway and they haven't got the manpower to put someone on her 24/7. If they were taking it seriously – which I'm not sure they are."

"What do you need from me?"

"Personal Protection, what else?"

"Dean, I'm not sure I can…"

"Randall, she didn't die because you weren't doing your job."

"It doesn't feel that way."

"You've just spent the last ten days in hospital paying the

price for your devotion to duty and love. Stop beating yourself up and get back on the horse. The business needs the money. I can't do it. I'm not qualified and I don't have the aptitude. You might just have come into money but you still have to work for a living. I need your help."

There it was. I've never turned down someone who asked for help and I wasn't about to start now. Especially since the one asking was my friend. And business partner. And always there for me when I really needed him.

"Personal Protection?"

"Yep. She wanted the best. I told her she'd come to the right place. Was I wrong?"

"I suppose we'll just have to find out."

More action-packed crime novels
from Crème de la Crime

If It Bleeds — Bernie Crosthwaite
ISBN: 0-9547634-3-2

There's only one rule in the callous world of newspapers: violence excites, death sells – so if it bleeds, it leads.

When hardened press photographer Jude Baxendale is despatched to snap a young woman's bloody body discovered in a local park she reckons it's a grisly but routine job – but she's horrifyingly, perilously wrong. For the murdered girl is her own son's girlfriend, and in a single chilling moment she realises nothing in her life is ever going to be the same again.

Why was Lara killed? Who stabbed and mutilated her? Who hated her enough to dump her body in full public gaze? Jude has to find out. Teaming up with reporter Matt Dryden, she begins to unravel the layers of the girl's complex past. But she soon learns that nothing about Lara was as it seemed…

Soon finding the truth will risk Jude's job, her health, her sanity – and place her squarely in the sights of a killer with a fanatical mission. And some deadly truths are best left uncovered. **Publication date April 2005.**

Also available:

Working Girls — Maureen Carter
ISBN: 0-9547634-0-8

No Peace for the Wicked — Adrian Magson
ISBN: 0-9547634-2-4

A Kind of Puritan — Penny Deacon
ISBN: 0-9547634-1-6

More gripping titles available later this year from Crème de la Crime

No Help for the Dying
Adrian Magson

ISBN: 0-9547634-7-5

Runaway kids are dying on the streets of London. Investigative reporter Riley Gavin and ex military cop Frank Palmer want to know why.

They uncover a sub-culture involving a shadowy church, a grieving father and a brutal framework for blackmail, reaching not only into the highest echelons of society, but also into Riley's own past.

The second fast-moving adventure in Magson's popular Gavin/Palmer series.

Available September 05

A Thankless Child
Penny Deacon

ISBN: 0-9547634-8-3

Life gets more dangerous for loner Humility. Her boat is damaged, her niece has run away from the commune, and the man who blames her for his brother's death wants her to investigate a suicide. She's faced with corporate intrigue and girl gangs, and most terrifying of all, she's expected to enjoy the festivities to celebrate the opening of the upmarket new Midway marina complex.

Things can only get worse.

A follow-up to *A Kind of Puritan*, Deacon's acclaimed first genre-busting future crime novel.

Available September 05